A Memory of War and Solace

Also by K. N. Brindle

Paths of Memory

A Memory of Blood and Magic

A Memory of War and Solace

Discover and follow at

www.knbrindle.com

A Memory of War and Solace

K.N. Brindle

A MEMORY OF WAR AND SOLACE

Library of Congress Control Number: 2024915670

ISBN: 978-1-965275-03-0

For Deanna, Kris, and Kathryn, who taught me so much, and who continue to hold the line.

And for T and S, who will carry the banner forward for us all.

Author's Note

If you've already read A Memory of Blood and Magic (and if you haven't, what are you doing reading the second book of a duology first?! Please go back and read book one—there is much in this volume which won't make as much sense if you haven't), then you already know how difficult Arin's early life was and how difficult their world can be. This book explores parts of Arin's world that are rife with discrimination and prejudice. In the first book, Arin grew enough into their own power and agency that they're no longer subject to the whims of others, but they are still one person in a very large, sometimes very ugly world.

This story doesn't mince at the pain and suffering felt by marginalized people. There are references to sexual assault, survival sex, depictions of physical abuse, and what we would today call hate crimes. There is discrimination, verbal abuse, and use of in-world epithets. As always, I tried hard to ensure that these depictions are meaningful and necessary to the story and that nothing is gratuitous.

Despite the word "war" in the title, this *still* isn't a story about fateful quests or chosen ones or dark lords. It is *still* a story about people, and the difficulties they face, the challenges they make for themselves and others, and the pain that drives people to make terrible choices that change lives forever.

Most importantly, this is a story about trauma. About pain and healing, and about how all the people in our lives contribute to either or both of those things. And it is about finding within ourselves the strength and self-kindness that we need to heal.

If you are reading this some time after having read the beginning of Arin's story (or if you have picked up this book by happenstance and don't know Arin yet), I offer this brief recap of the events that precede the novel you are about to read.

Please understand that the following comes nowhere close to doing justice to Arin's story.

— K. N. Brindle

A brief synopsis of

book one of the Paths of Memory duology:

A Memory of Blood and Magic

A hedge witch, called to aid in a breech birth, declared the child would be a *nyssa* (nonbinary) and a witch. Raised as a girl on an isolated farm, Arin was confused by gender expectations and their own emerging powers, even as a young child.

After ten-year-old Arin loses control of their power during a confrontation with powerful neighbors, the family was driven from their home. They fled to a new life, but a gang of brigands led by a criminal named Cal murdered Arin's family and sold Arin into servitude in the city of Anbress in the southern Freelands.

Fearful of worse mistreatment if it became known they are *nyssa*, Arin pretended to be a girl. But instead of abuse and indignity, Arin found a new home and family in the brothel run by the stern but kind matriarch, Ma'am. Arin worked as a housekeeper for two years, until an attack by a drunk patron awakened their magic again.

While recovering from a severe facial laceration received at the hands of the drunk, Arin overheard Ma'am—who had discovered that Arin is a *nyssa*—proposing to trade Arin to someone named Savat.

Before the trade could happen, a heavily scarred *nyssa* called Sem visited the house and demanded to talk to Arin. Refused by Ma'am, Sem returned and attacked the house guard, easily breaking through their defenses. To forestall more violence, Arin agreed to travel with Sem to Reft, a place of refuge for witches.

On the long journey north through the wilds, Sem taught Arin how to control their power by embracing pain. When they reached Reft, Sem left Arin in the care of its citizens, departing back into the wilderness.

In Reft, Arin made friends with young *nyssén* Kari, Migs, and Chan, and received counseling from Turin, a senior *nyssa* and member of the Reft Council.

As Arin adapted to life in Reft, they encountered the young and influential Viscount Tamar Savat of Fall and his servant Eelie, a *nyssa* and former citizen of Reft. Savat visited Reft several times for meetings with the Council, traveling by Eelie's magic.

While Savat seemed genial and friendly to the *nyssén*, Eelie was bitter, resentful, and manipulative, going so far as to attempt to magically coerce Arin into a relationship. Arin was able to rebuff their power.

Over the next few years, in the protective and nurturing society of Reft, Arin came to terms with the deaths of their family, and formed a new found family among their friends. They learned the arts of healing and warfare, and became a respected citizen. Arin, Kari, and a third *nyssa* named Fanti developed an intimate relationship.

Years since their last visit, Savat and Eelie returned to Reft and Arin was asked by the Council to help find a thief who had stolen from Savat. They joined their magic with others to locate him, and in a shocking turn, Arin recognized the thief as Cal.

Triggered by the shock of seeing him after so many years and reeling in a dissociative state, Arin used their power from the pain of their family's deaths to kill Cal. Although they tried to hide what they had done, Arin was eventually accused of the murder by Eelie.

Facing judgment by the Council of Reft for abusing their position and in despair at losing their family again, Arin opened a magical Bridge and left Reft to find their own way in the world.

"Summer's heavy rains;
poems taken down from walls
have left traces"

—Matsuo Bashō,
upon leaving the House of Fallen Persimmons

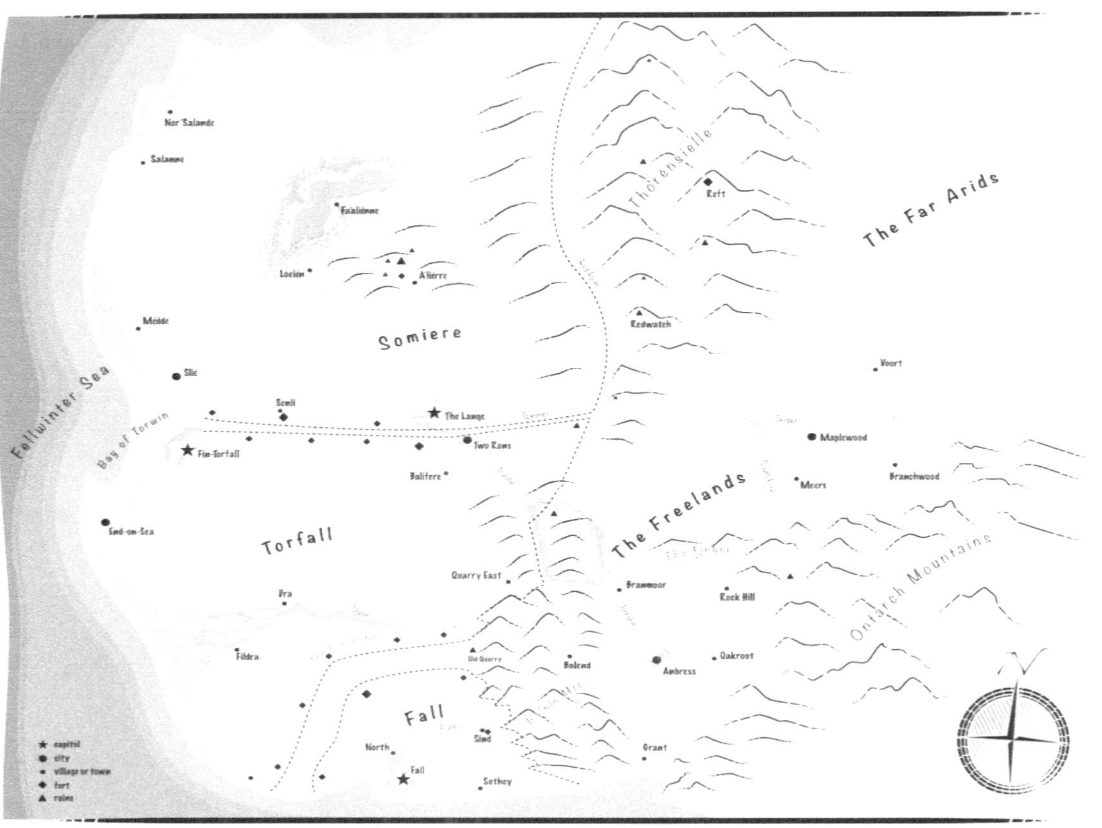

Nor-Salande
Salanne
Falalionne
Locien
Aliorre
Medde
Somiere
Thörensielle
Reft
The Far Arids
Redwatch
Voort
Sliz
Scmli
The Lamge
Two Rows
Maplewood
Meers
Branchwood
Fin-Torfall
Balifere
Bay of Torwin
Fellwinter Sea
End-on-Sea
Torfall
The Freelands
Quarry East
Brammoor
Rock Hill
Ontarch Mountains
Pra
Fildra
Old Quarry
Balend
Ambress
Oakroot
Fall
North
Fall
Simd
Sothey
Grant
capitol
city
village or town
fort
ruins

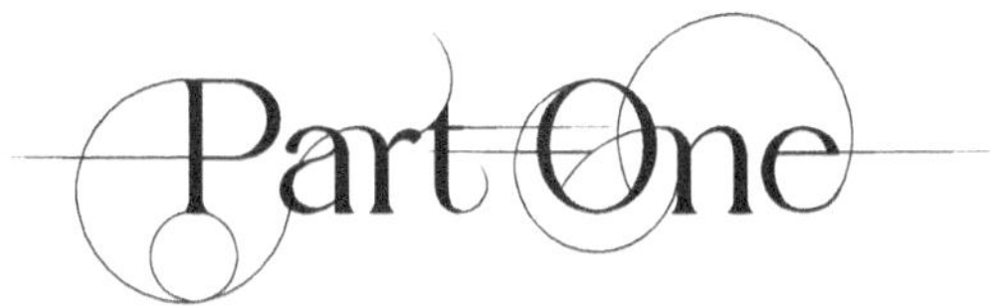

Part One

THERE ARE SOME choices that haunt us long after the decision is set; a stone laid down in a path that leads us inexorably into our future.

We spend our lives haunted by the most difficult choices we can't take back. But a day passes, and we find we can survive another day. Weeks pass and we find we can, after all, live with the dull persistent ache of heartbreak. Months go by and we dwell in the consequences of our choices. Years soften the ache into a discomfort, allowing us to move on, though the ghost of that choice returns ever to torture us.

In Reft, I learned that to draw on another's pain requires great empathy. The closer we come to true compassion, the more readily their pain can feed our power, but at the risk of entangling ourselves irrevocably in their lives. Sometimes, the only possible response to this entanglement is to live at as great a remove as possible.

Distance and solitude was the salve I chose.

A long day's walk east from the Balshin, and three days southeast of Two Runs in the northern foothills of the Balnin mountains, lies the secluded village of Evans Hill. On maps drawn up by the Lords of Torfall, the Torfall border cuts just to the east of the outlying farmsteads, but you're unlikely to meet anyone on either side of that line who believes they owe any fealty to lords of a distant capital. The isolation cuts both ways: no tax collector has been seen there for a handful of generations, and the name isn't even marked on many maps.

Walk due south of Evans Hill for a half-day or so, and you will find yourself in a dense wood that sprawls untouched for leagues, spreading west and south to encroach on the river. The wood's boundaries extend well into the desolate moors of the Freelands to the southeast, and south right up to the banks of the Bresnin, where it joins its larger sister. Intrepid boatmen might follow the smaller branch upriver to reach the Freelands town of Branmoor, or go even further to reach Anbress, where the river breaks into a great tumbling sweep of rapids.

In the local tradition, this forest is haunted. Everyone calls it simply "the wood"—names are for places people travel to or from. It is a place of creeping ivy and dense, low cloisters formed from the interlocking boughs of ancient trees. A place of dark thoughts and tangled imagination. A place of wounded memory and loss.

For the last two years, the specter haunting that wood was mine.

One

No few families in Evans Hill owed the existence of their lineage to Efanne himself, though hardly any know the true history of this place. By all I had read of the storied general of antiquity who had orchestrated the greatest strategic retreat in written history, he would have enjoyed the joke.

To have a place bear his name, and yet still no one remember him... a grand joke indeed.

Moving an army of six-thousand across the uneven wilderness where no roads marked the land and maps were sketched from horseback by outriders no more than a day ahead of the main body of troops was itself an undertaking worthy of renown. Shepherding a population of twenty-thousand through that same wilderness—adults and children seeking freedom from the quicksilver whims of a monarch rapidly descending into madness—should have been enough to cement his legacy.

Ultimately though, what clinched his place in history, as

obscure as it is, was the precisely controlled withdrawal through the Balnin and his final stand here in these forgotten hills. Mentions of his strategic brilliance exist in various texts, and all cite the five long weeks he held back an army thrice the size of his own while his people escaped across the mountains and dispersed into what is now known as the Freelands.

Never mind that he finally fell, on one hill or another—unlikely it was the actual hill the town occupied. He had won because he had succeeded, and the people were free. He had won because the army of the Mad King had been decimated, chipped down into fragments by intricate and deliberate application of strength to weakness.

Eight-hundred-year-old bones of tens of thousands of fallen soldiers nourished the land for miles around. It was fitting that the farmers of Evans Hill survived the stark lonely winters in plenty. It was no wonder the wood was deep and rich and fecund. It was no wonder the locals thought they saw ancient ghosts and spirits walking under its darkened eaves.

Rolling grassy hills vanished off to the horizon, the feathery tops gone blue-gray in the afternoon sun. I leaned on my walking stick and scanned the sky. Clouds hid the ragged tops of the distant mountains to the south, but the southern sky was always shrouded in clouds. The rest of the sky was a deep, clear blue that promised a crisp night and endless stars. A hawk circled over a hayfield some way off.

As I continued my circumambulation, I passed east of the last farmstead before the hills grew rough with scrub and the wood loomed ahead. In the distance, I could see a herd of cattle grazing the grassy hill, and west further still a gentle plume of smoke from a goodwife's hearth.

I had no worries of being seen by the farmer's family. The path I walked was well trod by me over the years, and with each days-long circuit—once each moon—I reinforced the Warding that shed casual eyes and led attention to wander.

The day was waning as I neared the edge of the wood. The tangle of creeper and low foliage that intertwined the lesser trees along the perimeter was as imposing a barrier as the rumors of ghosts. Despite its appearance though, there was a narrow footpath that wound through into the darkness within. It took walking my Warding line to see it.

The nature of a dense forest is deception. Standing at any point beneath the arched canopy, the wood beguiles with imagined paths leading away, just straight and clear enough to hint at an exit, winding just enough that that exit is forever out of sight. Truly though, few of these are paths; the natural rhythm of shadow and light tricks the eye into seeing order in the chaos.

I strode between the trees with the same confidence that the farmers north of me walked their fields. The transition from grass and earth to the thick, damp mat of dead leaves under my bare feet was comforting. This wood was my home.

Deep in the heart of the wood, protected by its own more forceful and more *aware* Warding, was a shambling ruin of stone and moss atop a low hill. The foundations of some watchtower or fort that had burned centuries ago—and had stood for centuries before that—was now a low mound of tumbled stone, overgrown and decrepit. I was confident no one alive remembered it. Only the oldest and most obscure maps I knew of marked it, and those only with a simple sign that meant "ruins." It made a perfect home for the dark and mysterious hedge-witch who roamed the haunted hills.

As the stone mound became visible between the trees, I smiled as always at the dense shrub perched precariously over the shadowed entrance. I had taken it as an omen and a welcome when I had found it, tending and encouraging the fierce roots in their struggle to grapple with the crumbling stonework and survive.

My hedge.

A flutter of wings drew my attention and I paused. A flash of brown and white, and a finch alighted on a branch close to my face. It peered directly at me with one eye and squawked three times. Then it shivered, ruffled its feathers and preened for a moment before a quick hop to a further branch and a panicked burst of flight back into the canopy.

I stood still, watching. My breathing slowed to the pace of the earth and I made myself as still as the stone atop the rise. My cloak of drab homespun wool, caught and snagged with brown leaves and twigs and brush as it was, was ample camouflage for anyone who might have braved the ghosts of this place.

I closed my eyes and reached out with my mind. I drew on the pain that resided ever in my heart, that limitless well of self-inflicted pain born of the devastation I had wrought on those I loved.

This wood was full of life; full of memory. A quick skim of the surface memories of that life showed me the face of the intruder into my domain. Seeing the world through the mind of an animal, even for the briefest moment, is disorienting and vertiginous. For all that the biological structures may resemble ours, there is nothing alike in mind or perception. Seeing through dozens of minds at once... well, I was practiced at it, and still it was a struggle to avoid losing my own perception of self.

I sighed as I let go my brief touch on those alien minds. I continued up the hill to my home.

I stepped down the weathered stone steps under the low lintel. I pushed open the wooden door, rotted and ruinous on the outside, and clean and polished inside. Despite the outward appearance, I had expended considerable efforts to refine my remote home into a comfortable, if austere, space.

I had reworked the interior of the ruins, drawing living stone from the earth beneath me to reinforce the crumbling foundations, dividing the space into four distinct rooms. The door I had made myself with fresh timber, scrubbing the inner surface with sand and oiling it to a smooth luster while encouraging lichen and moss and fungus to occupy the outer surface.

The stone ceiling of my home broke into multiple layers, each placed strategically so that one slab of stone, which from the outside looked to have fallen in rot and ruin, formed a clerestory, letting a soft, dappled light filter through, even in the gloaming.

As I closed the door behind me, I shrugged out of my cloak and hung it on a peg beside the door, leaning my walking stick in the corner, and noting the large pack that already rested there. The satchel of herbs and mushrooms I had gleaned on my encirclement of Evans Hill and surrounding lands, I lifted over my head and began to unpack. I carefully laid each find into appropriate jars or baskets filling a low shelf along the far wall. When the satchel was empty but for a couple of small wrinkled apples, I hung it on the peg beside my cloak. I didn't immediately look at my visitor, but spoke to them with resignation and not a little annoyance in my voice.

"Why are you here, Sem?"

Sem turned from their unselfconscious examination of my home. They looked me up and down, their flat expression revealing nothing of what they thought of me. I regarded them in turn.

The years had changed little in Sem. Their hair had more silver than black now, their face carried more wrinkles, and their body more scars. Their grimy trousers of myriad pleats might well be the same they had worn years ago for all I knew. The cloth looked old and worn enough. They wore a different jacket of the same style, sleeveless and open in a deep V down their chest. They had replaced their sandals, the wooden slabs no longer tied to their feet with strips cut from my old dresses.

But their eyes were the same. Lively and sharp, with a tension that spoke of a deep hidden well of emotion held in reserve, never to be shared.

That I was now taller than them was disorienting. They were like a visitation from a past life. A ghost of my childhood. Haunted woods indeed.

"You didn't come on me by chance," I prompted.

When they spoke, their voice had the same reedy timbre I remembered. Almost fragile. "I nearly didn't come here at all. Your Warding of this place is impressive. I think I tasted the style of Old Jae, no?"

I sighed. "Yes, I stumbled upon Jae, and they taught me their way of Warding. Will you tell me why?"

"No one 'stumbles upon' Jae Anten," Sem said, their face blank. They didn't pursue the issue yet, predictably opening a different front. "When I was scouting your boundary I watched a trio of rough-looking men walk a wide circle—I don't doubt they went dozens of miles out of their way to avoid that little collection of huts and barns on the hill up north. Despite the swords on their hips and their fingers itching to use them, they didn't even seem to realize what they were doing. Do they know what you do for them, this village?"

"They don't have any need to know."

"Then why do it?"

"Because I can. Because they deserve whatever peace they can have. Their children deserve to grow up without fear of brigands and highwaymen."

"And because it gives you a place into which you can disappear?"

I turned away from them. "I suppose it will be dark before you answer my question. I'm afraid you'll have to accept a meager dinner. I was not planning on guests."

Dinner was a cold mash I had left soaking before my Warding walk, flavored with some chopped bits of wrinkled apple, the last of a rind of hard yellow cheese made from sheep milk, and a heel of bread. Split two ways, it was enough, but only just.

The complication was that I only had bowl and mug for one. Sem pulled their travel bowl and a tin cup from their pack. We ate in silence for a long time, washing the meal down with cold water dipped from a stone cistern fed from a nearby spring.

Years of solitude makes one comfortable with silence, even in company. I had asked my question, and I could wait as long as necessary for the answer. Sem had never been talkative, but I had confidence that I could outlast them.

"Why did you leave Reft?" they asked, finally breaking the silence.

I closed my eyes, feeling the pain of loss roiling in my heart anew. There was an easy answer that I knew would not satisfy them. There was a more difficult answer that I knew I couldn't articulate. There was no answer at all, and no language existed to even frame the thoughts.

"You know what I did," I said quietly.

Sem grunted. "You think you're the first to lash out in rage and violence at someone who caused such pain? You don't think those in Reft would have forgiven you?"

I shook my head. How could I explain? That I feared that response in myself. That I had within me the same violent and selfish potential that Eelie had.

"Everyone who knew Eelie saw in them the rot that chewed away at their being. The void that swirled where their moral center should be. Those same people were ready to forgive me." I shook my head. "Is it up to me to take a life? To kill in retribution for violence I suffered? I knew it was wrong, knew it was hate and malice and rage, and I did it anyway. If I let them forgive me, if I allowed them to let me back into their society carrying that within me... Then *I* become the rot eating away at the center of Reft."

Sem sighed. "So, what then? You disappear into the wilds? Take everything good that you learned, every good thing that you've become and... take it out of the world? How does that serve anyone?"

I shrugged. "I serve Evans Hill well enough. The families go unmolested by robbers. Babes are born hale and with little pain. Sickness rarely troubles them. When the seasonal peddlers come they forget their plans to cheat the poor farmers."

"You sit here like a spider in your web, playing games with your little pets."

I flinched back as if slapped.

"What do you think will happen to your precious village in fifty years or so when you begin to be too old to walk your perimeter; when you begin to wither and death stalks you? Or when your isolation drives you as mad as Old Honfry and your mind turns childlike and mercurial?"

I turned away, but they continued, pressing their point. "Do you think they'll thank you on that day when sickness returns and they have forgotten their own herbalism? When brigands discover that a town exists where they never thought to look, and the villagers have forgotten how to protect themselves?"

"What would you have me do?" I whispered.

"Rejoin the world. Go back to Reft. Or if that's too much civilization and luxury—if you need hardship, doubtful comforts, and miserable weather to help you flog your guilty conscience, you can come with me. There are people—children—out there who really *do* need your help." Their gaze went absent for a moment, and their voice vague. "There's something brewing out in the world, and I don't like the stench of it."

I stood from the table and moved to take the satchel and my cloak from the peg and stick from the corner, pulling the door open. I stepped out into the darkening forest. The last light of the evening filtered through the dense canopy, making a mosaic of greens, browns, and yellows on the littered ground.

The smell of the forest was rich and evocative. Loam and leaf mold and green life. Some small animal scratched through the brush somewhere in the distance and birds called to each other from the branches above. I held my breath for a few moments and could just hear the gurgle of the spring.

I moved to the crumbling stone outcrop beside the door and sat. Sem came out beside me, taking in the shadows and scents of the living forest. For a time we simply breathed it in.

"When you Reshaped your body," they asked, "why didn't you remove the scar?"

Leave it to Sem to ask an intrusive question, apropos of nothing.

"Why have you never done a Reshaping for yourself?" I asked. How to explain that the scar on my face was part of me in a way that mere breasts had never been? I'd lived with it so long that I would hardly know the feel of my own face without it—the slight tension on my cheek when I smiled; the rippled texture I felt against my teeth when I moved my jaw. It was a constant physical reminder that I was myself.

Sem looked deeply into the distant labyrinth of trees for several moments, silent.

"There is a well of pain I have never felt the need to tap," they said finally. "It is a... comfort... to know it's there."

My eyes widened. I was not expecting an answer. The Sem I had known years ago would not have answered such an intimate question so bluntly put. It seemed we had both changed in the time since last we traveled together.

As if they could read my thoughts, they pressed. "Whatever you were when I found you in that brothel, you became something more in Reft. Not something *else*; something *more*. Deny it all you like. Hide it in the ends of the earth or bury it in this grave in the middle of your haunted forest. The seeds of that violence you survived as a child are in you and always will be. In Reft, you learned to tend those seeds and grow something nourishing from them."

They turned to look to the north. "Now you've come here and taken your skills and power—power that could change the world—and you've used it to make... an ornamental garden. Some pretty little stand of flowers for the birds to play in. It's lovely. Never mind that outside the boundaries of your little paradise the ground is littered with corpses you might have fed."

They shook their head. "I expected more from you, Arin."

I was shocked and hurt at the anger in their voice. I stood up. "Who are you to come here and tell me that I'm running away from who I am; that I owe anyone anything? Why are you not still training the Watch? Why are *you* not still living in Reft?

Maybe if you had been there—if you had stayed with me instead of handing me off like a sack of beans—" I turned away from them, unwilling to finish the thought aloud. "Stay the night, if you like. You can take the bed—I don't sleep much these days." I settled the cloak over my shoulders, and strode out into the forest twilight.

Between my bare feet and the soft, damp leaf litter soil of the forest, I was silent as a ghost as I walked through the descending darkness. Cicadas and crickets began their evening music. The frenzied buzzing and cheerful chirps filled the night air. Before long I reached a wide glade where the canopy opened out into an irregular perimeter revealing the darkening sky.

Near the edge, a pair of mules were grazing, leather hobbles preventing them from wandering far. I smiled at seeing the sorrel and clucked twice, the signal she had been trained to. Beatrice lifted her head and shuffled closer. I pulled the apples from my satchel and held one out to her. She took it from my hand with a dextrous curl of lip. I rubbed her forehead and scratched her cheek.

"Hey there old friend," I said softly.

Not to be left out, the gray mulled over and nudged my shoulder. Sem had never named the animal that I knew. The other apple disappeared just as readily from my hand. After a few moments of hopeful prodding, they both dismissed me and began their grazing again.

I stroked both mules' flanks and murmured nonsense to them as I scanned the sky. Darkness was settling heavy over the forest and the stars were coming out in the clear night. I let myself go still for a long while, letting the sounds and smells of the wood wash over and through me.

Sem's words churned in my gut. Of course, I could not deny

the truth of them. I had run away from the world, and we both knew it. I was hiding—hiding myself; hiding from myself.

But... a spider in a web? Was what I had done so despicable? I had spoken the truth: My Wardings kept the village and local families safe. On my occasional trips into town for supplies I listened for news of illnesses and upcoming births and saw to both where I could to ensure good health throughout Evans Hill. My monthly walks on the Warding line meant that some of its power clung to me—I was rarely remembered within its circle, even by those who spoke to me.

I moved through the wood like a shade, still lost in my thoughts. I paused here and there to examine a troop of mushrooms or a sprig of herbs. Some of these went into my satchel, others I left to mature longer before picking.

A glistening silvery trail of slime caught my eye, sparkling in the dappled moonlight that filtered through the trees. I stopped to watch a snail skate its way slowly across a flat stone as large as my leg.

The problem—the deep flaw in what I was doing here that Sem had seen immediately—was clear and simple now that they had spoken it. I had taken on the lives of Evans Hill, taken responsibility for them, and I had done it without their consent. I had diminished the choices of an entire village without consulting them, taking their very ability to choose out of their hands. And they didn't even know it.

I sighed to myself, continuing on my evening ramble. A vixen cried somewhere to the south. Its howls were eerily human, sounding like a woman screaming for her life.

Of course, had they known—had I offered, certainly they would have refused. Refused and likely chased me out with violence despite the cost to themselves. It was not only in Meers that the name "witch" was an epithet.

My wanderings led me down a hill into a crowded dell, where the trees were thinner, but the forest floor more varied. The soil here was rockier and the leaves lay sparsely on the ground. A low fog clung to the earth and swallowed the sounds of the wood. Shadows lurked around me as I moved through it, resolving into low stone plinths that marked ancient barrows.

I could feel the age of this place, a weight that hung heavily on my shoulders. If there was any kernel of truth to the legends of hauntings in this wood, certainly these graves were it. I had spent days examining the markers when I first came here, trying to determine their history. They bore the remnants of engravings, but so little had survived the centuries of erosion that even the nature of those marks was lost. Were they names? Dates? Prayers? Chan might know.

I remembered my tall, willowy friend who was so enamored of language that they learned even the long-dead precursors to what we thought of today as Freelander and Somiri. Thinking of them inevitably took my thoughts to Migs, to Kari and Fanti, and all the others I had left behind in Reft without any word or gesture of goodbye.

I sat down on a broad stone beside one of the markers. More than a thousand years ago, it might have been a bench placed near a loved one's burial mound so that family could sit as they visited their departed kin. It was half buried and spiderwebbed with cracks—now occupied by weeds and moss.

The fox cried again, and in the chill it was easy to imagine this place teeming with ghosts. Someone had built these barrows, mounding stone and earth to make monuments to the dead. Perhaps some of these graves held those very someones, their own tombs raised by yet more hands, testament to their respect and visions of some future that may or may not have ever been found.

I peered around the dell, my eyes finding dozens of markers in the mist. Each one held a life, a story. But whatever their stories, they had been lost to the inexorable tread of time. Not for the last time, I wondered what it said of me that I found immense comfort in this place. That it existed at all, that those long-ago people had found some kind of peace in an orderly interment of their dead.

I knew the motivation that had driven me to settle here, to take on the village of Evans Hill and shepherd its people in their lives. The need to feel a part of something, even if it was illusory. I could pretend I knew the people of the village and was involved in their lives, and at the same time not risk actually living in their society.

I leaned back and rested my head against the marker. In reality, this was my society. The long-dead, who could neither speak nor feel nor reject me. I closed my eyes and felt the fog close around me like an embrace.

Two

The next morning, I returned to my home to find Sem gone, either earlier than the sun which was only just lightening the sky, or the previous night after I had walked off into the wood. The only sign they had been there was a scrap of paper on the table, weighed down by a handful of silver pennies. I moved the stack of coins and lifted the paper to read the words penned in a surprisingly elegant hand: "Walking west. Took some food." Nothing more.

I sighed aloud and shook my head. A quick scan of my larder showed me that Sem had taken enough that I now needed a trip into Evans Hill if I was to eat tonight. I pocketed the coins and strode back into the wood, grabbing my walking stick as I passed the door. I hadn't even shed my cloak or dropped my bag yet.

If I left now, I could reach the village by just after mid-day, walking fast. Under the arched boughs of the trees I pushed hard, moving as quickly as I could. When I broke out of the wood into the rolling hills the sun was only a hand or so above the eastern horizon, the hills taking on an orange glow over the tops of grasses waving in the morning breeze.

My route curved easterly to avoid the bulk of the Borwith farm, the southernmost of the outlying farmsteads. By now, they would be out in the fields and I had no wish to test my Warding this far from the center and off the line itself. Further into the center of the circle, the power was strong enough to shield me from close observation. Near the edge... I wasn't so sure.

As the sun rose steadily, the day warmed and burned off the morning dew and my bare feet became caked in dust. Despite the rising heat, I kept the hood of my cloak up, shadowing my face and making me even more anonymous to any passerby.

The village of Evans Hill was spread out in a semi-circle at the base of the rolling rise that was the source of its name. The road was an unpaved dirt path, and the houses were a mixture of river stone foundations and timber, much like the buildings I remembered from my childhood. The roofs were red clay tile instead of thatch, but otherwise any house here might have been the one I grew up in.

There was no grocer or chandler in Evans Hill, and it was days yet before the harvest market—a small affair that spread out on the common green for villagers and farmers to trade their goods. But there was a public house where villagers could share pints of ale after the day's hard work. The owner kept a room to let to traveling peddlers, and not knowing when they would come, kept a larder stocked with enough food to offer.

I walked around to the kitchen door—under a lean-to shed attached to the rear wall of the house—and knocked three times. And waited.

Some minutes passed before I heard steps and the door

opened. The owner's wife and cook for the house stood within, one hand holding a large wooden spoon, the other clutching a towel and planted firmly on hip. Pinala was short and plump, brown hair going gray at the temples and plaited in a long braid over her shoulder. She tried to see me, her face going vague and perplexed as her stare warred between the shadow under my cowl and the dusty path behind me.

This confusion was one effect of the Warding line I walked. Even those who saw me didn't see me.

"Excuse me for interrupting. May I bother you for some onions, lentils, and grain?" I held out three of the silver pennies that Sem had left me, more than enough for what I asked.

At my voice, she seemed to startle and her eyes went to the glint of coin in my palm. There, they could focus, and she gave herself a little shake.

"Oh, aye. Come in, come in. Sun's getting powerful hot these days, no sense you standing out in the heat, 'specially you in that old cloak..." she seemed to hunt for a name, something familiar to hang on the idea of me in her mind that she couldn't quite pin down.

"Marga," I said. "Don't you know your old Marga?"

Pinala shook her head and smiled ruefully, "Of course I know you, Marga! Why-ever would you think I could forget you! Just the afternoon heat an' the hearth fire... made me loopy for a breath. Onions and lentils and grain, is it? Let me get you some sacks." She scooped the coins from my hand as she turned, tucking them safely into her apron pocket.

I stepped into the small kitchen as she bustled around, filling a small sack with onions from a basket in the corner, then hunting around on a shelf for another for dried red lentils that filled a large clay urn.

As I waited, I could hear voices from the public room

through the door. Pinala's husband Forth seemed to be arguing something with another man. There was little enough I could make out, especially with her shifting pots and stacks of plates here and there, and the fire crackling beside me.

She spoke absently as she worked, "Don't mind ol' Forth, he's just all of a lather with the peddler." She shook her head. "Coming in here talking talk of war and battles and Dukes! As if wars was a thing we had any care of here in Evans Hill. I mean! Can you imagine? Dukes and lances and swords—ha! Swords! Have you ever heard such nonsense?"

I stepped closer to the open door so that I could hear more of her husband's talk and less of Pinala's.

"...won't be reaching you, I'm sure. Not here out in the nowheres as you are. But mind: Anywhere west, an' prices are getting higher and the roads less and less safe. You watch an' I'll tell you, this goes on any longer and this time next year won't be any peddlers making the trek this far out. Won't be no profit in it for us. I'll give you a good price for those last casks of that liquor you make from buckwheat down here. Ain't no-one else going to give you better. It's harsh stuff and not suitable for drinking anywhere but here...but I'm thinking maybe it'll do for some thirsty soldiers..."

"Aye, talk talk talk is all those men do," Pinala said next to me. I turned and she pressed a basket into my hands: onions, lentils, and a sack of buckwheat just as I asked. There was also a small sweet loaf tucked in. "For the road," she said kindly. "Now, you get on back home to..." her face took on another look of confusion, and I knew it was time for me to go. The power of the Warding line clung to me, but if she fixed me in her mind, she might not let the memory go. I thanked her and took my leave of the cramped, hot kitchen.

I walked back behind the line of houses, not looking to meet anyone else before I could make the road. But as I turned past the edge of the second-to-last house, I saw a small, dirty face peek out from behind the corner.

I knelt down in the dusty path and pulled my hood back a bit. I guessed the child was no older than five but was small even at that, and was dressed in a ragged homespun dress that had not seen a wash in days, perhaps longer. Matted and tangled curly brown hair framed a narrow face that showed dried streaks of tears through dirt and dust that no parent would have stood for. From the urchin's thin, boney shoulders and sunken eyes, it seemed that food had been in as short supply as washing for the last several days.

"What's your name, little mushroom?" I asked quietly, my voice light and full of humor that I did not feel.

"I'm not a mushroom, I'm a little girl," she said, indignant and proud. "I'm Deala. You're Marga—I heard Pinna say your name."

"You're Andia's little one, aren't you?" I asked. "Deala, you live down southwest by the Hasser farm, right? That's miles off. What brings you to town and peeking between the houses?"

She looked down, hands and feet fidgeting. With her face down to the ground, I couldn't see the tears flowing anew, but I could hear them in her voice. "I'm sorry. I don' wanna bother you. But momma's sick, an' no one can help."

I held out my hand to the child. "Let's see about that."

As we walked, I tore a hunk off the end of the loaf for the girl, who took it shyly and began gnawing on it. We crossed the green and set off southwest. For the most part, I followed

Deala's lead. As well as I could reckon, we were heading in the right direction, but I didn't know our destination well. I passed by the orchards on my monthly encirclement but had never had any need to come close, and never through the village.

From what I had gathered from overheard town gossip, Andia and Deala lived alone in the small cottage by an apple orchard—Deala's father had died some time before I arrived in Evans Hill. They tended the apple trees and brought in their meager harvest to sell on market days, but otherwise kept to themselves.

It wasn't long before Deala's steps began to flag, and not wanting to push her past exhaustion, I stopped and picked her up, balancing her weight on my hip. She curled against my body and wrapped her arms around my neck, laying her head on my shoulder. The sudden intimacy was discomfiting to me, who had never held a child before, aside from the handful of births I had aided.

As I carried her along the rough path that cut across the rolling land, a memory of my mother's voice came to me unbidden, crooning a meandering melody. I found myself humming the tune absently, almost more of an intoned breath in my chest than voiced singing. Deala hugged me tighter.

At the pace I set, it was only half an hour or so before I could see the orchard in the distance, and soon we were among the trees. There were signs I noted immediately. Fruit fallen on the ground and uncollected, crawling with ants. A cluster of baskets by the trunk of a tree, not only empty, but with the beginnings of weeds growing through them. A sense of dread crept up my spine, and I spoke to the child with some trepidation.

"How long has your momma been sick, Deala?"

I felt her whole body shrug in response, and she buried her face further in my shoulder.

I set her down on her feet beside the baskets and rooted through the stack, finding one that looked intact. I handed the basket to the girl and gave her a little pat. "Here. Gather as many of the fallen apples as you can that are still good while I go see to your mother."

I watched her for a moment, then turned to the house. It was a snug little cottage, reminding me much of the little one-room house I had grown up in. The boards were whitewashed, neat and trim, though there were signs of neglect in the thatch. As I reached the door, I placed a hand against the latch and paused, worried at what I might find within.

A soft moan came from inside, and I released a breath I hadn't realized I was holding. A worry left my shoulders. I would at least not need to tell the child that her mother was already dead. I pushed the door open and entered.

As I expected, the interior was a single room, though what should have been cozy and homey was close and unpleasant. The two windows were shuttered, leaving the air stifling and the room in a deep twilight.

Andia was curled up in the one bed tangled in sweat-stained blankets and her face crumpled in pain. I set my basket and satchel down and moved about opening both windows to let in light and catch the slight breeze, and came to sit beside her on the bed.

Sweat beaded on her brow and her face was flushed and hot. Her lips were dry and cracked. I worried about dehydration, but before letting her drink I wanted to find out what had brought her to this. A sour smell came from the chamber pot—old vomit. It wasn't enough to cover the rich scent of blood. I gently pulled back the blankets and uncovered her body. Her thighs and the blanket wound around her was stained with black dried blood and fresh red.

Her response to my every touch was to curl more tightly around her abdomen, clearly the source of her pain. I began to suspect the nature of her illness.

In Birth Magic, one draws on the pain of the patient. It is a profound well of power, and that makes the work relatively easy, if one can open oneself to it. For me, it is easy enough to find the empathy required. It would take very little to have gone a different way in my life to find myself here where she lay. Had I been slower at knowing my own mind, or better at keeping it to myself, I might have grown up in my parents' house and eventually wed. Had I been a little older when Cal took me, I might have been inducted into a different kind of service in Ma'am's house or some other, with similar consequences.

I placed my hands on her, shrugging off Andia's weakened attempts to fend me off. I drew in her pain and spun it into threads to find its source, scanning her body with power that was somehow both eyes and fingers. Through these ethereal senses, I could see the problem immediately.

She was pregnant. But it had gone wrong in the way that such things sometimes did. The mass of almost-life was there, growing fast, becoming something more than a collection of undifferentiated tissue. But it was in the wrong place. Instead of implanting in her womb it had begun to grow in the passage to it. Such a thing was known to the healers of Reft, and easily resolved by them if caught early.

But this was not early. The growth had caused enough damage already to her mother's body that Deala was now unlikely to ever have this sibling or any other, and may still lose her mother in the bargain. I didn't have the skills or knowledge of Atua and the healers, and I knew I probably couldn't save the pregnancy.

Whether I could save Deala's mother was the question at hand. From the state of her heart, I could see there were only moments left to act.

Still, I agonized over the decision. I knew Andia was not conscious enough to make the choice, and she had little time left. Here and now, in this circumstance, I was at a crossroads where I had to choose for her. A small part of my mind took a grim satisfaction at my predicament. I had taken on responsibility for the whole village without their consent. And now the hard consequences had become real.

In the end, it was the thought of Deala outside, needing and expecting her mother to come back to her that decided me.

It took very little of the power I could draw from her to separate the bundle of tissue and urge the ruptures in her body to close. There would be scarring within. Likely enough to prevent any future pregnancies from taking root, for good or ill.

Blood flowed from her womb, and as her insides continued to knit I moved on to the damage and infection impacting nearby organs. I could sense her heartbeat steadying and calming. I stayed beside her long enough to be sure that she was stabilized, then stood and moved to the door, taking up the washing tub and the soiled chamber pot.

A brief look down at my own clothes showed me that I had not escaped my work unstained. I didn't want Deala to see me covered with her mother's blood. I remembered my horror at seeing my own mother's crumpled body and drew on that pain, turning the dark red stains gray to match my tunic for a time.

As I emerged from the house, I could see Deala standing some ways off, gripping the basket with both hands and on the verge of tears. I gestured her to come to me. She abandoned the basket and came at a run. I knelt down and held out my hands to catch her before she could touch my clothes. Though hidden, her mother's blood was still wet upon me.

"Your mother is going to be okay, little one. She needs plenty of rest now, and lots to drink. Where is your well?"

Deala led me along a narrow path behind the house to a low stone ring. Along the way, I tipped out the noisome mess of the chamber pot. At the wellhead I dropped the bucket down on its line and hauled it up, once, twice, and thrice. With the washing tub half full, I dropped the bucket twice more to sluice out the chamber pot and then carried them back to the house. At the door, I admonished the girl to stay close, but remain outside for now.

"I'll call you in when your mother is well enough to see you."

That she obeyed was, I think, more a testament to her desperation and exhaustion than to my persuasion.

Back inside, I checked Andia's heartbeat and breathing again, and having satisfied myself that she remained stable, I moved to start a fire in the small hearth. I dipped the kettle full of water from the washtub and hung it over the flames, then set to work stripping the blankets and her clothes, using them to wipe blood from her body as best I could. These went to soak in the washtub while I found a fresh dressing gown on a peg and got Andia into it.

A quick scan of the room showed that I had cleaned enough of the evidence of her mother's trauma that it was safe for Deala to enter. The child entered slowly, trepidation showing in her features. When her mother sighed and shifted, with no sign of the previous pain and illness, Deala ran to the bed and made to climb in.

"Wait little mushroom. Let's clean you up first. What would your mother say about tracking such dirt into the blankets?"

Deala silently suffered me to strip off her filthy clothes and drop them in the washtub. With the corner of an apron dipped into the kettle of warming water, I wiped the worst of the grime from her face, hair, hands, and feet. Finally, she was willing to wait no longer, and slipped away from me and up into the bed beside her mother.

I spent the next hour setting a stew of lentils and buckwheat to bubble over the fire—both of them would need food, and lots of it—and scrubbing the blood-soiled clothes. After some time, I looked up to find Deala asleep, and Andia staring at me. She worked her lips, trying to speak for a few moments before finally finding enough moisture for her throat and lips.

"I don't know you." There was suspicion and a hint of fear in her voice. So much for my Wardings. I had lingered here too long by far to hide in their shadow.

"I'm Marga. Deala brought me to you," I said, making my voice light. "I was in the village for some trading." I tried an easy diversion. "She thought I might be able to help. As it happens, I know something of herbs—"

"No herbs could have helped me," Andia interrupted. "I know what..." Her eyes darted to my scar, down to my bare arms and the crosshatching of fine scars there. She looked away from me and wouldn't meet my eyes. "There's no herbs could have helped."

I moved to stand, and saw her reflexively draw back in fear and loathing at what she guessed I was, pulling Deala's still-sleeping form protectively away from me.

So be it.

I nodded. "I'll leave you now. Take care standing at first, and eat as much as you can bear. Your body needs the nutrition."

Without looking back at her, I picked up my satchel and the remains of the food I had bought, and walked out into the dwindling light.

On reaching home, I absentmindedly put the food away. Onions, buckwheat, lentils—barely half what I had bought from Pinala—some more wrinkled apples I had picked up leaving the orchard, and a handful of mushrooms I'd foraged on my walk back through the wood.

I was exhausted and disheartened by the day's work. I shed my clothes, sticky now with Andia's dried blood, and left them to soak in a wooden tub.

A quarter-hour walk from my home of crumbling stone was a deep pool accumulating in a cleft of rock as it tumbled down a steep gully. It was formed by the waters of the same spring that fed my cistern.

The whole wood was my personal world. I walked naked and barefoot down to my bathing pool. I could tell from the evening sounds of the wood that I was alone under that living canopy. The crisp air against my skin felt good; bracing.

As I reached the gully and stepped into the frigid water, I felt it traverse my skin like a line of fire burning my nerves from toes to ankles to calves to thighs. I was heedless of my own pain even as the icy waters of the earth took my breath. When it reached over my hips and touched my abdomen, I shuddered with it—so cold that it felt like searing heat. I forced myself to duck the rest of the way under the surface, traversing for a moment from the world of sunlight and living wood to a world of ice and stillness and death.

From a fold of rippled stone along the edge of the pool I scooped a handful of fine white sand, the remnants of quartz pummeled by eons of the tumbling stream. I scrubbed my skin with it, something enough like soap to clean my body, rubbing some color back into my cold-grayed skin.

There was only so long I could stand the frigid bath before my body began to rebel, my muscles losing control and my teeth rattling. I ducked my head once more and scrubbed my scalp under the water before climbing out, shivering on the wet rocks.

I dried as I walked back to my home under the moonlight, warming enough that the shakes had stopped by the time I pushed the wooden door open and stepped inside. I didn't even bother to eat. I was tired beyond any meaningful measure. I rolled myself in my blankets, exhausted.

And I dreamed.

It began in violence—a raging tumult of sound and light and fear. War. There was clashing and burning and screams of the dying, and in the center of it all, I walked.

I moved barefoot through the din, my mind turning from one scene of pain to another, trying to pick any detail from the morass of agony around me. The ground was churned to a welter of mud and blood and white-foamed water that thrashed at my feet in waves and swells—somehow I stood at a sea shore, though armies flailed around me.

Now and then as I walked I caught a glimpse of the distant horizon through breaks in the melee. It was a startling sunset of orange and yellow, glowing like embers in the sky and fading to a darkness above streaked with luminous purples and blues. That sky caught my eyes and though I did not falter, I spared no thought to my footing. I was lost in the infinity of colors, and the pandemonium around me faded to silence.

When I brought my eyes back from the horizon, I felt small and vulnerable in that silence. The battle around me had diminished to nothing, and all I could see or hear or feel was the swells of the waves at my feet. They throbbed like a heartbeat, slowing and calming until they too were nearly still, only echoing distantly from the far shore. The light of the sunset dimmed and the sky above me settled into a deep oppressive darkness. It had weight. It pressed down on my shoulders like a reminder that I had more to do than simply bear witness to this end.

As the light faded, there was no sign of the great fray that had thrashed around me. I knew the ground should have been piled with the bodies of the slain, but there was nothing, not even bones. The mud I had trod was choked and smothered in the endless remains of all that I knew—it was a fine dust that had settled so thick upon the land that nothing could ever grow again.

Darkness settled into a night so absolute that there was no longer any sight. My senses strained for something to orient to, but there were no stars, no flicker of moon, and neither smell nor touch. The distant forlorn sounds of the sea faded into a final silence and my senses were utterly bereft.

All I knew then was a vague memory of the taste of ashes.

I woke with a gasp of breath and an unshakable disquiet. I rarely remembered my dreams so well as I did that one, and the vast emptiness filled me with a dread and heartache that I could not name. I sat up in my blankets and held my head in my hands. A deep, weary pain had settled there, just behind my eyes.

I shouldn't have been shocked at Andia's reaction. I knew when I settled here that the people of Evans Hill were unlikely to ever welcome me, a witch, into their society.

But it still hurt.

And if I hadn't been here, if I hadn't been keeping watch over the village, Andia would have died and Deala might have starved to death for all I knew. Hadn't my presence changed that fate?

In my mind, I heard the counterargument Sem would have made: It was only luck that I was in town to spot Deala yesterday. Had Sem not visited and taken my food, had I not needed to buy from Pinala...

But I *had* kept watch, and I *was* there to save her. No one else had come. There had been no whispers for me to catch of her illness or even gossip of who she had slept with to become pregnant. None of her neighbors had known anything was wrong. None of them had visited to check on her.

My stomach churned in a cold lump of worry. No one had known she was ill. No one had checked on her. Yes, such illnesses did come on suddenly, but there had been time for Deala to wander clear across from the orchard to the center of the village, and no one had had the curiosity to ask why she was alone?

Isolated villages like Evans Hill were insular and interconnected. Everyone knew everyone else's business. Someone *should* have noticed.

Again, my mind supplied Sem's dry response. Yes, villagers kept track of each other and checked in on one another's health and doings... because they had to. They were insular and interconnected because they *had to be to survive.* That was how a village like Evans Hill's natural defenses *functioned.*

And over the last two years, I had undermined that interlocking system of mutual support, usurping the very fabric of community that they depended on for survival, like a disease that first diminishes the body's defense. What had happened to Andia and Deala may well be only the first cracks. But small cracks were often the first sign of a crumbling foundation.

Of course Sem had been right. I buried my face in my hands and sighed. Years of absence from my life, and now they returned and were still teaching me new lessons.

I threw my head back and screamed in frustration, letting my vexation and discouragement radiate out through the stone and wood around me. I held nothing back. When I was spent,

I sat with my frustration, letting it roil under my skin and dissipate until my breathing returned to normal.

I could let my Warding around the village fade. If I stopped walking the line, its power would last for some time longer, growing gradually weaker. It would be perhaps half a year before all traces were gone. Would the people be able to rebuild their sense of community?

Waiting longer wouldn't help them recover from what I had done any sooner or more easily.

First one, then two.

I rose and dressed, not really planning. I was curious to see what I would do next.

What I did was to move to the table in my main room and pick up the scrap of paper that Sem had left. I stared at the few words there for some minutes. *Walking west.*

Well. West was a short word for a very large idea. When I was a child, Father used to thrill us with stories of exotic adventures that involved *west*. But where west? Two Runs? The Lange? Somewhere farther in Somiere or Torfall? What was I meant to do with "west"?

Sem would not have left me word without knowing that I could make some use of it. From their words, clearly I was meant to follow. I could wander a lifetime looking for them as they moved.

My eyes drifted to the doorway where Sem had stood when I had come home. The simple arch led to a small storeroom. Just inside and leaning against the wall was the short wooden sword that Sem had carved from a length of firewood all those years ago. One of the handful of items that I treasured.

It was not where I normally kept it.

A challenge? I moved to take up the sword. I had not held it since tucking it away in a wooden chest in the corner. An object like this, imbued with meaning and emotion by the two of us, could easily anchor a Finding.

I had not done a Finding since *that* night. The night I killed Cal. A part of my mind rebelled at the idea, but I pushed those thoughts roughly aside, my frustrations with myself bubbling up once more.

I held the sword before me and drew on my deep well of pain, adding in the shame and self-blame I felt at what I had done in Evans Hill for spice. The power raged within me and I let it swirl, struggling to find my center, to find a calm and steady place in my mind.

It took far longer than it should have. I should have waited—only started once I had reached a state of calm—but having decided, I was impatient to act. I held the power back as I breathed, slowing my mind, slowing my heartbeat, slowing my breath until I could start to feel the texture of the wood beneath my fingers.

I let my mind wander. The days of my journey north with Sem. The sense of wonder I had felt for the first time exploring the wider world. Sem's daily carving on mule-back using the small hatchet. The day they had set the challenge for me to take the sword. First one. Then two. The pain and struggle for days and days as I tried to reach it. The thrill of pride and victory when I finally did, Sem lying on their back laughing at their broken sandals.

As I felt my consciousness slip into that moment, lost in memory, I felt the emotions of that moment fill me. The lines between now and then blurred in my being and I was *there*.

I grasped the power and directed it into that memory of Sem, their head thrown back in laughter. An awareness flared to life in my mind, and I could feel them far to the northwest among the lonely hilly scrublands that stretched between

Evans Hill and the rest of the world.

They were well ahead of me and I could chase them now, knowing exactly where they were. But I could also guess where they were headed. The first town of any size in the direction Sem travelled was Two Runs. As much as Sem wished to avoid large population centers, the food they had taken from me would not last long. They would have to stop there.

And Two Runs lay at the confluence of the Sommíre and the Balshin, whose waters passed the western boundary of my wood. I could reach the river in only a few hours' walk.

I had little to pack beyond food and clothes. I still intended to return to this place. Even if I was leaving the Warding to dissipate, this wood was still my home. I would not forget that while someone was more likely to have checked on her had I not imposed my protection on the village, Andia likely still would have died without me. Despite everything else in the balance, I *had* saved a life.

With my walking stick in hand, my satchel, and my cloak, I left my home of stone and moss. I ambled in a circle around the ruins three times, laying a strong Warding that I was sure would turn any eye away for a long time to come. I held the wooden sword as I paced, centering the Warding upon its weight and carefully crafted form. On my third pass, I returned to the door and thrust the sword point-down deep into the loose soil just outside the stone threshold. It would hold the Warding until the wood rotted.

Satisfied that I had done what I could, I set out due west through the wood.

I made good time under the canopy. I breakfasted on an apple and some foraged berries as I walked, and well before midday, I could hear the rippling of the Balshin. I emerged from the dense wood along its banks and sat for a few moments. I let my feet trail in the cool water as I eyed the trees along the riverbank.

A chestnut tree a few dozen paces away had a broad, thick trunk. Some decades-old damage or sickness had left it with a deep cleft along its length. It was leaning precariously over the bank. I could see that it was unlikely to last another decade—erosion of the riverbank would bring it down into the water in a handful of years. It looked just about right for my travel downstream.

I was by no means a master of woodworking, but my brief time assisting the carpenters in Reft had taught me enough for this. Drawing deeply on my power, I widened and lengthened the fold in the trunk and tapered the trunk on either end. The chestnut shed its canopy and separated itself from its roots but for a single wrist-thick tendril which bent as the weight of the remaining wood lowered the bole into the water.

A siphon of power into the surface and the bark withered and slipped away into the rushing water. The wood smoothed and hardened, and the lines sharpened along the length of the hull. I tossed my walking stick and satchel into the boat.

I placed my hand on one of the fallen branches, shaping it into a paddle beneath my hand. A short hop from the bank into what was now a narrow boat, and I released the final limb tying it to its root system. The river currents took me and soon the woods were flowing past on either side.

Off to my right, I could sense Sem somewhere beyond the rolling hills. They were stopped again for the night and were making time far more slowly than my flight downriver. I was already nearly halfway to Two Runs, and by morning, I would be in sight of the town.

I'd spent some time on the water experimenting with the shape of my little boat, and now it was stable enough in the current that I felt reasonably safe to let the river carry me unguided. This part of the Balshin was deep and the current kept me towards the center. It rushed me down to its joining with the Sommíre.

I was able to make a small Warding around me and the boat to assure I stayed centered and upright. It was very weak, as I couldn't pace the circle myself, but I was hopeful it would be enough. I curled up in my cloak to sleep through the night. Between the stars overhead and the soft shushing and slapping sounds of the river reverberating on the hull, sleep came easy to me.

If I dreamt, I do not remember it. I woke with the first rays of sun on my face, and I rose in my little boat to find the low roofs of Two Runs in the distance. I put paddle to water and soon was grounding the bow on the sandy bank. I splashed through the shallows and hauled my boat out onto the bank.

I stretched my back and took my bearings. The town was an easy hour's walk further downriver. Sem was still a day or more off to the southeast. They hadn't yet started off from their camp.

After pulling the boat further up onto the high bank, I rolled it over to sit on and took stock. Between my satchel and pockets in my trousers and the lining of my cloak, I had most of the contents of my pantry, my bowl, spoon, and cup, one silver penny, a change of clothes, and my folding knife.

I ate an apple while I decided on a course of action. It made little sense to sit here camping, waiting for Sem to catch up. If I went into Two Runs, I could see about additional supplies and perhaps gain some news of the world that I had missed in my isolation.

For sure, I would need shoes if I was going to go far. I had little money to trade, but I thought I might find someone to buy my boat, even if I was unlikely to get a fair price for it.

Decision made, I rolled the boat back upright and pushed it into the water. The day was promising to be warm, and already between the morning sun and my efforts at paddling along the shoreline I was sweating. I shed my cloak, preferring to let the sun darken my skin in exchange for feeling the breeze along the water.

It wasn't long before I began to hear the sounds of the active docks of Two Runs. Fishermen and merchants and dockworkers called out to each other in a rough, clipped vernacular: an odd patois of Freelander and Somiri.

The river flowed under a broad timber bridge anchored to either bank with massive stone foundations, and supported at intervals with stout wooden pilings. I passed under one of these gaps and into Two Runs.

The docks themselves were a sight. A vast assemblage of floating platforms, jetties, and piers, interconnected with a confused labyrinth of precarious planks and gangways that stretched well out over the water. Vessels of all sizes and configurations filled every conceivable space in seeming disarray as people swarmed over and around, hauling ropes and moving myriad crates and baskets here and there.

The town was a fair ways off the water, and those buildings I could see were all rough timber with low roofs of red clay tile. I took a moment to don my cloak and pull up the hood to cover my face and arms.

I picked a smaller, less busy landing to pull my little boat into, and as I neared I was assailed by the smells. Old fish, rotting water weeds, and mud. I had never before realized that mud has a smell.

With the paddle, I brought the boat near a low landing and awkwardly climbed out. Once I was on the relatively stable wooden planks, I used the paddle to pull the boat close enough that I could kneel down and lift it out of the water. Being grown from a single bough with power and not tooled and fitted, it was lighter than it might have been.

Content that it was secure enough for a time, I walked up the plank, intending to go deeper into the maze of the docks in search of a buyer. I didn't get far before an angry call stopped me.

"Oy, no one ties up 'ere without what pays the docking fee!"

I turned to see a rough-looking man standing on a plank above me. He wore a threadbare pair of trousers tied at the waist with a blue sash. A silver chain about his neck held a large silver disk in the shape of a compass. It had the look of a symbol of office, and whatever splendor it might have held was diminished by the ratty straw hat upon his head and the crude knotty beard that fanned out across his bare sun-darkened chest.

"It's not tied," I said, simply.

"What did you say?" The four words held menace and threat, meant to instill fear and respect.

I felt neither, but I was aware enough to realize that antagonizing him would get me nowhere. I tried for a tone of conciliation. "Please, I'm just trying to sell it for enough coin to travel overland."

The dock master glanced at the little boat in disdain, then turned the sneer on me. "Dock fee's a copper each day," he said. "That thing ain't worth what you'll pay me to leave it here." He hopped down to the plank I was on, his bare feet spread firmly to catch his bulk, and the wood beneath us wobbled. He stepped forward intending to loom.

"Now, you'll pay, or you'll—"

He halted suddenly as I slowly pulled back the hood of my cloak. I saw his eyes widen as he took in the scars on my face and forearms, my short fuzz of hair. His eyes ran down my body, my flat chest, broad shoulders, and round hips. I could see him taking in anew my rough-spun cloak and bare feet.

"Price for you is ten pennies a day, or off with you!" He held out his hand, expecting the money.

I simply looked at him, saying nothing, not moving.

He shook his head in disgust. He turned and took several steps down to my boat and casually kicked it over into the water, then came back up and brushed roughly past me, nearly pushing me off the plank. As he passed, he turned and spoke under his breath. "Get 'ye gone, witch, or you'll be in the drink beside it."

I felt the bouncing of the plank as he walked up back into the criss-crossing gangways, already cursing at some other boatman.

I walked slowly back down and knelt by the edge to grab the boat before the current carried it away.

"A fine boat, he is."

I looked up to see a wrinkled old face squinting at me from a nearby plank. Like many on the docks, he wore trousers and a hat and little else. He was handing a fishing net down to a child who sat in a boat that was broader and longer than mine. The child wore similar trousers and hat, and also a billowy blouse tied high above the waist.

I was amused by the gendering of the boat. "Why do you say 'he?'"

The old fisherman grinned, a gap-toothed smile that nonetheless lit up his face. "Ah well, it don't matter none. Some say 'she' for the romance and joy a boat brings. My boat brings fish. Not much romance in that." He climbed down into the boat slowly, using his hands to feel at the edges of the dock, and I noted the child helped him aboard. "Hard, hot work, is fishing. And smelly if you work it too long. Seems like 'he' makes as much sense."

Between the two of them paddling, their boat crossed the narrow waterway to where I sat, my feet dangling over the edge to hold my boat in place. Close up, I could see the old man's eyes were filmed with white cataracts.

"Been looking for a good boat for my granddaughter. Two boats will net us more fish. She says yours looks fine and trim."

I glanced at the girl, who leaned forward and put a hand on his arm, whispered something in his ear. Her eyes were wide and fixed on me.

He shrugged and patted her hand. "There's lots who look down on us fisherfolk round here. Call us dirty and smelly, and try their best to cheat us. Never mind that most everyone here survives on the fish we catch." I wasn't sure if he was talking to me or to her.

He turned his head generally in my direction. "Can't give you much for him. Not sure what you need to make your journey..."

"I don't need much," I said, "and would be far happier to know he's helping you bring in more fish. He *is* a good boat and won't let you down."

"We could spare half a lum," he said.

That was about twenty copper pennies in Torfallin currency. I nodded without haggling. It would be enough, somehow. Then I realized he couldn't see my nod. "Deal," I said.

The fisherman whispered something to the girl, who pulled her gaze away from me and dug her hand into a small pouch she wore around her neck, tucked into her loose blouse. She came out with a brown metal cylinder the length and width of her thumb. She stretched her arm out, offering me the copper rod by one end. I reached out to take it. As soon as my fingers closed upon the metal, she snatched hers back, as if worried I might touch her.

The lump of copper was solid and weighty, stamped on one end with the coinage mark and the other with a seal of weight. I tucked it in my pocket and lifted my feet from the boat.

As soon as I released it, the girl slipped easily over the side from the larger boat to her new one. I handed her the paddle and watched as she maneuvered away from the dock. She moved the boat through the water as if it was a part of her. She paddled a quick circle around her grandfather's boat and a smile half-formed on her face.

"Thank you," I said to the old fisherman. "Good luck with your catch."

He smiled and began paddling away.

I collected my satchel and stick, and walked away from the water to find the market of Two Runs. As I crossed the maze of planks, I noted the dock master arguing with someone, hands flailing and voices raised. I grimaced to myself as I passed, wanting to topple *him* into the water, but I knew there would be no profit in it. I had been living so long isolated that I had apparently forgotten the casual cruelties and hatreds that the outside world held for people like me.

The transition from docks to fish market to general market was gradual and demarcated mostly by smells. The pungent odors of working docks gave way to the milder scents of fish and shellfish, and eventually to the spices, grain, and leather smells of a bustling market.

Two Runs was a trading hub between west and east, north

and south, and though it was on the Torfall side of the river, the merchants thrived on the exchange of goods between Torfall, Somiere, and the Freelands. In that crush of people, I kept my hood up despite the heat, hoping for some anonymity.

Shoes were my first priority. I passed a market stall selling wooden sandals much like the ones Sem favored, but decided I preferred real shoes. Whether by design or convenience, the various merchants and craftspeople had generally organized themselves into little districts, and it wasn't long before I found a cobbler amongst a cluster of leather goods stalls.

The shoemaker eyed me askance as I approached, her eyes darting to my bare, mud-crusted feet. If she thought anything at the sight of me, she held her tongue at least. I looked over her wares and my eyes widened at the posted prices, marked in chalk on a slate beside her bench. A whole silver mark for a simple pair of shoes; more for anything finer than boar hide. A pair of boots in supple cowhide were marked at ten silver marks.

I moved on before she decided to chase me away.

Two other stalls sold shoes and both were priced nearly as dearly. One hard-used pair of shoes looked like they might fit me, but the aged leather was cracked and some of the stitching was frayed. The vendor wanted twenty-five copper pennies for them which would be nearly all of my money.

I didn't bother trying to haggle. I knew by his sneer that the price wouldn't come down for me.

Resigned, I returned to the first stall and traded ten coppers for a pair of the sandals. The seller took my half lum and returned ten pennies. I carried the sandals back to the edge of the docks to rinse my feet off in the river before donning them.

First priority accomplished, I returned to the market. The sandals made a soft slap-slap as I walked. My gait was awkward; each step required some concentration to avoid kicking the things off. I wondered how Sem managed to fight so well in them.

The stalls selling food were all arranged on the main thoroughfare, and here too, the prices were high enough to give me pause. I remembered the conversation between the peddler and Pinala's husband about prices going up and rumors of war. I suddenly worried that I might not have enough for even common staples.

Surprisingly, rice seemed to be the least expensive among the grain merchants—I had always thought of it as a rare and exotic treat—but even so, two pounds of it was going to cost most of my remaining coin. I waited in the short line for the vendor and listened to the banter around me. Two men in line behind me were discussing the war to the west.

"I heard 'e's won again."

"He never. Can't the Lords of Fall field a decent general?"

"They did. All las' year, they sent their best generals one after another. They lost, each one. The Duke jus' marched 'is armies out and knocked 'em flat; lums up and pennies down."

The matron ahead of me traded her coin and left. I stepped up, and asked for my rice, placing the silver penny on the counter. I regretted over-paying Pinala for the food, and was beginning to regret leaving half of it for Andia and Deala. I watched the vendor measure out the weight, scooping the dark brown rice from a large sack into a smaller.

"It'll spill over, wait and see," the first man said darkly. "I heard he plans to roll up the west and then set 'is eyes on us."

The merchant counted out three copper pennies and slid them across with the small sack of rice. I thanked him and turned to go.

"Duke Savat ain't going to stop 'till he's put himself over the

Torfall Council and sits as Lord of the Freelands too. See if 'e don't."

I stopped short and turned to the man who spoke. "Who did you say?"

He looked at me for a moment, annoyed that I would interrupt into his conversation, but his need to gossip triumphed. "Duke Savat."

"Tamar Savat?" I asked. "He's a Viscount."

The man leaned close and spoke conspiratorially. "*Was* a Viscount. Named hisself Duke last year—and don't think the lords of Torfall were 'appy about that!—an' now he's got his eyes on 'Lord o' Everything.'" He looked me over again, leaning down to peer under my hood, and scowled. "An' what do you care?" He shouldered roughly past me and he and his friend dismissed me, moving up to the vendor.

I moved off in thought, absently looking for other affordable foodstuffs, but mostly considering what I had heard.

Four

About four miles west of the joining of the Balshin to the Sommíre, the Torfall road drew close enough to overlook a broad grassy plain rolling down to the wide river. On the northern bank of the river, some miles away and sprawling to the horizon was The Lange, the great capital of Somiere.

The road had once been paved in ancient stones, but this far east most of it was a dusty track, wide enough for wagons but a rutted and stoney trap for ankles. Most of the traffic between Two Runs and the western cities traveled by water.

A cairn of crumbling stone beside the road—perhaps some ancient marker or statue—made for a good spot to rest and wait. It took a few tries to find the right position of flat stone for a seat and smooth and high enough stone to lean back against, but I found it, and let my body relax. I pulled my hood low for shade and scanned the view of The Lange.

I had read so much of the city and its people, part of me longed to go there. From what I could see, there were broad roads and a multitude of great domes and spires, crowded with smaller buildings nestled between. Even in the haze of distance and heat, the city was a riot of color, with various banners and pennants. The city was built of stone from several different quarries. The buildings shimmered in pale ivory marble, rich reds, sienna and cobalt and deep, ebony basalt against the blue of the sky.

Someday, I thought to myself, I would go there and visit the great library and the *Gruende*, famous repository of medical knowledge.

A steady breeze that blew through the river basin and up and over the hill helped disrupt the mosquitos that tried to bite me. The sounds of the broad, slow water occasionally reached me, and otherwise there was nothing but the knot in my mind from the Finding; that persistent sense of Sem's location.

I could feel them still to the east but closing the distance between us. I hadn't been sure that they would take the road and not the river, but now I could clearly tell they were coming overland, the mules steadily nearing.

I had nearly an hour's respite before they appeared in the distance, swaying back and forth with the gray mule's gait and trailing a low cloud of dust. It was another quarter hour before they reached me and pulled the gray to a halt. Their face was placid, but I noticed a small quirk of their lips that was either a smile or a grimace. That was as much emotion as I expected from Sem at finding me here, well ahead of their path.

They clucked twice and the sorrel came forward. Sem moved their pack from her back and settled it behind them on the gray as I stood and scratched Beatrice's forehead. I felt the awareness of Sem's location from the Finding fade as I approached. I came around and mounted, and Sem nudged the gray on again.

We rode for a time in silence. I closed my eyes for a while, feeling the play of the mule's muscles under my legs, her grassy smell, the sound of her whuffing breath and the rhythmic plod of her hooves. I wondered that this didn't bring me back to my journey to Reft, didn't send me into my memories more than six years ago. I suppose I had changed too much.

"Where are we going?" I finally asked.

Sem didn't respond at first. They looked away south, then turned to the north to stare at The Lange.

I knew to simply wait them out. They would answer in time.

"Somewhere south of here, on the road to Quarry East, there's a town—much like your 'Hill. Fourteen years ago, a child was born." They stopped talking to adjust the pack behind them.

I waited. I knew Sem would not be speaking of this child if they were a boy or a girl, and safe.

"When I was in the east, word came to me that this child needed help in reaching Reft. The people of central Torfall hold the *nyssén* in lower regard than even your parents' backwards little village, if you can imagine that." Sem's lips twisted into an ugly sneer for a moment, then relaxed. "Ash does their best to keep to themself, but what they've told me of this village..." They turned to me. "Are you sure you're up to this?"

I nodded. I wanted to ask who Ash was, but refrained.

"It may come to bloodshed," Sem warned. "You need to be resolute. We go there to save a life. That sometimes requires pain. If it comes to us or them, I would rather it be those that want to do us harm that are hurt. You understand?"

I thought of Father and Mother and Ranji, and our flight into death; of abandoning the home I grew up in because the Geoffs and their ilk wouldn't suffer someone like me to live in peace. I remembered Andia and her visceral fear and loathing at what I was, never mind that I had just saved her life. I found Chan's memory—still lurking in my mind from the Circle we had formed in my Reshaping—their father's rage and fury and violence, preferring a dead son to a living child happy as they were.

"I understand," I said levelly. "We will do what we must." I had every intention of doing just that, even if it meant working to temper Sem's more violent reflexes.

Sem grunted.

We continued to ride, both content not to speak as the mules stepped out the miles. I let my mind wander, and found myself recalling the maps I had studied in Reft. The road we followed continued on steadily west all the way to Fin-Torfall, the capitol on the sea. The Torfallin border all along the Sommíre was dotted with forts and towers, garrisoned year-round, though the Somiri had never made war across the river since the Torfallin first landed on the southern shores. Each of these had grown into small towns and villages, though they still retained their original military character. I didn't think they would welcome us.

If I remembered correctly, there was a road south to Quarry East, though we wouldn't join it until the first outpost. In a few more miles, I thought we might cut south cross-country and rejoin the road. Thoughts of the garrisons and towers brought my mind to what I had overheard in Two Runs.

"So Savat is a Duke now," I said finally, "and it seems no one can defeat his armies."

Sem grunted. "Rumors are he has recruited *nyssén* to his cause, and they march into battle alongside his soldiers."

I took some time to digest this news. If true, it certainly would not improve our acceptance by the people of Torfall. Even if the rumors were empty, they would have the same effect. "What *is* his cause? Why would he be waging war at all? And against whom?"

Sem glanced at me for a moment before speaking. "The first is an excellent question, and knowing that will help to answer the second. As to who he is fighting... that appears to be anyone who will meet his armies in battle." They lifted their left foot up over the gray's back, slipping off the sandal and idly scratched the sole of their foot. "First, he rolled up the other lords of Fall and accepted their allegiance. That explains his new Ducal status. Now he threatens the southern Torfallin border outposts."

Sem replaced their sandal and straightened their posture on the mule. "But do you care why? Are you back in the world to stay?"

I thought of Savat and his polished, gentle demeanor and kind words. I thought of Eelie, and their intensity and bitterness. The idea that Eelie might be somewhere among armies, helping to wage war and kill people knotted my stomach.

"It doesn't smell right," I said, echoing Sem's words from the night they first came to my woods.

Sem grunted in agreement.

As I expected, we left the road some miles short of the first garrison town. Sem turned the gray southward and we set off cross-country. The mules didn't seem to mind the hilly terrain. They kept a steady pace and soon we were well beyond sight of the road behind us.

As the sun began to set, Sem found us a campsite between two hills. It was a shallow depression, large enough for the hobbled mules to graze, with water from a narrow creek and a grassy knoll with a shallow-enough slope to be comfortable while remaining dry. We unpacked the mules and set up camp.

As we ate a dinner of boiled grain with lentils, mushrooms, and herbs—the last of what they had taken from my pantry, I noted—I told Sem about bringing Deala home and saving her mother. I spoke about my realization that my silent protection had undermined the fabric of the village. They had the grace to avoid reminding me that they had been right, only listening to my story and sighing when I reached the end.

"It's a narrow path to walk," they said. "Living on the edge of their society, accepting the crumbs of humanity they deign to grant us. Knowing that you have it in your hands to save them, or destroy them." They looked to the horizon, to the setting sun. "I've never had the stomach for it. For now, there's enough empty space in the world to leave them to theirs."

I thought this over for a time. "Is that all there is then?" I asked. "To choose between salvation or destruction or indifference?"

"What more do you want?" they asked, shrugging.

We let the fire die out and neither of us said any more.

I woke early the following morning. The sun was just lightening the sky when I returned from the privy trench and climbed to the top of the near hill. I chose an empty-hand technique for my exercises, starting slow and speeding up as I went. I felt clumsy in the sandals, unaccustomed to the way they slipped over my feet and slid in the dirt. I nearly kicked them off—I was far more comfortable barefoot—but I decided that the need to learn to move in them was greater than my need for comfort.

Partway through, I could smell the campfire, and when I finished, I returned to the campsite to find Sem making tea and warming the remains of last night's meal. They split the mash between our bowls and we settled to breakfast.

"Tell me about the child," I said between mouthfuls.

"I don't know much," Sem replied. "They call themself Benni. Ash came here some years ago to keep an eye on them after they heard a traveler's tale of how this village treated the child."

I thought this through for a moment before understanding. "It wouldn't be worth a story if the child wasn't being mistreated."

Sem grunted. "Their family is a typical Torfallin family, mind. They set great store by their history, by their place within their village, their society. I sometimes think it's because Torfall, as a people, fled their homeland so long ago that no one fully remembers the real reason. What they can hold to of their history—lineage and ancestry—colors their actions and beliefs. It's more important than any one person."

Sem and I finished our food and began cleaning up and breaking camp as they continued. "They pass their ancestry down through the male line, you know. And so in their mind, a child who rejects that mantle... it's a betrayal of their family and their history. They have no place in their world for those like us, *especially* one of us who they see as a boy. It's as bad here for *aiyssén* as it is for *nyssén*."

I shook my head at this analysis. "Their line matters more than their child?"

Sem hesitated a moment. "For some. Not all Torfallin are so. But even those who would act differently... act under the pressures of their society. And these tenets are all tangled with Torfallin folklore of demons and tricksters that even now some still believe. The fact that we can wield a power they don't understand only fuels their fear of us."

We continued southward, letting the mules set the pace

through the hilly scrubland. Some time before noon, we crested a hill and could see the Quarry Road flowing south far ahead of us like a dry riverbed.

Sem decided that we should stay in the hills and off the road for as long as the mules could handle the terrain. I concurred. Whether by some sense of foreboding from the morning conversation or simply caution at the unknown situation, we both seemed to want to avoid traveling too much in the open.

It was coming on evening when we reached the top of a hill to find the village Balifere spread out below us. The road crossed to one side of the village, with a common green on the other. Low buildings framed in thick timbers infilled with stone spread out east of the road all the way up to the lee of a dense wood sprawling away to the both east and west.

There were some outlying farms visible, but it was clear that the villagers made much of their living by the quarry traffic. We could see at least two smithies and a large wainwright's yard with several low, heavy-timbered wagons in various states of construction or repair. A taller stone building with two floors and many windows and an attached stables was surely an inn.

On the green across the road was a large camp of tents. A pennant of blue and yellow flew over the largest tent, though I couldn't make out the device. For all of the gossip and rumors of war, seeing soldiers camped beside the village filled me with unease, and not a little bit of excitement.

I looked to Sem to take the lead, and we descended the hill towards the road. I kept my eyes moving, taking in the soldiers' encampment and the evening foot traffic between buildings of the town.

On closer inspection, I could see the flag over the camp carried a charge of a stylized beetle in black and a yellow chevron over a blue field. The soldiers by and large were ignoring the town, focused instead on their evening meal and camp chores—some were still erecting their tents. They all wore gray, with the same blue and yellow flashing on their tunics. I didn't think much of their watch—if we had wanted, we could likely have crept straight into their camp without raising an alarm.

By the time we were abreast of the first buildings of Balifere, I started to sense a distinct tension. I could tell Sem was aware of it, and even the mules seemed to be picking up on it, their steps turning hesitant. I scanned the visible townsfolk and saw them watching us with furtive glances. We kept the mules on the road and moving steadily until we reached the inn.

Most of the people on the street had their eyes locked on Sem, tracing the scars that covered their body and eyeing their swords. With so little attention on me, I stayed quiet, content to sit upon Beatrice and observe.

After growing up first in the Freelands and then in Reft, I was startled by how alike the people looked. I had known that the people of Torfall were of a type, pale-skinned and smooth light hair, but to see a whole village who had the same coloring and sharp features as Eelie was disconcerting. The men were all dressed alike, their trousers and coats in somber colors, and wore hair and beards long. Fewer women were about, but they all seemed to braid their hair and while their dresses were more colorful than the mens' clothes, they seemed to all be cut from the same pattern.

I found myself fixating on variations: this woman had her hair braided in a more complex pattern than any others I could see. One man stood out for his large pot belly and bald head.

None of them smiled.

A large man wearing a blue sash over his coat came out of the inn and confronted us. The others seemed relieved that he stepped forward. When he spoke, his voice was gruff and firm.

"I don't know what you think you're here for, but we have nothing here for the likes of you. Please leave."

Sem pulled the gray to a halt and Beatrice stopped as well. Sem looked the man up and down for a moment before speaking.

"A strange greeting for an innkeeper to give to travelers on the road," they said quietly.

"Inn's full," the innkeeper said.

I glanced up at the several dark windows in the upper floor.

Whether he saw my look or simply felt the weight of his own lie, the innkeeper blushed before speaking again. "We don't want any more trouble. Would you please just go on your way?"

I looked out at the handful of people that had gathered behind the innkeeper and saw their eyes averted, their shoulders hunched. *Any* more *trouble.* There was something going on here beyond their fear and hatred of us, but I couldn't quite piece it together. I felt like I was missing something critical.

A man with huge arms and shoulders came up from behind the innkeeper. He wore a leather apron and carried a large hammer with a heavy iron head. He, at least, seemed willing to meet Sem's eyes. His face carried a grim expression.

"We don't want you here!" called a feminine voice plaintively from somewhere within the crowd.

"You'll get the same that—" someone else began angrily, before he was shushed by others nearby.

I kept my eyes scanning the crowd and the road ahead and behind. The townsfolk were not boxing us in yet, but between the blacksmith and a handful of other village men with hate in their eyes, I began to worry what spark might set tempers alight. Despite the innkeeper's words, there seemed to be plenty of opportunity for more trouble here.

I glanced back at the soldiers' camp, but they seemed to have no interest in the goings on. My skin began to crawl with the sense of impending action. The gathered villagers were no longer silent... there was a low current of murmur and unease.

A newcomer dressed in a gray tunic slashed with blue and yellow stepped out of the inn common room and pushed forward through the crowd to reach the innkeeper. All I saw was pale blonde hair tied back in a tail over a sun-baked face, and then the newcomer was grabbing the innkeeper's arm and speaking urgently in his ear. I saw Sem's hand shift slightly towards their sword.

The innkeeper turned sharply to the soldier and shook his head, a small movement. "Soldier, I don't care what your commander said. This is our town."

The soldier took a step back and drew himself up sharply. "Mayor," he said formally, and loud enough for the whole crowd to hear, "I'll thank you to refer to me by my rank, never mind that I've supped in your hall. It's in my company's standing orders to keep the peace. If any of you choose to break it this night, you can begin by testing our blades. We'll have no brawling in the street!"

The innkeeper and mayor shied back as if slapped, and turned his eyes down to his feet, then looked out over the townsfolk. He didn't look at us.

I watched as the soldier scanned the crowd then turned his eyes to us. I saw him flinch slightly at Sem's scars, linger thoughtfully on their swords, and then turn to me. His gaze lingered on my scar and then he saw me watching him and turned away.

He was younger than I first had thought. His sun-burned forehead and nose made him appear weathered and hard, but he wore no beard and I guessed his age at no more than twenty.

On the shoulder of his tunic was sewn a short red ribbon fixed with a silver badge that I thought indicated an officer's rank, though I couldn't guess what. He wore a sword at his waist and silver-worked boots.

I could see him deciding which of us to address. Ultimately, he turned to Sem as the elder of the two of us. "My men and I have no quarrel with you, and will defend your right to walk the public roads. But it may be safer for everyone if you did move on." He seemed embarrassed at this speech, but stood his ground.

Sem said nothing more, simply nodded and nudged their gray back to moving. Beatrice and I followed, though she had picked up on my tension and whickered softly, her steps quick and her eyes rolling.

We kept a steady pace down the road that passed along the village. I was well aware of the eyes that traced our progress. Despite the soldier's warnings, the blacksmith followed us all the way to the edge of the town, as if making sure we didn't steal any coppers on the way out.

As we descended the next rise and the village and its eyes were well out of sight, Sem turned off the road towards the woods that covered the rolling hills to the eastern horizon. I hadn't lost the tension in my shoulders, and we were among the trees before I felt I could take an unencumbered breath.

"Were you expecting that reaction from them?" I asked.

"Something stinks in that town," Sem said.

I didn't ask them where they were leading us, but I started to spot signs of a trail. I doubt I would have noticed except for my years living in my wood. It was nothing so blatant as a worn path or broken branches... it was only a subtle difference in the fabric of the wood. There were none of the telltales of a Warding or other protections.

We rode for another hour, with Sem turning here and there under the shadowed canopy. We were riding now only by whatever starlight and moonlight filtered through the leaves above and would soon need to camp, if only to let the mules rest.

I was about to suggest a stop when I smelled it.

It was not a strong scent. Not wafting smoke or the warming smell of hot coals. This was a faint acrid odor of cold charred wood; of wet ash and weathered desolation and something else. It might have been a day-old campfire, except that I could smell it filtering through the wood and not yet see a trace. The mules were restive.

We rounded a low rise into a narrow glade and halted. Charred timbers stood checked and crumbling in a blackened circle amidst the litter of the forest floor.

I held Beatrice still with the tension in my back, and scanned the ruins and the surrounding wood. Sem and I both dismounted and I took the gray and Beatrice to the edge of the glade where I set their hobbles and feed bags. They were both spooked and unhappy.

I returned to stand beside Sem, stepping gingerly and still searching for some hint as to what we had found. Sem wore a look as dark as a storm, their brow was pinched and their lips a hard line.

My eyes were already well-adjusted to the darkness, but it still took some time before I could make sense of what I saw. It had been a small building, little more than a hut. Beside the burned and broken remains of the hut was a fire pit, and now I began to understand the shapes I was seeing, I noted the iron cook pot tumbled on its side, the scatter of split firewood that was once neatly stacked, weeds just beginning their inevitable encroachment across the charred earth.

And I saw the bodies.

There was nothing to be done for them. All of this had happened days ago, perhaps weeks ago. The only consolation I could find was that there was little enough left to rot. The fire had seen to that.

My eyes darted to Sem's face and I could see them fixed upon the bodies. The larger of the two burned corpses had been an adult. I stepped into the burned circle and knelt beside them.

Without touching the remains, I could still see some evidence of violence. The skull had been smashed, probably before the fire had been set. They lay on their side, curled slightly with one arm stretched out towards the smaller body.

I had to calm my breathing before I could look at the smaller one. I can't imagine the child could have been fourteen—they looked so small and helpless. Sem's words came to me unbidden: *They have no place in their world for those like us.* The child's body was curled tightly into a posture of pain and fear. Their arms covered their head and their legs were drawn up in a futile attempt to defend themself from whoever had come for them, but I could see they too bore signs of a vicious blow to the face.

I stood, wiping tears from my eyes, and moved back away to the edge of the glade. I took several deep breaths. Neither of us spoke much that night, but by silent accord we moved the mules further into the wood before setting a makeshift camp. I couldn't stomach the idea of a fire and it seemed Sem felt the same. I had no appetite in any case, so we simply curled up in our cloaks.

I spent most of the night watching Sem's eyes staring into the distant darkness. After some hours, I began to feel the need for sleep, so I stood and stepped out a circle of Warding around our small campsite. I didn't trust the villagers' fear of us enough to leave our safety to chance tonight.

Even so, my sleep was fitful and restless. A part of me was filled with rage at what had been done, and I wanted nothing short of violent, wrathful retribution. Another part of me was bone-tired and full of sorrow and dejection.

It all amounted to a wearying sense of frustration and help-lessness. We had reached the end of our quest, and there was nothing we could do now for either of them.

As the first light of dawn was filtering through the trees, we buried Benni and Ash. Sem did the work, cutting across their forearm with their short sword and letting the pain fill them. The ground parted and swallowed the two bodies deep into the earth where they had fallen. Sem left the burned remains of Ash's hut as they were. They said nothing, spoke no words and the anger I had seen on their face last night was gone. They walked back to the mules, silently tying a strip of cloth around their arm to staunch the blood.

We mounted and rode together deeper through the wood, no particular destination and no deliberate direction other than away from that place. We were moving eastward and a little southward, and the terrain was rising steadily, growing more hilly as the wood thinned. It was mostly pine now, with large boles towering over us and spreading their branches into the sky. The ground the mules covered was a deep, spongy peat of rust-brown pine needles.

It was early afternoon when hunger and exhaustion caught up with us. We had eaten nearly the last of our apples as we rode, but they were small and wrinkled, and not enough to sustain us. In perfect accord, we stopped the mules and dismounted in a low depression near the top of a hill. A copse of pines shaded our campsite and gave us a source of fallen wood. I carried our cook pot down hill, following a shallow ditch and the faint sounds of water.

Talkative was not an accusation that could be made against Sem, but I was beginning to be concerned and frustrated at their silence. As I hunted for the water source that I could hear, I determined to push them to speak to me about what we had seen.

Between an outcrop of pale gray stone and a steep grade of clay, I found the narrow trickle of a creek. It took some labor, shifting stones and breaking up the clay boundary, until the water ran clear enough and deep enough to fill the pot without silt. Once done, I walked back to our campsite, catching the smell of smoke.

Whether due to the pine wood, the bright light of midday, or simply distance, the smell was cleaner somehow, and I was glad to find that it didn't carry any hints of the horror we had found the previous night. Sem was squatting by the small fire set in a ring of clay they had cleared of the soft loam of the forest floor.

I set the pot by the fire to boil and sat down a few steps away watching them for a moment. They didn't look up at me; didn't acknowledge me, and I decided I had had enough.

"Tell me of Ash," I said firmly.

Sem looked up at me sharply, then off to the horizon.

I waited. It was a skill I had learned from Turin. I centered myself, breathing steadily and slowly. I felt a slight breeze through the pines and listened to the crackle of the fire. I let my fingers comb the mulch of the forest floor.

It took a long, long time before Sem spoke. When they did it was quiet, nearly a whisper. "Ash and I met in the early days of Reft. It was hardly more than a circle of tents in those days, and we hadn't yet found the Vale or the mountain. We moved from place to place, trying to find a home, but also trying to find what we could be."

I said nothing. I simply listened.

"Ash was never going to be one to settle. They were too contrary. Always... *taniéne ket i batte*. You know the saying? 'An ember in the thatch.'"

I struggled to avoid any expression of surprise. I felt a pang of sadness that I would never know the person that *Sem* labeled a contrary firebrand.

"Those mountains are full of old forts like Redwatch, and we found them and some wanted to stay and make them ours. But Ash always argued that if we found a place that others had built, then others must know of it, and would come back to take it from us someday."

Sem's eyes came back to the fire, watching the flames dance. "It was the Vale we found first, you know. We knew that it could be a haven for us and for all the others like us. We weren't there ten days before Ash decided to leave. To return here to Torfall where they had been mistreated and hated and chased out."

They looked at me then. "That was Ash. They could have gone to the Freelands or to Somiere. There was need for us there too, and far less pain and animosity waiting." Sem grinned. "But Ash settled here *because* they knew people would spit on them and hate them and fear them all the more for being a Torfallin *nyssa*."

Sem sighed; a long, exhausted-sounding breath. It was as if the weight of rage and sorrow of last night was leaving their body in a stream of tainted air. Instead of deflating, they seemed to be strengthened by the release. Their shoulders straightened and their head lifted.

They peered at me suspiciously and then grunted softly. Sem stood and began preparing our meal, dipping the small tea kettle into the pot of water and setting it aside before pouring a measure of rice into the bubbling water. They stretched and pulled the small shovel from their pack, starting off down the hill to dig a privy trench.

After a time, I moved to the cooking pot and stirred the rice. The water for tea was bubbling, so I pulled it further from the fire and tossed in a handful of leaves from a small pouch in Sem's pack. A bird trilled somewhere from over the hill, and another answered.

Something—I don't know what it was I felt—made the muscles in my back tense. I looked to the place where I had laid down my pack and walking stick, and stood, moving slowly to pick up the stick and don my ratty cloak. I let my mind and heart visit the pain I carried always at leaving Kari and Fanti behind in Reft without a word.

Footsteps came rapidly up the hill, and I recognized Sem's gait. They came up from behind a low snarl of trees and moved directly to the fire, upending the cook pot over the coals, half-cooked rice and all.

They exchanged the shovel for their swords, and we moved quietly up the hill from the cover of one tree to the next. I let Sem take the lead as it seemed they understood more of what we were both feeling than I.

The closer we came to the crest of the hill the lower they crouched in their movement. I had a harder time of it, being taller. I was glad of my daily exercises by the time we were peering down the other side.

We waited tensely, neither of us making a sound. I was still not sure what we waited for, but after a few minutes of near silence—the wood around us was still alive with all those subtle shifts and skitters of a living forest—I heard the bird trill a third time.

It came from someplace further away at the bottom of the hill, in a low valley that ran east and west. This time, I could tell it was no bird. Someone was giving some covert signal.

We had little enough cover where we were, but a few paces below us there was a dense and tangled thicket of holly. I tapped Sem's shoulder and pointed. They nodded, and we slowly made our way to it. Closer, I could see it had a nearly hollow center, its branches leggy and sparse. I dug out my pocket knife and carefully cut away the low outer stems so that we could wiggle in under its prickly leaves.

We waited.

After a time, Sem tapped my shoulder and nodded with their head, pointing me to a horse and rider moving slowly through the valley below us. They were far enough away that the forest canopy and soft, peaty floor were swallowing the sound of horse and harness. Only their movement gave them away.

The trill came again, and all at once an arrow took the rider in the chest, toppling them from the saddle. The black horse was well-trained and didn't panic, only moved slowly towards a dense cluster of trees. The rider's boot was tangled in the stirrup, and the body was dragged behind through the pine needles.

We held still, though my immediate reflex was to run down to try to save a life. I felt Sem's hand on my back—whether intended as comfort or restraint, I couldn't tell.

Slowly, cautiously, four soldiers emerged from cover and converged on the downed rider. They wore black clothing that had been carefully disguised with branches. They checked the rider, and then skulked away further along the valley to the west.

When they were out of sight, I shrugged Sem's hand off and carefully extracted myself from the bush. They looked at me for a moment, and shook their head. I closed my eyes and drew on the well of pain inside me and wove an Aversion—similar to a Warding, it would keep eyes from fixing on me as I moved.

Sem sighed. They knew as well as I did that it was imperfect and would not last long.

I descended as quietly and carefully as possible, moving from cover to cover, and kept my eyes seeking for danger, checking my surroundings to make sure my stick didn't catch and make noise. As I used the tree trunks, shrubs, and low folds of ground to hide my movement, I made sure to glance up at the trees I passed—many historical defeats could be traced ultimately to a failure to recognize *all* of a battle's terrain.

I reached the rider without incident. Under the mottled hood, I found long pale hair and a short beard over parchment-white skin and an angular, masculine face. But more, he wore a gray tunic similar to those I had seen on the Torfallin soldiers camped outside Balifere. I pressed my fingers beside his throat as Ciala had taught me. There was no pulse, and the position of the arrow told me that there was no help for him.

I glanced back up and around, and saw Sem moving towards me in a low crouch, their short sword drawn. They reached me beside the fallen rider, and leaned in close.

"Before you do another foolish thing like that, we need to have a talk about how long you desire to live," they whispered harshly. They reached down and flipped back a fold of the rider's cloak, exposing a horseman's short sword and a black beetle device over blue and yellow on the sleeve. Sem grunted. "Torfallin soldier. Probably an outrider for that company we saw in Balifere."

I took in the uniform, the sword, the riding boots. The cloak that hid his colors and the lack of barding or device on the horse tack. "Moving in stealth. His foes were also. But black... does any lord other than Savat use that color?"

Sem shook their head. "Not in this part of the world." They paused in thought for a moment. "Those four were on a mission. This was no chance encounter; they were lying in wait for this one."

I thought this through. Soldiers—and those who write of soldiers—often glorify the battlefield: the cavalry charge driven by ringing trumpets. Epic clashes between armies in great formations trading blows under rippling banners. Indeed, some battles are fought so.

But the *winning* of battles... those commanders who made their name in the histories employed tactics that were carefully crafted to ensure victory even before the first horn was sounded. Tactics such as silent, coordinated attacks on an army's scouts to keep the larger body of soldiers blind to a coming assault. I looked up to the crest of the next hill.

Sem grabbed my forearm. "Don't," they said.

I shook them off and moved swiftly up the hill, kicking off my wooden sandals as I went. The forest floor was soft, and my steps quieter and my footing surer without them. This side of the valley was steeper and higher, and when I reached the top, the wood was thinner as well. A broad vista of rolling hills stretched out to the south. The horizon was rippled in wooded mountains that merged into a haze of blue.

To the west, I could see far down the hill towards the heart of the wood, and a gap in that canopy that ran north and south through it. It was the Quarry Road, and a faint bloom of dust in the northwest told me that the Torfallin troops marched along it. They would have outriders ahead and in the woods to either side of the road to warn of dangers, and Savat's men seemed to be picking them off with precision.

I held myself still and focused on the southernmost part of that wood. It was miles off, and the dust and heat of the day played games with my eyes. I let my breath settle into a slow, steady rhythm. If my guess was right, there were soldiers lying in wait to ambush the Torfallin.

I'm not sure I understood in that moment why I cared. The Torfallin were no friends of mine, and this conflict between Savat's armies and his neighbor's had no claim on my concern or loyalties. Perhaps it was as simple as the thought of a young soldier, sun-burned and travel weary, trying to do his best to avert needless violence and choosing to stand up for two strangers who he had no reason to protect. Or maybe I could tell myself that as an outsider to the immediate conflict, I felt the need to save as many lives as possible.

Honor and foolishness are both built of such choices.

Movement in the distant tree line caught my eye. I held my breath, trying to reduce my own motion even further. I caught another hint of someone lurking among the trees.

I was close to cursing myself for my imagination when I saw two black-clad figures step out from the eaves of the wood. They peered southward down the road, shading their eyes with gloved hands, then turned to scan the hills to the south and east. One of them looked straight at my hilltop, making me glad I was holding still. The two conferred, then turned and skulked back into the cover of the trees.

I let out the breath I held. I spent a few moments taking in the terrain, memorizing the hills and valleys as best I could, and then picked my way back down the hill to where I had left Sem and the fallen soldier.

When I reached them, Sem fixed me with a hard stare. "Saw what you needed to know, did you?"

I looked at them levelly. "Those soldiers we saw on the green are marching into a massacre."

I was expecting them to scoff, or to shrug it away, or to tell me it was no business of mine. We were unwanted and despised in this land. What pain and death these people wrought between themselves was nothing we needed care about.

Sem sighed. "You think you can help them?"

I nodded. The terrain was clear, a rough sequence of move and countermove had already played out in my mind as I came down the hill. Any more certainty could only come when I had seen the disposition of forces. I looked down at the soldier's body, which Sem had pulled free from the stirrup and straightened, and at the horse which they had tied to a nearby branch. Beatrice was steady and reliable, but speed mattered now.

They sighed and nodded.

"Why?" I asked. I couldn't say myself why this had become important to do. I hoped they could help me understand, or talk me out of it, or tell me I was being a fool.

"This war stinks. It makes no sense... and that means it makes a very specific kind of sense that may not be good for us in the long run. These particular soldiers don't matter much in the wider world, but I wouldn't mind getting a closer look." They reached out and took my arm by the shoulder. "Before you go haring off, we should Pair."

I gave them a steady look, then nodded.

We each drew on our pain—me with my memories of Kari

and Fanti, of Father and Ranji and Mother; Sem with blade and blood. We stepped into a Circle together and power and pain and memory surged between us.

I did my best to hold myself back from them—it was considered a courtesy to others in a Circle to hold oneself in tight control, so that the deep well of pain and raw emotions didn't flood too strongly into the others' minds. But some blending was inevitable. It was tied too tightly with the goal, after all.

What I felt from Sem was pain. Raw, fierce pain like a burn; hot and ice-cold at once. I wanted to grasp my forearm, though I knew mine was unhurt, the pain raged through me in waves. Somewhere in my mind, I was grateful for the simple, brilliant pain—clean, without the deeper well of hurt and sorrow that was the source of my own power.

I gasped with it and rode the flood for a moment, but the Circle was only the first step. Pairing was much like a Finding, but symmetrical, reciprocal. I had practiced it in Reft, and the forming of it was always uncomfortable to me. The blurring of self that came with a Circle was one thing, but deliberately linking mind to mind was more intimate, more invasive.

It is difficult to describe it. It is a process of utmost intimacy, of perfect vulnerability. I was taught that the technique was first born between lovers, and it's easy to believe.

I found a place in my mind, a convenient corner that was easy to return to, and also not of foremost importance. Not a memory, not even a feeling... it was like reaching in and prising open a doorway into the self, and leaving it ajar. It was a feeling of sheer defenselessness; of consummate trust.

I reached out through the Circle and found the open vault in Sem's mind. I could feel them through the link reaching out to find mine. We each stepped through together in perfect symmetry. I reeled in a sense of vertigo, my mind seething with agony and rapture. It was dissociation and orgasm and singular focus all at once.

And then it was done.

That doorway into my mind pulled just to, not closed, but close. I could feel Sem there, resident inside my self. I could feel a part of myself in them. Until one or the other broke the connection, we could ride half the world away from each other and still would be connected and know precisely where the other was. We could share thoughts and experience instantaneously, like slipping a note beneath a door. I could open myself to their pain if I wished, and they could lend me their power. We would each know the exact moment of the other's death.

I took a deep breath, and let out a long, shaky sigh.

Sem looked at me sharply. "You ready to do this?"

I nodded with confidence I didn't feel.

"Then go. I'll do what I can."

I knelt down to strip the dead rider's boots off. He was bigger than me, but they would fit. I didn't look forward to a hard ride with my feet bare and my sandals wouldn't fit in the stirrups. After a moment, I unhooked the sword belt as well. I pulled on the boots and belted on the sword, then approached the black horse.

I had ridden horses in the Vale in my Watch trainings in Reft, but I wasn't especially comfortable on the animals. I dug my last apple out of a pocket in my cloak and offered it. The horse wrapped his lip over the apple and took it from my palm, munching happily.

I stroked its forehead and moved around to the side, planting my foot in the stirrup and pulling myself up by the saddle horn. The horse shifted as I settled myself, but wasn't fractious, so I pulled experimentally on the reins to turn his nose to the north, back up towards our campsite.

My scan of the terrain had left me with a sketch of an approach in my mind. Near where we had set our fire was a narrow gully running more or less westward, deep enough that no scout would ride it—They wouldn't be able to see more than the width of the steep walls.

Beatrice looked up at me reproachfully as I galloped past the mules, and soon I found the gully I remembered. The horse was hesitant to descend the bank at first, but after a few false starts found a spot he liked and made a startling leap down to the level floor. Soon we were covering ground, following the fold west to the road.

After an hour or so of hard riding, the forest floor softened, and the horse began to prefer the slightly higher ground along the edge. The walls of the defile were steeper here, and I could see evidence of water running through the soft soil. I pushed him as hard as I dared, but there came a time where I knew we would have to climb out to continue.

There was a tree fall ahead, with a morass of rotting trunks acting as a soil break, where natural actions had formed a berm and a narrow ramp up to the northern side. I dismounted and led the black horse up slowly, careful to peek over the ledge at the woods around us for any threat.

As we reached the top, I felt a pressure form in my mind, and took a measured peek into that place where Sem's consciousness rode within me. It was disorienting, dreamlike. A foreign perspective of sensations and awareness that couldn't find alignment with my own. I could taste the sounds and smell the images in the dappled light. Another downed scout. This one had been taken with two arrows, and one for the horse.

A moment later, a vertiginous burst of uncanny speed through a different wood and I was tasting Sem's short sword slicing through the belly of one black-clad soldier; smelling the crushing impact of a scabbarded longsword against the knees of another. I felt them pluck an arrow from the air and drive the fletched nock-end through the chest of the bowman who had shot it. They cut open the fourth man's throat, the color of his silent scream reverberating through my mind.

Sem was some miles to the south, and the sending filled me with confidence both for its confirmation of the enemy's tactics, and for the knowledge that the squad of Savat's men was not trailing me.

At the top of the berm, I remounted and galloped on, holding as best I could to where I guessed the column was. The texture and color of the wood changed, the sparse brown trunks and rust of the fallen needles filling in with low greenery and dense tangles of bramble and saplings. I descended the diminishing hills towards the broad lowland forest bisected by the Quarry Road.

I hated to do it, but I drove the horse with urgency, my heels in his ribs any time he flagged. If I didn't reach the column in time, they would be caught unawares by the ambush, and I would be stuck in the midst of the carnage. He was well-trained to the work, pushing relentlessly through the dense foliage, his footing sure and determined.

Shadows were lengthening when the trees thinned suddenly, and the road was visible ahead. I pulled back on the reins to slow the horse, and scanned north and south, hoping to spot the column. I nudged my mount forward, emerging from the treeline, and spotted a haze in the sky to the north. I had come out south of their march.

I drew on a trickle of power and changed my cloak and tunic to a gray to match what I remembered of the Torfallin soldiers' uniforms. I hoped it would keep a spear from my chest long enough to get their attention. I turned the horse's nose north, put my heels to his flanks, and he took off at a hard gallop.

We reached the vanguard and I called out as loud as I could, "Halt the column! Halt here! Urgent message for your captain!" I kept the horse at a gallop, fiercely hoping to get through the line of pikes without challenge.

The foot let me through, but the next squadron of mounted troops closed ranks, forcing me to pull up the reins.

"Who are you to order a halt?" called someone from behind the horse line, which loosened to let the speaker through. He was a grizzled veteran, barrel-chested and big-shouldered and his size seemed almost comical on a smaller than average mount. He drew close to me, eyeing my horse with a hard look. I could see the order to take me captive forming in his eyes.

Behind him rode the young officer from Balifere. He seemed to defer to the veteran, though the bigger man wore no symbol of rank beyond a knot of coarse jute on the shoulder.

I wasn't willing to leave the next few moments to chance. I reached out with a trickle of power and brushed aside the veteran's suspicion. It was a simple thing: his distrust rode at the surface of his mind. It took only a light touch, like sweeping dust from a floor.

I looked to the young officer. "There is a force lying in wait at the end of this road. They have killed your outriders to the east, and likely the west as well. They mean to ambush your column at the southern foot of the forest," I said calmly, now that I had an audience. "Take me to your commander. I know something of their disposition and can give information." I let my clothing fade back to its natural brown and mottle.

The young soldier's eyes widened, fear and indecision showing plainly in his eyes. It made him look even younger than I had first judged. He looked to the older soldier, whose lips twisted in a sour expression.

I glanced at the older soldier, questioning.

The veteran looked at me with a sneer, then at the young officer, then grunted. "I'm a sergeant. You are speaking to our commander," he said, his eyes darting to the younger man.

At a signal from the young commander, the sergeant pulled his horse back, and several other soldiers formed a space around us. The sergeant passed word down to halt the column. The commander looked ashen, his already pale face going a sickly tinge of gray.

"Say that again," he said.

"Your scouts are dead. There is an ambush awaiting you down this road." I saw his eyes darting between me, his sergeants, and the road ahead and behind. He licked his lips. I could see panic rising in his face. "What's your name?" I asked.

His eyes came back to me, danced to my scar, then back to my eyes, uncomprehending.

"Your name," I said, with more force. "What is your name."

"Uh, Feren. My name's Feren. Amital Feren."

"Amital Feren, well-met. I'm Arin. You know who I am? You recognize me from Balifere?"

He nodded. His eyes were showing whites all around.

I looked at the mounted men that surrounded us. "How long have you been in command, Feren?"

He swallowed, and took a deep breath trying to calm himself. "One day," he said quietly. "I'm just a lieutenant. We set off from Fin-Torfall, a month and a half gone. Captain Adona... he..." Feren gulped. "His horse trod on his foot in camp two weeks ago... It... blood poison set in. He told me to carry on. We are supposed to meet up with the Bluecaps in... down south. I... I'm just commanding the march... I don't know what to do..." The last was barely a whisper.

I felt a nudge from a place in my mind, and tasted Sem's voice: *Three-hundred afoot with swords. About fifty archers. Both sides of the road.* I could sense their position, several miles to the south.

"What troops do you have?" I asked. I needed to know what was possible. I also thought that keeping him focused on facts he could answer might keep him from outright panic.

"Two cohort of foot: one swords, one of pikes. One squadron of light cavalry."

I remembered a reference to Torfall's military organization. Each of their cohorts was eighty men. "How many in your cavalry squadron?"

"Thirty-two," he said, "but you said they killed...?"

"How many outriders did you have out?"

"Eight."

I closed my eyes for a moment. One-hundred and sixty foot and twenty-four horse. "Nearly twice your numbers wait for you to the south, hidden in the trees."

Feren's eyes were still wide with fear. "I... we need to turn around?"

I shook my head. "They almost certainly have eyes in the forest, even this far north," I said urgently, but quietly. "If you try to turn back now, they will only melt into the woods to either side and fall upon your flanks as you march. Even this halt cannot last too long, or they will assume a scout made it past their men."

Feren looked up at the sergeant, who nodded very slightly. I pretended not to notice, but the confirmation of my assessment was welcome.

"You have camp followers? Remounts? Anyone else?" I asked, my thoughts spinning into possibilities.

Feren licked his lips. "We have... a dozen or so farriers, armorers, and smiths. Some wagons, and remounts for the cavalry... That's all."

I sorted through every tactic I could remember, every gambit I had read of. We were at a significant disadvantage in terrain and force, but we had two critical advantages: we controlled the initiative, and they thought that they did. All we had to do was exploit them. I looked over the swordsmen who marched at the rear, their short, broad swords sheathed with thick shields on their left arms.

"Change the order of march. Half the sword cohort first, pikes second, then the remaining sword, horse at the rear. Leave your wagons and half the cavalry here, like they're seeing to some unexpected issues with the horses." I sensed the sergeant and the other veterans moving closer to listen. "Call forward all of your camp followers. We're going to set an ambush of our own."

For a tense few minutes, I laid out my ideas to Feren, making sure to check the sergeant's understanding of each point. I knew I had to convince him most of all, or there might well be a mutiny on top of the ambush. I looked back along the lines as I explained the plan that was taking shape in my mind.

Feren looked sick as I explained how the gambit would play

out. When I finished, he took a deep breath and turned to his sergeant, who grunted and nodded once, grudgingly.

"Do it," Feren said, turning to look at me while his sergeant started passing orders. "How…"

I was watching the cohorts reorganize and it was a moment before I understood he was asking me the question. "I've read a lot of books," I said absently, and almost laughed at the confusion that replaced fear on his face.

We were five miles further down the road, riding at the head of the remaining cavalry. Before us marched a mixed double-cohort of foot soldiers, though the last two ranks of fighters were interspersed with farriers, smiths, and armorers, carrying spare shields and weapons to blend in with the others.

We had left behind the soldiers they replaced—the best riders among them—with half of our cavalry and most of the remounts. The remaining cavalry trotted in a weaving pattern almost randomly, occasionally doubling back or charging forward as if losing control of a fractious mount. Our hope was these movements would confuse any eyes in the trees, and blind them to the numbers we had left behind.

With any luck, those were now making their way quickly southwest through the forest.

We had perhaps an hour before the plan came to completion, and little to do now but march and hope. I sent another update to Sem, forming the thought and pushing it through the open doorway in our minds: *Column still under march.* I heard them nod in response. They would know precisely where I was.

I was riding now alongside Feren. His sergeant—who had

the unlikely name of Mims—had ridden ahead to check on the vanguard.

"You're not the sort I expected to find commanding here," I said.

Feren took a moment before he answered. "Do you mean, because I'm too young?"

"You're not afraid of us."

Feren made a face, somewhere between a grimace and a rueful grin. "I'm more than a little afraid of your friend."

I shook my head, having trouble explaining what I meant. "I grew up hiding who I was. Most of the world I've seen hates us, or fears us, or treats us like the muck on the bottom of their boots. Or all three at once." I looked off to the horizon, remembering what I had seen the night before. "Someone in Balifere *murdered a child,* and the person who was trying to help that child. Burned their bodies and left them in the woods. The people of that town either looked the other way, or helped to do it. There will be no justice done, because in their minds it was." I looked at Feren. "That's your world. Your society at work."

Feren flinched but said nothing.

"Now I ride into your column, with a warning of what's coming. I'm honestly not sure why I did. I don't owe you or your men anything. And the people of Torfall would as soon cut my throat as sell me shoes. You have no reason to listen to me; to believe my warning. Yet you do. Why?"

The quick, steady rhythm of hoof and creaking harness filled the space between us as I waited for my answer. A pair of cavalrymen rode past at a disorganized gallop and then wheeled in a circle and returned to the back of the line.

When Feren finally spoke, it was a slow and rambling speech, as if he was picking out his words with care, but unsure where his thoughts were headed. "I grew up in Fin-Torfall. In the city, it's not like it is out here. Sure, I heard stories growing up about witches and the things..." his eyes darted quickly to my face and away, "...the things you do. But just because people tell the stories doesn't mean everyone believes them."

He shrugged uncomfortably. "I don't hate anyone. And most people I know don't hate anyone. But somehow that hatred you talk about... it exists like... like a cloud, a fume that you can smell only if you're not standing in it. I've seen it take root, like with that crowd outside the inn."

I listened to his words, trying to keep expression off my face. I could tell he was trying for respect and kindness and that he thought he was speaking it. But the more he talked, the more his words seemed to stir a seething anger deep inside me.

He looked down at his hands. "I didn't know about the child. But I could see that violence was there somehow, roiling between those townspeople and you, ready to erupt. I suppose you could have killed them all, or torn down the whole village. But you rode on, even though their treatment of you was offensive. I guess that's why I believed you. I saw you choose to avoid more violence."

It was the distance he was giving it, I realized. That he could speak of the hatred that had driven my family from their home, that had stolen their lives and my childhood, that had murdered Ash and fourteen-year-old Benni, as a force unrelated to the people that wielded it... it seemed to absolve those people of the consequences of their prejudice. His "somehow" seemed to imply that the townspeople were as much victims of the potential violence as we were.

"It wasn't a *fume* that crushed Benni's skull," I said coldly, and pulled roughly forward. I only managed to go a few yards before he caught up to me.

"I'm sorry. I said something wrong, and I didn't mean to be offensive. I... I don't always say the right things."

I sighed in frustration. I wanted to be angry. I wanted to rage, but I knew there was no point. He was not a reasonable target of my fury. In truth, I knew it was a delayed response to the meaningless murders in Balifere.

"When it's not directed at you," I said quietly, "it's easy to believe that people don't hate. When you see it only now and then: in an offhand remark or an ugly jest, you can believe that it's an unusual, uncommon occurrence."

I turned in the saddle to face him, catching his eyes in mine and holding them. "But when you look into someone's eyes and see the fear and hatred lurking within—whether they revel in it or are unaware of it—you cannot pretend that it is not there *for you*. When you see and hear and feel it so often that you are surprised only at its absence... then you know that its presence in society is welcome and comfortable and... *intentional*."

"And what do you see in my eyes?" Feren asked.

I looked away. "I see curiosity. I see questions." It was better than the alternative, I thought. "Ask. I promise I will not turn you into a newt."

"What's a newt?" Feren asked in confusion.

The earnest, innocent question made me laugh. "It's like a small lizard," I said.

We rode for a few moments more before he spoke again, haltingly. "What... how..." He glanced at me and shook his head, starting over. "When... How did... you know you were... what you are?"

I thought this question through before answering. "You mean that I'm *nyssa*? Or a witch?"

"I... I don't know what I mean. I just... I don't understand—

not that my understanding means anything—but…"

"When you were young," I asked, "what is your first memory of knowing that you were a boy? I don't mean, 'when did you first hear others say you were a boy?' Or 'when did you first know the difference between girls and boys?' Or even 'when did you first call yourself a boy?' When did you *know*?"

"I… I'm not sure I can answer that," he answered thoughtfully. "I don't know that I can think of a particular moment."

"I don't have this experience myself, but I think," I said in return, "that when your parents and neighbors and sibs all name you something that agrees with your own sense of yourself, then you maybe *don't* have any 'particular moment' of clarity." I stared out over the marching soldiers ahead of me, watching the pikes bob rhythmically. "My family had a notion of what I was, but my mother wanted—really desperately wanted—me to be her little girl. When she felt me drifting away from that fantasy she had made for herself, she tried to push me to it. That's when I knew. When that vision she had for me became clear, and it felt viscerally, violently wrong."

Feren's response was silence. I hoped he was thinking over what I had said.

I felt a gentle nudge in my mind, and smelled Sem's thoughts: *They can see you.*

"Signal Mims. We're nearly upon them." I felt for Sem's position, sensing them about half a mile further down the road. "About half a mile."

The others should be northwest of you by now, I sent back. I could feel Sem shifting position, staying in sight of the ambushers while moving to their western flank.

My calm and confidence had fled. At this point, we were well-committed to my plan, and it was all up to Feren's soldiers. If the foot moved too quickly or not in time, or if they broke under the coming attack... If the cavalry we had left behind were lost, or late, or struggled with the terrain... There were thousands of ways my plan could fail, and now I worried them all one by one as we rode.

Feren had assured me that his swordsmen knew how to form a tortoise, that his pikes were steadfast and would not break. That his horsemen were sure in the saddle and would time their counter well.

Mims rode back to us and reported to Feren. "I've got all the cavalry and the first rank of foot scanning the trees. The men are ready to give the signal at first sighting."

Feren nodded. "As soon as it sounds, we ride left—hard. I know your heart is with the foot, Mims, but we'll need you more than they will so long as they follow orders."

Mims grunted, and saluted his commander with a fist to chest, riding back to the right flank position.

I looked Feren over. "You seem to be full of confidence suddenly."

"My men know their jobs and are skilled," he said. "We just needed a plan." He glanced at me shyly. "*You* gave us that. I know I could not have. Now that we know *what* to do... watch us do it," he said, grinning.

Neither of us spoke more, the tension was too high, nerves wound too tight. I began to fret in the saddle. My body wanted to move, not just sit and let the horse carry me. It was agonizing, riding knowingly into an ambush. I kept my horse moving, but my eyes were deep in the trees, hunting for any sign of them. My shoulders were tense, and I tried to force them to relax. I shifted the sword on my hip, making sure it was ready to draw.

For all my years of reading, this would be my first real battle.

I'm not sure who spotted them first, but a shrill whistle

burst from among the pikes and swords, and to their credit they moved with speed and perfection. The men stopped their march mid-stride and the pikes dropped from their marching carriage into a fierce, bristling nest of steel pointing left, right, and forward. Even as the first arrows flew from the woods on both sides, the swordsmen mixed in with the pikes interlocked their shields into a wall of armor, with both cohorts tightening their ranks into a dense, solid mass of shield and pike.

The volley of arrows rattled against the formation, finding few chinks in that defense.

A second volley was in the air, still aimed at the foot soldiers—who held steadfast—as Feren, Mims, the remaining twelve cavalrymen, and I all charged our mounts hard to the left between the trees, wheeling wide to catch dozens of black-clad archers and swordsmen unprepared and ill-defended.

I could barely hear the tramp of hooves over the pounding of blood in my ears as we drove straight into the right flank of a mass of soldiers who were expecting to catch us confused and unawares and panicked. My sword was in my hand and I don't remember drawing it. I swung it in artless arcs, bludgeoning as much as cutting the enemy down.

My horse—a well-trained cavalry mount—was familiar with the business, and trampled more than one wide-eyed archer in our charge. I lost track of Feren and the others and for some moments it was all chaos and screams and violence.

The enemy soldiers weren't fools, however. They had lost most of their archers on this side in our initial charge, but the swordsmen were beginning to form up, and though we were mounted, we were only fifteen against many times that number.

Through the trees, I could see the formation of pikes and shields, still holding fast. But beyond them, more black-clad soldiers were emerging from the treeline, their archers peppering the wood and steel hedgehog with arrows shot at close-range. These were beginning to tell, where the volleys had failed. I could see several of our foot soldiers on the ground, dead or wounded.

Feren caught my eye and grinned wickedly, his face splashed with blood. I glanced around, wondering how long we could hold against them if they got their formation in order. Not long, I thought.

Before my thoughts could turn to fear or worry, a horn sounded clear and brash, and I heard a great shout carry over the battle from the other side of the road.

"TORFALL!"

The cavalry we had left behind galloped out of the far trees in a fearsome charge, more than twenty strong including the swordsmen who had joined their ranks. They had ridden southwest and circled the wood, riding hard all afternoon in secret to fall on the ambushers' left flank. They rode them down and broke the enemy formations into pockets of confusion.

I caught a glimpse of Sem moving through the trees west of the road—the briefest flashes of uncanny movement. Seeing them with my eyes while also feeling them within my own mind made my head spin so that I nearly tumbled from the saddle. My senses struggled to make sense of the smell of a blade severing a bowstring; the color of a grating scream as another bowman's arm was crushed by a sharp blow; the sound of blood spraying through the air from a severed hand. Sem was systematically removing the archers from the field.

With most of them down or scattered, now our foot soldiers' formation erupted, spreading to either side of the road, the pikes and swords flashing as they forced the churning mass of black-clad soldiers to choose between steel or hoof.

The violence and blood and screams was almost too much to bear, but then almost as quickly as it had begun, the battle was over. The ground was littered with the bodies of the fallen—mostly in black with orange and purple stripes on their tunics. But some here and there wore gray. The remaining enemy soldiers threw down their swords and bows, and were rounded up by Feren's men. Mims directed the pikemen to oversee the prisoners, while Feren sent half the horse out to circle the battlefield looking for stragglers or anyone fleeing.

The battle had lasted only half an hour or so, but I felt a great weight of exhaustion on my shoulders. I could barely lift my sword enough to clean and re-sheath it. I could feel Sem moving through the wood, perhaps unwilling to get too close to the Torfallin soldiers.

I climbed down off my horse and began to see what I could do for the wounded.

Are you going to come into camp? I asked Sem.

Feren's men had established a camp beside the road just south of the woods, and a smaller one further south for the prisoners. At first light, Feren sent half a cohort to escort the armorers and smiths back north to retrieve the wagons. Half the squadron of cavalry was still taking it in turns scouting the surrounding countryside in broad arcs to secure the camp and hunt down any enemies who had escaped through the woods.

Of the three hundred and fifty ambushers, fewer than one hundred remained alive, and only half of those had surrendered uninjured. We had lost only thirty nine. I had already seen to our injured immediately after the battle, and the worst of theirs this morning.

No, Sem thought back in reply. *I have no desire to keep that sort of company. I'll bring your things and follow.*

I could feel them moving northeast through the trees to retrieve the mules and all the things we had left at our campsite. I desperately wanted a bath and a change of clothes, but the only water nearby was a meager creek on the edge of the wood.

I was there now, bending by the muddy bank to wash blood off my hands in the shallow trickle. I was bone weary. I had healed nearly a dozen men with power drawn from the miasma of pain that permeated the battlefield. Even using the pain of others, I was so tired that I didn't trust myself to heal with power anymore, but still I had worked on through the night, my surgical skills saving many more.

I had finally eaten some time around midnight, when one of Feren's sergeants noticed me sway and nearly faint between seeing to injured soldiers. He had ordered me to sit down and eat a bowl of stew and a heel of bread, and had stood over me to watch that I did so.

It felt strange to be among so many who were not *nyssén* and who knew that I was. It was stranger still that they seemed to accept me without any overt hostility. If I heard soldiers casually refer to me as *mixie* or *witch* in my hearing, at least it was said without heat or anger. There *was* still a kind of fear and distance, as someone might be glad of the protection of a fierce dog, yet be hesitant to pet it. Word of my role had spread through the ranks in the aftermath of the battle, and some of the foot seemed to regard me as something of a talisman.

I heard steps behind me, and turned to see Feren approaching. He had cleaned himself of others' blood, and somehow his stature had changed. He looked the part of their commander. It seemed as if he had grown ten years older in the night.

"You ate breakfast, I hope?" he said.

"Yes," I said. I had eaten a crust of buttered bread. I was not used to the thick stews and thick porridge, always full of salted meat, that the soldiers seemed to eat mornings and nights.

"We're going to remain here for a day to let the wounded rest. But then we need to continue on to Quarry East. We're overdue to join up with the Bluecaps." A grin spread across his face. "I can't wait to see their faces when we march in with eighty prisoners." He squatted down beside me, suddenly thoughtful. "I thought that when you rode into our column and took charge of my troops that I had seen a marvel. Last night, when you put down your sword and took up the surgeon's knife and needle..." He shook his head and smiled again. "Books, was it?"

"I studied with a healer," I said. I didn't particularly want to discuss Reft or the Watch with him.

Feren seemed to let it go. "What are your plans now?" he asked almost tentatively.

I thought over the question. Sem seemed content to follow my lead for now, and I had nowhere in particular to go. I thought of my haunted wood to the east. It would be a comfort to return there. But then I thought of the look in Andia's eyes, and I sighed. There were still wounded among the men, and having started their care, I felt obligated to see it through.

"I will ride with you at least as far as Quarry East. I assume there will be surgeons, or a field hospital there?"

Feren nodded. "Likely. The Bluecaps are the elite of the Torfallin Army, and they've set up their field command there. They'll have turned the city into a fortress by now."

"Do you know why Savat began this war in the first place?" I asked, thoughtlessly.

"Duke Savat? I don't know much of his politics. It's mostly

above my station, but perhaps we can learn something when we reach Quarry East. General Hines's men will have some no-tion, I'm sure."

above my station, but perhaps we can learn something when we reach Quarry East. General Hines's men will have some no-tion, I'm sure."

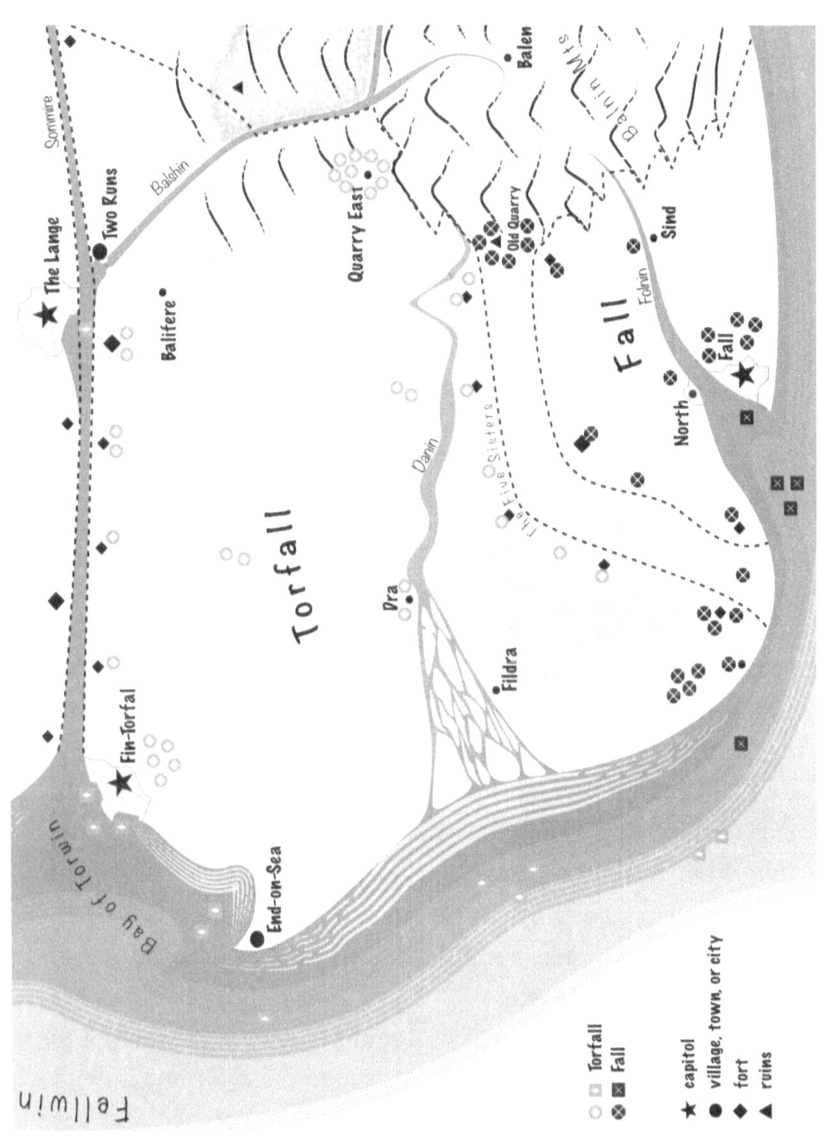
Fellwin
Bay of Torwin
Sonnire
The Lange
Two Runs
Balshin
Balifere
Fin-Torfal
Torfall
End-on-Sea
Dra
Fildra
Danin
The Five Sisters
Quarry East
Balen
Bajnin Mts
Old Quarry
Fohrin
Sind
Fall
North
Fall
Fall
Torfall
capitol
village, town, or city
fort
ruins

Seven

The horse's steady gait had become a comfort after miles under the late summer sun. Neither Feren nor his men had made any claim on the leggy black—who I had named Artem for his calm in battle and his sure step—so I considered him mine. The road stretched on before and behind us, dust pluming in the air from the tread of hundreds of feet and hoofs.

The column was led by half the sword cohort and a few of the cavalry, but our pace was held by the prisoners. They marched in hobbles made from their own tack and pack leather, surrounded by the pikemen. I rode with Feren and the rest of the horsemen behind, and the wagons and remaining foot brought up the rear.

Somewhere off to the east, I could feel Sem shadowing the column. They were not far off, but since their journey north to retrieve the mules, they had held a steady distance and kept out of sight. I had informed Feren of their location to avoid any misunderstandings between them and the company's outriders. Now, I felt them pressing forward, moving well ahead of us.

The soldiers' practice was to eat their midday meal on the march: strips of dried meat and a hard flavorless biscuit, washed down with water. Even Feren and his sergeants ate the same, so I felt I couldn't complain, though it was supremely unappetizing after the first day. Breakfast each day was a gluey porridge with flecks of ham, and the evening meal always the same thick stew. I wondered how they survived without vegetables. I found myself looking at the grass with some craving.

The heat of the afternoon rose and the dust of the column was sticking to my sweaty brow. By what I could see of the other faces, I was sure mine was filthy. My skin itched, and I longed to submerge myself in water. To say I had begun to dream about bathing was no exaggeration.

I felt something change in my mind, and then a new awareness bloomed there. I still could feel Sem's location, slowing so that we began to catch up to them. But now, I had a new certainty of place in my mind. I realized suddenly that Sem had performed a Finding, and *pushed* it to me through our Pairing. I had no idea such a thing was possible.

I could feel it now, shining like the brightest star. It was slightly off the road to the southeast, about two miles ahead and a mile east.

"Something wrong, Arin?" Feren asked.

I realized then I had pulled up short. "Nothing wrong," I said absently, still feeling the location Sem had sent me. "I need to leave the column for a time. I'll return before long."

Feren didn't question me with words, but I could see on his face that he wondered.

"I will return," I said again. "My friend has left me something I need to collect."

I rode away without giving him time to object or question. I pulled slowly through the marching soldiers, careful not to disrupt the column. When I reached a smooth verge along the left side of the road, I pulled Artem off and across country. I gave him his head and he sprang to a gallop, letting go his pent-up energy in a joyous burst.

He maintained his footing despite the rougher terrain, and it didn't take long before I sensed we were approaching the marker that Sem had planted in my mind. We topped a low rise, and then I saw it: my walking stick speared vertically into the rocky soil, with my satchel next to it. I smiled.

Artem overshot and I pulled him around in a tight circle before dismounting. He stepped lively, but didn't wander. Perhaps a bath was still out of reach, but I could change my clothes at least. I had been wearing the same for days.

I dug out my other tunic and trousers and then kicked off the boots and stripped down to the skin. Once they were off my body, I shuddered at the feel of the sweat-stained clothes. Blood and mud and dust had dried into a cracking paste so that parts of the tunic I shed were stiffened. I desperately wished I could bathe, even eyeing the gritty soil, wondering if I could manage a sand-bath, but dismissed the idea—too much clay and not enough sand.

Nonetheless, I stretched and basked for a moment with the hot sun and dry breeze on my naked skin. I spread my toes and felt the dry grass and sharp pebbles beneath my feet. I had forgotten how quiet and peaceful the world could be, after days in the company of over a hundred soldiers.

I stood there for several minutes before I sighed and pulled the clean clothes over my sweaty body. I promised myself that my first priority on reaching Quarry East was a bath and freshly laundered clothing. When I lifted my satchel to tie it to

Artem's saddle, I saw that Sem had found my sandals also, tucking them underneath. Now that I wore clean clothes and felt marginally more myself, I couldn't bring myself to put on the dead soldier's boots.

"You won't step on my foot, will you?" I asked the horse. He whuffed at me, which I took for agreement. I found a bit of leather strap and ran it through the finger loop at the top of the boots, then stuffed my sandals into the satchel and strapped that down as well. I pulled my staff from the ground and tucked it under my cloak which was rolled and tied behind the cantle.

Artem nosed my hand, looking for food. I stroked his forehead and pushed him away affectionately. "I have nothing for you."

I pulled myself back into the saddle, settling my bare feet into the stirrups with only a little awkwardness, then clucked and nudged him gently forward. We turned back towards the road, but I kept him to a slow walk. I had no urgent desire to return to the noise and smell and not-so-subtle stares of Feren's men.

Quarry East was indeed a fortress. Smaller than Anbress, but larger than any rural town, it was a hub of bustle and activity. We saw first a great palisade that appeared to entirely encircle the city a full mile from its low stone wall. The nearby mountains looked shorn nearly bare of trees for miles.

I nodded to myself, admiring the fortification. It served a dual purpose: the wooden wall of tightly planted stakes—each hewn solid from a tree trunk and sharpened to points—stood twice the height of a man, and would slow any attacking force well before they approached striking distance of the main defenses. The denuding of the nearby hills to build it also denied cover to any attacking force.

We were hailed by the garrison as we approached, and Mims rode ahead to answer. Once our identity was established, a group of soldiers emerged to take charge of our prisoners, and our column was led along the palisade a short way until we reached a narrow alley running along the circumference. It was barely the width of a wagon, so we were forced to march double-file between the wooden spikes. Along the inside, the trunks were spaced just enough to allow for defenders to thrust a pike or sword or to shoot arrows between them.

The field between wooden and stone fortifications was crowded with tents laid out in strict grids. Thousands of soldiers camped in organized clusters, each its own self-contained village. We rode along the road, maintaining our double-file march through several choke-points and barricades and reached the stone wall of Quarry East.

It was not much in terms of defense, only coming chest-high to a mounted soldier, but it was wide enough to act as a causeway, giving the soldiers who garrisoned the town and stood atop it clear visibility over the surrounding terrain and an easy, defensible perimeter to patrol. A stout wooden gate made of steel-pinned timbers—each as thick as a man—stood open.

Mims directed the corporals to seek the quartermaster and see the men established. As the column moved off, Feren and Mims rode into the town, and I followed. The older man still made every effort to ignore me entirely.

Now without the column around me, I could feel the eyes of everyone we passed. There was a curiosity in those looks, and in any that saw close enough to guess at what I was, unveiled hostility.

As one would expect, the town itself was stone. The quarry that gave its name and wealth to the people here also gave its body. The buildings were all of a peculiar grayish-blue granite, largely uniform in cut and color, though with the occasional vein of brown or amber. Even the roads were cobbled with the same stone.

It made for a vaguely disorienting ride, especially as many of the townspeople on the street wore clothes stained with dust the same color. I had to look up to the clear sky for some relief of the monochrome life around me.

As we rode, there were more and more of the soldiers who wore blue-lacquered helms. They looked sharper and more serious than those who camped outside. Some were in gleaming mail and all wore their blue and yellow prominently. These must be the Bluecaps which impressed Feren so.

In time, we arrived at a large building with standing pennants beside the open door. The flags carried golden chevrons over a light blue field, with three stylized trees in black and an eagle in deep blue. Feren led us inside.

I would not call the common room raucous, with a dozen men standing around various tables, or crowded around the cold hearth, debating and arguing over maps and lists in low voices. But as we stood among them, Feren waiting to be acknowledged by a ranking officer, a hush descended in a patchwork of attention and silence until all seemed to be watching us.

Watching me.

I returned the looks, as coldly and calmly as I could. My shoulders were knotting up under the weight of the stares.

One of the men beckoned Feren over to his table, and they conversed quietly for a time. The seated commander fixed me with a hard stare as he listened, Feren making his report while gesturing to me and the map unrolled between them. He dug from his pouch a fistful of tokens taken from the dead and captured commanders of the ambush, placing them on the table.

Mims ignored me as usual, standing a full pace away, turned half towards me but staring over my head, as if he could not decide between guarding me as a threat and pretending I wasn't there.

After a time, the consultation finished and Feren returned, sending Mims off with messages for the troops, then turning to me.

"Captain Nesh has set aside rooms upstairs for us." He looked at me for a moment, seeing my tension and seeming confused at it. "It's okay, Arin, this is the best fortified location outside of Fin-Torfall." He turned and waved over a serving maid, "Take the Lady—" he cut himself off short, his face turning crimson. "Take... er... please um... to... uh... a free room." He turned back to me, his eyes down. "I'm very, very sorry..." he muttered, and scurried away.

My face was hot, all the more for his effusive apology. I took a deep breath, determined to let the unintended slight go. The maid looked confused and uncomfortable, but also looked me over critically, taking in my tunic and trousers, dusty from the road; my stout belt and sword and satchel; my bare feet and my hips and my short fuzz of hair and scarred face. She clearly had no idea what to make of me. She solved this by turning and walking wordlessly towards the corner stairs.

I followed.

The second floor was of thick wooden planks, stained a dark gray with age and pipe smoke. She led me down a narrow hall and under a low lintel to a crossing hallway before we reached a wooden door.

The room was small, but comfortable. A bed against one wall, small fireplace on the other, a window and washstand directly across from the door, and pegs along the entry wall to hang belongings. There was a stiff-backed chair against one wall and a thick rug on the floor, though what color it might have been originally, I couldn't say.

Having brought me to the room, she turned to leave, but I caught her arm.

"I would very much like a bath."

She looked startled, and her eyes danced in sudden nerves.

"Is there a bathing chamber in the Inn?" I asked helpfully.

"There is, but... the soldiers make constant use of it."

"Well then, take me to it. I rode here with a column of soldiers, I might as well number among them."

The maid's eyes went wide and her face turned nearly purple. "You couldn't possibly! They're all men... and you, you're... uh... It wouldn't be right!" She shook herself and tried again. "For ladies, we bring a tub here to your room. I can tell the chambermaid to warm the water and prepare a tub. It can be ready for you in an hour or so."

I tried to keep the frustration from my face. "I am not a lady."

She seemed to ignore this rebuke, nodding. "I'll tell the chambermaid to prepare a bath."

I sighed, realizing I would never win for arguing with her.

"Another thing," I said, ignoring her flinch. "Is there someone who can launder my clothes? And perhaps something clean to wear while I wait? I've been riding for days with only two changes, and both filthy."

She nodded and scurried out, promising that she would send the chambermaid who would supply all my wants.

I hung my satchel, cloak, and sword belt on the pegs, then moved to the washstand, determining at least to clean the dust and road grime from my face and hands while I waited. I caught a fleeting sense of Sem somewhere to the east, bathing in a cold forest pool and I wished briefly that I had gone with them.

It was nearly a quarter hour, and I was almost fuming before a tentative knock at the door brought the chambermaid. She gave me the same sort of appraisal as the earlier maid, part confusion, part fear, part disapproval, before promising to bring me a bath and a pair of shifts to wear while my clothes were laundered. She was good enough to keep it from her face, but I could hear the grimace in her voice at the state of my clothes.

Another long wait before she returned with two other maids dragging a copper tub. They rolled up the rug and placed the tub in the center of the room, then began a slow procession of trips back and forth to the kitchens, bringing buckets of hot water, two at a time. The chambermaid watched me all the while, and only when the water was half to the rim, she placed a folded towel, two white linen shifts, and a lump of soap on the bed.

I stripped off my clothes, combined them with the other items I had pulled from my satchel and piled them in the basket she carried. She looked at the clothes with obvious disapproval, whether at the smell or the cut, I wasn't sure. She nodded to me and departed, all the while avoiding looking at me.

I soaped and scrubbed myself at the washstand, getting most of the grime from my skin before settling in the tub. I did my best to bend over and scrub my hair. It was not an especially comforting bath. The water was hot enough, but there was not enough of it and the tub was cramped. Still, it was a relief to feel clean. I stayed in it until the water had gone cold.

Once cleaned and dried, I pulled on one of the shifts and lay down on the bed, not bothering to pull back the covers. The bed at least was soft and comforting.

I was not expecting to sleep, but I must have, for when I next opened my eyes, a soft blanket was draped over me and the window showed the muted light of late afternoon. I stood, stretching out my stiff limbs, to see the tub was gone, the rug unrolled, and my cleaned clothes were folded and neatly stacked on the chair.

I put on the better of the clothes I had: a deep blue tunic that reminded me—in color if not in quality—of the one Fanti had made for me years ago, and the wide, bell-shaped gray trousers. The launderers had ironed its multitude of pleats to crisp perfection.

I was about to venture to the common room, when a knock sounded at the door. I expected a chambermaid, but it was an old man's face that greeted me as I opened it. He was thin and wiry, with short-cropped white hair and a trim beard. His clothes were finely made, but subdued, as if he dressed to fade into the background.

He gave me a slight bow, hardly more than a nod of the head. "General Hines would like to meet you."

I followed him through the narrow hall and we descended the stairs. By the fading light through my window, I had expected the common room to be busy with dinner service, but the room was mostly empty. Feren was standing by the fireplace in close counsel with a man wearing an elaborate uniform. Feren caught my eye and nodded to me as we descended, but they continued talking.

The old man led me to a table on the far side of the room to wait, then stepped back out of the way. Despite the lamps and crackling fire and the afternoon light through the windows, the common room had a dim, quiet feeling. One end of the table was piled with dispatches, lists, and rolled papers. A single large parchment was unrolled over most of the other.

I leaned over it, examining the intricate map inked upon it. It was a map of the southwest of the continent, from the Sommíre south to the sea. Laid upon it were small wooden markers, lacquered in blue and black. There were square tokens marking ships at sea, and discs over the terrain, each carrying a sigil and some annotations I took for cohort counts. A dense cluster of blues were stacked beside Quarry East. A road ran southwest from the town, crossing the Danin river and running westward to connect a string of forts all the way to the western coast. There were some blue tokens marking each fort along the chain.

Beneath these were a number of black tokens, radiating outwards from Fall and their own fortifications. Between the two strings of forts lay a broad frontier, a curving buffer claimed by neither side on the map.

Judging by the black tokens, Savat's armies had ventured across the border, with one significant mass of discs just south of us near a mark on the map bearing the name Old Quarry. A second thrust had broken through the western line and had taken the westernmost fort and occupied a village hard on the coast. Its mark on the map wasn't even named.

"What do you think of our position?" the old man asked softly from over my shoulder. He moved up to stand beside me and look down on the map with me.

"We seem well secure here for now," I temporized. "What do you know of the 'why' of this war?" I asked him. "How did it start? Why do they fight?"

He shook his head. "It began so fast, even Fall's own embassy in Fin-Torfall knew nothing of it. I hear there wasn't even a formal declaration until troops flying Duke Savat's colors crossed the line and besieged the Fifth Sister."

"How old are these positions?"

He answered carefully. "The units marked here at Quarry East and nearby are updated hourly. Others as the dispatch riders can reach us. These," he indicated the clusters far to the west, "Are two weeks old at most."

I traced my finger along the line of forts called the Five Sisters and the blue markers placed there. "These are in imminent danger."

"Oh? How do you read that?" he asked. "Are the forts not well garrisoned?" He seemed genuinely curious.

My mind had run ahead of conscious thought, and I paused a moment to let myself catch up, speaking slowly. "Savat's men to our south... are meant only to hold us here. They threaten incursion along the Balnin foothills, but they will not move against us while the western frontier holds." I moved my hand to indicate the dense cluster of black discs occupying the west. "These though. They mean to envelop the defenses, cutting them off from supply and to maneuver to this point." I touched the narrowest point of the Danin, where a quirk of the terrain made the river twist suddenly north then back south, forming a chevron. I guessed this was where the cohorts that tried to ambush us had crossed. "There they will cross, with their flanks covered by the armies encamped south of us."

The man grunted. "They march west to go east?" he said, a hint of disdain in his question.

"They have no other reason to have taken the west but to encircle the southern fortifications. Your sea power can repel any threat on the water. There can be nothing more than fishermen waiting for them in this village. They cannot move north from their position—these marshes may as well be a mountain range for the difficulty they will have trying to cross. The entire incursion can have only one goal. If you move south without attention to that western enemy, you'll find them on your right flank."

"You seem to see much. How then would you counter such a maneuver?" He asked softly.

My mind worked the problem, envisioning move and counter, sorting and discarding ideas. "Cede the western forts. Pull back all the Torfallin forces to the First and Second Sisters, here," I pointed to the easternmost forts of the line. "Bring half the forces out of Quarry East, and move across the Danin. Between those from the western forts and the ones from here, you have..." I quickly added up the numbers, "more than eight-thousand foot and three-thousand cavalry against their seven and two. Crush them quickly and decisively enough, and you can regroup and entrench to repel the western forces, with reinforcements from the northern brigades, if needed."

"But... cede the western fortifications?"

"You will have defeated a quarter of Savat's troops, and strengthened Torfall's hold on the gateway to the north. And they will have gained... what? A few fortifications that guard a sprawling marshland in a dead-end corner of the country. Once we've taken Old Quarry and established a substantial army there, we can push south into the heart of Fall while the reserves hold off any encirclement here."

I looked up, then, realizing everything I had said and how I had said it. I was an interloper here and despised. Feren and the other man had approached the table while I spoke and were listening.

The elaborately decorated officer said to the old man,

"Well, General Hines? What do you think?"

I stiffened, turning suddenly to reappraise the gaunt white-haired man standing beside me. He wore an expression that was somewhere between thoughtfulness and amusement. When he spoke, it was first to Feren.

"Young Feren, I commend your instincts. This young person does indeed have an excellent military mind." General Hines now faced me. "Arin, they call you, yes?"

"Yes."

"Feren here has received a promotion and a new command. *Captain* Feren will lead a special detachment to coordinate the strategic withdrawal from the western Sisters. Will you join him?" The three men looked at me impassively, waiting for an answer.

Feren's eyes held a question and... a hope?

"I will," I said. It would get me out of this town and out from the stares at least. There was another reason, though: Looking at the map, something had become clear to me. By the numbers and the terrain, there was no way Savat could win this war, even with some *nyssén* fighting on his side. Cause pain, yes. Suffering and deprivation, yes. His troops could bloody the Torfallin, and maybe even push the border north, but he couldn't hope to hold it. The whole thing made even less sense as I examined the troop positions.

I still wanted to know what this war was about. The battlefield was the most likely place to learn it.

"And your mysterious and absent friend?" the general asked softly.

My eyes darted between Feren and the other men. "I can't speak for them," I said. I took in the map once more, noting the positions of each unit and the lay of the terrain. I committed as much of it as I could to memory, and pushed the memory through the doorway in my mind to Sem. "But... probably. Though they will not place themselves under any command."

Eight

The tower of the central keep of the Third Sister stood proudly against the lowering sun as our column descended the low hill. Mims called a halt to the company as we waited for the scouts to return. I could see them now leaving the main gate of the outer walls and galloping their horses up the hill towards us.

Our modified company made excellent time. We were organized for speed: two squadrons of light cavalry and a mixed cohort of mounted archers and sword. We had crossed the Danin and left Captain Tomrin—the officer who had been in counsel with Feren the night I met General Hines—at First Sister with three full divisions from the muster at Quarry East. After a week of hard riding along the Sisters Road, we had already brought the new orders to the garrison at Second Sister and the Golden Corps who were camped along the road behind us. By now, both should be marching east to rendezvous with Tomrin's divisions.

Our mission was to continue west as far as Fourth Sister, bringing the order to redeploy eastward. When we reached the last defended fort, we would ride back with its garrison.

Feren was well-settled into his new rank and role. It showed in his confidence and posture, but also in the way his sergeants looked to him. He was no longer the young, accidental commander.

My role as advisor was awkward though, not fitting neatly into the normal chains of command the sergeants were accustomed to. With me, Mims was mostly still struggling to find some balance point between toleration and indifference. That I was wearing a new tunic in Torfallin colors seemed not to matter to him. I was growing accustomed to his looking past me, and I tried to ignore the occasional glare of suspicion. The other two sergeants, Bergin and Joff, were more accepting, having survived their injuries at the ambush in no small part due to my skills.

The real surprise was in the rank and file. The half cohort of sword and several of the cavalry squadron were veterans of our surprise attack on the would-be ambushers north of Quarry East. They had insisted on staying under Feren's command, and had wasted no time in regaling the others with stories of the feat. My role in the fray was magnified and expanded in the retelling, and soon I could not move through our evening camps without feeling wide eyes follow me. Better awe than fear, I suppose.

The scouts arrived and Feren and his sergeants pulled close to hear their report. I heeled Artem forward to join the circle, feeling more comfortable in the saddle now in my correctly-sized riding boots requisitioned for me by Feren. As I approached, I picked up the scout's report mid-sentence.

"—almost two-hundred injured, just arrived from the west.

They're in dire shape, sir. The surgeon's train was hit by archers in the retreat. There's only a junior medic left in the garrison."

Feren looked at me, guessing at my urge to ride down as soon as possible. "Wait, Arin, we'll all ride down together. You'll spend hours alone trying to convince them you can help." He turned back to the scout. "How many at the Sister?" Feren asked.

"Nineteen-hundred, mixed cohorts and the townsfolk. It's the garrison, plus all that's left of the Winter Corps, and they pulled the villagers behind the wall when word came of the attack out west."

"And General Pern?"

"Dead," the scout said grimly. "He and his two captains. The garrison commander has taken charge. By what I could learn, the general and one captain were wounded in the initial attack, and the remaining captain was conferring with them in the wounded wagons when they were ambushed. It was a rout, they say—they were overconfident and unprepared."

"Well," Mims said, "They've paid for it, haven't they."

Feren looked up sharply at Mims. "Prepare the column. We move at once. Have the bannermen unfurl the pennants so they know who is riding down on them." He turned back to the scout. "Jaem, you ride back ahead and tell them I'm coming in to take command."

With the orders given, we descended the hill at a trot. I kept pace with Feren as he doled out more instruction to Mims and the other sergeants.

"When we reach them, Mims, I want you to gather anyone of rank who's left from Pern's men. Find out what happened to them and who might be left to the west. Joff, look to the state of the garrison defenses and shore them up if needed. You can supplement them with squads of our archers, but keep our men together as much as possible. Bergin, gather a squad and stick with Arin; help them organize the wounded. Make sure they have everything they need. Knock heads if you need to." Feren looked to me next. "Arin, do what you can."

I nodded.

The Five Sisters were all built on a common design from the same blue-gray stone quarried from the mountains to the east. A keep with square towers on each corner occupied the center of a square bailey, the outer wall wide enough to house barracks, smithy, stables, and other necessities. The wall enclosed a parade field, and outside it was a deep, stone-lined dry moat to discourage undermining and ladders. Access was a single narrow span, specially prepared on the inward side so it could be collapsed in case of a siege.

They had stood for hundreds of years, most of which were tense but peaceful. In the intervening time, something like villages had grown along the outside of the moat like mushrooms on a fallen log. The men who maintained the long, lonely watches of the forts—in Torfall all soldiers were men—encouraged the establishment of these almost-villages: there was always demand for gambling and drink and lustful adventure. Whether the commanders tolerated or enjoyed the houses of vice and recreation in these so-called "Little Sisters," there was a long-standing policy that these structures had to be built of wood. At need, they could be fired to deny an enemy useful cover. We rode now between the shabby wooden structures, all standing abandoned in the emergency.

We crossed the narrow bridge double-file and entered into the Third Sister.

A field hospital has a smell. It is an odor layered with the rich metal scent of blood, a thick, cloying stench of febrile sweat and waste, and a subtle top-note of wounds gone bad. It's a smell of horror and pain and misery. Men lay on a sea of cots and blankets that filled the parade ground between the bailey and the keep. The regimented order of the wounded and dying somehow made the scene more gut-churning.

A harried soldier, his gray tunic smeared with blood from other men stopped short in front of us. His hair was brushed back from his face and frozen in place with a stiff crust of dried blood. Smears of it ran along his temples, no doubt from his own hands.

"If you can walk, I have no time for you. Please go," he said tiredly. He didn't even look at us, moving his arm as if to brush us aside.

I caught his wrist and held him firmly. "We are here to help," I said. "What's your name?"

"My name? I'm Winten, and you're in my way." Now he looked up at us, his eyes going slightly wild at the sight of me in my clean gray trousers and tunic, Bergin in his blue and yellow-slashed uniform at my side, and the five swordsmen arrayed behind us. He looked from one of us to the other before fixing on me doubtfully. "Who are you?"

Bergin spoke for us, in his low, rumbling voice. "Sergeant Bergin, attached to the Bluecaps out of Fin-Torfall," he said with a slight nod, "and this is Arin, who is a field surgeon. We're your watch relief. You in charge?"

Winten nodded slowly. "Corporal. Medic. But..." he spread his arms wide, taking in the grim horror of the endless wounded.

I couldn't let him fall into despair—I still needed him for a time. "Bergin, put out a muster for ten from the garrison—or the townsfolk. Find anyone who has any knowledge of herbalism, healing, animal husbandry, or even caring for a sick family member. Anyone who won't wilt at this work. Tell them to report here to me." I took Winten by the shoulder as Bergin took two of our men away on the errand. "You've done as well as you could here on your own. Tell me where things stand..."

We walked slowly down the aisle between injured soldiers as he gave halting answers to my questions. What was the process for triage and organization of patients? Little and none. What was the status of medical supplies? Low on everything. I looked grimly over the men laid out on blankets, holding their own wounds closed or lying unconscious. Winten was clearly operating by rote. Utterly defeated.

"Take me to the worst wounded," I said.

He looked at me, startled. "Over here," he said slowly.

Winten led us down to the end of one aisle, where a soldier lay insensate on a blanket. His shirt and trousers had been cut away and used for wadding to pack and bandage the gaping wound across his belly. The bleeding had slowed, but the man was dying nonetheless. The mixed stench of feces and blood told me his bowels were cut through. There was nothing a surgeon could do for him, and I was surprised the man was still alive.

As if reading my thoughts, Winten tried to explain, looking wide-eyed between me and the three soldiers behind me. "I would have eased his passing, but we've nothing to give him, and he's not conscious enough to take it anyway." He looked down in defeat. "I thought of the knife, but I was needed elsewhere..." He trailed off.

"Bring water," I said, putting as much command as I could muster into my voice. I knelt down beside the man. Seeing the state of him, I wasn't sure I could do what I meant to try. But there was such a maelstrom of pain and hurt surrounding me, it was urging me on. I could almost *taste* the power surging around us. It reminded me of that day, long ago, when Sem had begun their assault on Ma'am's house. I remembered watching them pace between the broken men that littered the street, drawing power from their pain. I remembered Turin's distaste at my description of Sem's actions. Dire, some called it.

Winten returned with a bucket of cold water drawn from the well and set it beside me. "What...?" he started to ask.

Without waiting to explain or to doubt myself, I reached out with both hands and pulled away the bandages to reveal the raw butchery that was the soldier's abdomen. The man thrashed and wailed in pain, but I leaned over and pushed him down, right hand on his chest and left on his thigh. He was too weak to fight me.

His blood was flowing again, and the smell of his torn viscera was overpowering. I could vaguely hear a cry of shock and dismay from Winten and sensed a struggle as one of my swordsmen held him back, but I was already drawing on the sea of pain that roiled in the makeshift hospital. I pushed that power and my awareness into his injuries, feeling my way along the serpentine tissues, finding each cut and tear and *willing* them to knit, to bond, to heal.

With the bowels and internal organs becoming whole, I released him and picked up the bucket, sluicing the foul ordure out of his still-gaping abdomen. The cold shock of the water made him flail again, but now I was closing the gut wound, letting the flow of his own blood force out the last of the contamination. The edges of the wound writhed as they came together, the tissues finding their affinity across the divide, becoming one again.

When it was done, I used the last of the water to rinse the

streaks of blood from his body and from my hands. He was breathing deeply and steadily now, the healthful unconsciousness of long-needed sleep. His torn body was repaired, but he would need days yet of rest and then a great deal of food.

I stood, turning to find Winten staring in horror and confusion. I caught a rueful smile from Raad, who still held Winten by the shoulders. The squad that Bergin had picked out were all veterans from the ambush in the Balifere wood, and of those, these were the most ardent in their approval of me. I had saved each of them from wounds nearly as dire as the one I had just healed.

"Wha... What? What *are* you?" Winten begged, somewhere between tears and revulsion. His face took on a gray tinge.

It was Boon who answered, clapping Winten on the back and smiling, "Arin's our witch and healer, and they're here to help." He winked at me. "Now, you're going to gulp down your stomach, and you're going to stand up straight, and you're going to do everything they say, and together, we're going to save these men's lives, yes?" Raad released the man, and Boon led him away to inventory and organize surgical supplies.

I nodded my thanks to Raad, and between him and Deremin, the three of us began walking slowly down the lines of wounded, taking stock of the injuries, and looking for any whose wounds were mortal. Of these we found many, and I set to healing the ones who could not wait. We also found too many who had already succumbed, and those the two soldiers lifted in their blankets and carried to the far side of the field.

In time, Boon returned with Winten, each carrying baskets of bandages, medicines and surgical supplies. Little enough indeed to care for so many. As they arrived, so too did Bergin and the others, trailing eleven men in hard-worn uniforms and four women of the town. In addition to the skills I had asked for,

Bergin had also thought to recruit a handful of soldiers to help carry and reorder the wounded.

With more hands, the work of triaging the injured moved quickly, even if it took time to organize teams and educate them on their jobs. Soon enough, they were moving through the rows of blankets checking injuries and reordering according to seriousness. The worst injuries were brought to me near the well, where we had set up a field surgery upon three wooden tables taken from the dining hall.

One soldier whose blood-covered face and chest had amounted to a shallow scalp wound—which I quickly stitched—I put to work rotating great tubs of water. One was water boiled in large kettles over an open fire, one cold from the well, both replaced frequently.

I lost track of the hours and the bodies as I worked. I tried to avoid drawing too much on the power, balancing its mental and emotional exhaustion with the work of my hands. Winten and a soldier from the garrison named Gordin Dane, who had some skill with a needle, had joined me at the tables and were bloodied to their forearms along with me.

It was hard, filthy work, and the air was humid and close. At some point I came to realize that I was seeing by the light of torches and lanterns instead of the sun, and knew that I needed a rest. I stretched and knuckled my back, easing the tension that I always carried there.

There were no more injured in immediate danger, so I scrubbed my arms in the hot water tub and stripped off my blood-stained tunic, wiping myself down and changing it for another from my pack. Feeling better for the clean shirt, I looked up to see Feren and Winten standing a few feet away, their faces flushed in deep reds and their eyes desperately averted.

To his credit, Feren found his voice quickly enough. "Arin, if you have a moment, I need a word with you."

I nodded, and we walked away from the surgery to the keep.

Feren glanced back at the dwindling bustle of the field hospital as we walked. "Well done here. It looks like things are well in hand." We passed through the steel-banded gate and up one of the narrow stairs. Feren led me through a warren of passages to another tight spiral ascending until we emerged at the top of the tower. He didn't speak again until we reached the northeast corner.

He looked up at the night sky, at the moon-lit clouds scudding across the stars. "I've spoken to the remaining officers of Pern's army who are here. It looks like when they were initially attacked, the army split, with some retreating to the garrison at Fourth Sister." He scowled. "Pern was a fool. They were the larger force, but so complacent that he had contradictory standing orders. When they were attacked in the night, their discipline collapsed."

"It may not have been all his fault," I said slowly. "You know we've heard rumors that Savat has recruited *nyssén* to fight with his armies. A single *Grim* could do unimaginable damage to a force, no matter the size."

Feren looked thoughtful for a moment, no doubt remembering Sem's participation in the ambush. "I take it your friend is still far from here?"

Sem had made their own way south from Quarry East through the mountains. I could sense them almost due east of us, more than a week's hard ride. I felt a glimpse of a long narrow valley from above, of crumbling stone buildings, of dusty streets filled with a tent city. Black-clad soldiers blended in with the shadows, carrying crossbows and pikes.

"I think they're in the mountains above Old Quarry, watching the enemy encampment there."

Feren nodded absently. He drew a leather-bound spyglass from his belt pouch and extended it, peering into the distant, dark horizon. He handed it to me then, and pointed to the north.

I leaned my elbows on the parapet to steady the spyglass and put it to my eye. I could see the edge of a broad forest to the left, a darkened shadow that thinned to a lighter grassland. It was difficult to make anything out in the night, but there was just enough light from stars and moon to catch a sea of movement to the east of the wood. Shapes darker than the darkened terrain. An army on the move, black-clad, emerging from the treeline and winding in a great arc encircling our position. In no more than two days, they would block our retreat east.

"They mean to cut us off," I said.

Feren nodded again. "The scouts came in an hour ago. They count two thousand in that army, and another similar force closing in from the south."

I added up the numbers, and they pointed to disaster for us.

He spoke quietly, steadily, as if still convincing himself. "I'm going to take most of our company, and the remains of the Winter Corps' cavalry, and ride west to try to bring out the garrison at Fourth Sister. If we can break whatever besieges them there and pull them out, we should have sufficient numbers to return in force and break through."

It seemed a tenuous hope to me. "If they're still there. If we can reach them and break the siege. If we can return without falling prey to the same destruction Pern faced."

Feren sighed. "Arin, we're full to bursting here. The fortress was never provisioned to hold against a siege with the numbers we have now. At the worst... Taking away half the men and horse will give you more time to figure out some miracle."

I looked at him sharply. "Give me?"

"I'm leaving you in command of the Third Sister."

I said nothing for a long moment. "They will not like that."

"You'll have Bergin and Joff, and all of your men," he said with a grim smile. The joke—that those fervent advocates whom I had saved after the ambush were mine—felt bittersweet. It was an admission of the chances of his success.

Feren left and the days passed interminably as we watched the agonizing approach and encirclement by the Fallian army. I was right about one thing: The remaining members of the garrison did not like being left under my command. The only good news was that there were some few who didn't object, or at least weren't as vocal.

Winten was one. He did not endorse me as far as I knew, but he did not speak against me either. With the worst of the wounded healed or healing, and with my new responsibilities trying to organize the defenses and resources of the Third Sister, I had little time to return to the surgery. I formally gave him charge of the care of the remaining wounded, placing all those helpers we had recruited on the first day under his command.

In the days following Feren's departure west, some of those whose lives I had saved were returning to light duty, and some of them seemed generally well-disposed to me. I had Bergin assign them and several of my men to work alongside the wider garrison, in the hopes that they could encourage some degree of acceptance of who and what I was, or at least respect for the chain of command.

Feren had formally placed me in charge in the presence of the garrison officers who were remaining, to make his decision unambiguous. They took it stoically for the most part, though I made a mental note to speak to each individually when I had time. The soldiers were accustomed to taking orders from someone of higher rank. Feren had given me that rank, and so they could find respect for my authority even if they were skeptical of my person.

I called a council of the garrison commander and our sergeants in my war room—previously the officers' mess hall—to plan the defenses. We gathered maps and lists of men and supplies, and the mood was grim. The list of supplies was woefully short, and the list of men too long for the available food. The garrison commander, a man named Holder, was competent and respectful, if cold. It was in the conference that he raised the notion of burning the Little Sister outside the wall, to deny the enemy cover for the siege. I immediately took this advice and sent Bergin to assemble a salvage party of trusted soldiers to enter the abandoned village, strip it of material and supplies, and fire the buildings. Foreseeing that the townsfolk would object, we determined to keep them uninformed until the smoke gave away the plan.

Thereafter they were a world of trouble.

I had largely gone unnoticed in the wider population of the fortress that first day. Spending my time with the wounded, I was invisible to most everyone else. But now, with the plumes of black smoke filtering over the wall and through arrow slits, the townsfolk's tempers boiled over.

My appointment raised awareness of who and what I was and made me more the target of their ire. Having no inherent habit of respect for officers, and holding the prejudices that seemed endemic to Torfallin village life, they were openly hateful and showed every disregard for my authority. Along with the regular dire updates of our envelopment by the Fallian forces, Joff brought me daily reports of townspeople shirking assigned duties, flouting the rationing I had imposed in expectation of the coming siege, and openly disparaging "the vile witch" that dared direct their lives.

I'll admit that I was sorely tempted to take action against the worst of them, but there wasn't any unused space within the fortress for imprisonment, I couldn't put them outside the wall for fear they would reveal our numbers and disposition to the approaching army, and I wouldn't impose any harsher sentence.

And then there was Dane.

He came to my war room on the third evening after Feren left. I was stewing over the maps spread over the wide table, trying to find a way to maneuver out of the trap Savat's army had put us in. I had improvised tokens from the table to represent the various forces: a pair of saltcellars for the two Fallian armies, thumb-sized cordial glasses for Torfallin forces that I could be reasonably sure of. I had stared too long at the maps; A deep, throbbing pain pulsed between my eyes with each heartbeat. I rested my hand on one glass, wondering where it could safely move.

"Early for hard drink, is it not?"

I looked up and it took me a moment to place him. His tunic was clean of blood and his hair washed and pulled back in a short tail. "Dane, yes?" He was the garrison soldier who had joined me and Winten in the surgery. "How are the wounded?"

"Pained," he replied. A slight smirk twisted his lips. "I'm sorry, should I call you sir?"

"Call me what you like. I've been called worse," I said, returning to the map and willing him to leave. "What do you need?"

He approached the table and stood for a moment, studying

it. He reached out and idly shifted one of the saltcellars.

I was about to chastise him, but immediately saw that he was right. It had been in the wrong place.

"It's a pickle we're in," he said, still wearing that smirk.

I looked at him now, my eyes narrowed. "One I'm trying to get us out of. You have some insight to share with me?" I couldn't keep the sharpness from my voice.

His face softened, the smirk shifting slightly to a more engaging smile. "Marki and Ciala say that if anyone can find a way out of this, it's you."

I didn't register the comment for a long moment. It was too foreign to my current context.

When I finally did understand the words, I sat down hard on the wooden chair behind me. Hearing those names, here in this place, years since my departure from Reft was the deepest, most profound shock—ghosts out of the life I thought I had left behind.

"Who are you?" I asked when I found my voice.

"You know who I am. I am Gordin Dane, of the Torfallin militia. I am also Gordin Dane of the Watch of Reft." They nodded to me in respect. "And you are Arin, out of Anbress, formerly of the Watch, and now... a Grim? A wielder of Dire Magic at the least. And... a Captain of Torfall?" Their eyebrow quirked up in a question. "I admit that I wonder where your loyalties lie."

Over the next few days, Dane's revelation filled my mind with new possibilities. A connection to their Paring partner in Reft, and through them to other members of the Watch in the field was an incredible strategic advantage. But that advantage was held just out of my grasp. Dane resisted my attempts to communicate through them to the network of watchers, still unsure of my ultimate goals.

They insisted that my use of the sea of pain in the field hospital—unconsenting—in the healing of the worst injuries constituted Dire Magic, regardless of my motivations of saving lives. It was a sour point between us. That we both wore Torfallin colors was another: They wore the gray as a cover to hide their identity, while I was an open ally and held rank despite my being a *nyssa* and a witch.

I consulted Sem for some clue as to how to influence them, but Dane was too young, having joined the Watch well after Sem's departure from Reft. All they could tell me was what I knew already: That I should try to enlist them to our aid. That I must find a way to escape the trap that held us in its grip.

I hoped that it would be enough that I was trying to extricate us from the siege, but Dane seemed to place a higher value on the secrecy of the Watch network than on their own survival. That they had announced themself to me at all was a dramatic gamble and, they said, a gesture of trust. They made a habit of finding me when there was no one near enough to hear and posing sharp questions, so that I was always on edge. I felt like a buck being stalked by a wolf.

"Where did you go when you left Reft?"

I sighed and leaned against the parapet. I didn't need to turn around; the voice was by now all too familiar. I took one last look through the spyglass at the camps arrayed to the east and south to double check the scouts' final counts, before I turned to face Dane. The army coming up from the south had joined with the first force and now fully cut off any hope of our returning east. I didn't dare send any more scouting parties out of the fortress—the enemy was too close. We were stuck fast.

A sea of tents and pennants cut cleanly across the road. Several poles rose above the peaks of the largest tents, rippling in the warm breeze with broad flags showing a split field of lavender and orange. Three diamonds in black on the lavender and a hawk rampant over the orange, clutching a serpent by the head in its beak. The serpent trailed in a sinuous line back from the hawk's head like a trailing crest. It was the first time I had seen Savat's ducal banner in the clear daylight. It filled me with disquiet.

Even atop the keep tower, I could still smell the char and soot of the burning of the Little Sister, though the fires had long-since reduced the buildings to blackened twisted ruins. It was an acrid stink that reminded me too-well of the burned cottage south of Balifere, and the death and horror Sem and I had found there. It left me in a foul mood.

"Where did I go?" I said, finally replying. "I went into exile."

"That was not to be your punishment," they said mildly.

"It was not for the Council of Reft to punish me. Whatever *they* thought of my deeds, *I* knew the nature of my actions."

"Turin grieved for your loss. As did others."

I turned away and stared out to the horizon, seeing nothing. Sharp questions and sharper truths.

"As do I," I said softly. Too softly for them to hear. "I traveled," I said aloud. "Reft taught me much, but I needed to learn something else: How to give myself kindness and forgiveness." My lips twisted into a rueful grimace. "Sem would say I hid myself away in the world."

"Would you go back there? Rejoin the Circle? As much as you may think your bridges burned, I know many would welcome you back."

I became suddenly alert at their words. Something in what they said had brought me sharply to attention, my mind vibrating like a plucked string. Before I could form whatever thought was trying to make itself known, a shout drew my attention and the moment was lost. We both turned and moved to the far side of the tower, looking south over the bailey wall to see a rider pushing his mount hard. The watchman on the wall below us called out to open the gate, and the rider crossed the moat bridge at a hard gallop, not pulling short until he was well within the walls.

Forcing myself to hold to a swift but steady walk, I wound my way down the stairs and halls and more stairs until I reached the bailey. Dane followed, saying nothing. A crowd of soldiers and townspeople had gathered around the rider, and they seemed to ignore my arrival, clamoring for word of outside the walls.

It wasn't until Bergin appeared beside me and started shoving and cursing that they parted, forming an alley through to the rider, who was dismounting and taking off his helmet. It was one of Feren's scouts. He nodded when he saw me.

"They're on the way, sir. Two days behind at least, but they're coming," he said.

Feren must have nearly killed the horses to ride so fast. "How? Did you make it to Fourth Sister?"

The scout shook his head. "We was about halfway there when we found them all already coming back this way. The garrison of the Fourth, and some scraps of the Winter Corps. Near enough about two thousand men. They'd spotted that lot moving through the wood west of the road," he said, throwing his arm out towards the eastern wall. "As no one was attacking them, the captain of the Fourth figured out what they was up to. Brought 'em all out."

I grabbed Bergin's arm and whispered to him, "Get the archers and spotters up on the walls. I want to know the moment ours are spotted and when the Fallians move." They would. There was no chance they had missed the rider coming in. It was an even bet whether they would close in to prevent our reinforcement, or wait for us to double our numbers within the fortress before beginning the siege. In their place, I would have waited, but I knew our supply status: With two thousand more troops joining us, we would have a scant week of supply left. "You," I said to the scout. "Come with me."

I led him back through the crush into the keep and up to my war room. The map was still spread over the broad table, the saltcellars and cordial glasses replaced with wooden tokens whittled by one of the wounded men who was still idled by his splinted legs. They were marked on one face with a crude etching of the Third Sister—little more than a pair of straight notches, and on the other with odd wiggling lines that suggested Savat's hawk and serpent.

I picked up two of the markers, turning them to show the tower. "Where did you leave the column?"

For the next several minutes, I watched as the scout examined the map, tracing with his finger, walking around the table to better understand the terrain features. "Here," he said finally, pointing to a point where the road turned sharply south and passed through a narrow depression between two hills. "Left them two days gone."

I put the two markers in line on the spot. "How fast were they traveling?"

"Captain had them riding hard," he thought aloud. "No wounded to speak of, and they left camp followers behind to follow as they might. Roads are good and packed." He shifted the tokens forward along the road a measured distance. "I think they'll be about here."

I nodded, letting myself take in the new information. "Go get some food and a billet. Get some rest," I said absently.

It was three days before a plume of dust rolling from the horizon to the south announced the arrival of Feren's troop. A runner found me on my morning rounds of the bailey wall—I was reviewing the archers on the northern stretch, the keep rising between me and the view of the southern road. I sprinted eastward around the wall, taking note of the changes to the enemy muster as I ran. They were preparing to move, either to cut off the new arrivals or to close around us.

As I rounded the last corner, I could see the truth of what the spotter had reported... They were coming in far too fast even for a forced march, and the pall of dust rising from the road was too broad, too high to come from two-thousand horse even at a hard gallop.

Feren and his army were riding too hard. There was an even larger army hard on their heels.

I called out orders as I ran, "Archers to the southern wall! Clear the bailey! Raise the gate and prepare to collapse the bridge!"

My soldiers scrambled to their tasks, and by the time I reached my chosen position above the gate between two squads of archers, all was in readiness. We waited, my eyes tracking the dust cloud that slowly, agonizingly resolved into an army driving their horses to their limits in desperation. They were beyond any semblance of order or discipline, columns lost in the chaos of a hard retreat.

The archers to either side of me were calling out encouragement as if they were watching a horse race. Perhaps they were. I took my spyglass from my belt pouch and leaned forward on the parapet to steady it. I couldn't yet see the pursuers for all the dust Feren's horses were raising, but now and then, I saw a volley of arrows land amongst them, horses and men disappearing suddenly to be trampled beneath the seething mass as some shafts hit home.

I gritted my teeth in frustration and drew on my memories of other arrows stealing the life from Ranji, from Mother. When the next flight was loosed, I pushed that pain and power into a wave of intense heat, rolling like a breaker through the air over the heads of the galloping horses.

It was something like lighting a fire, but more diffuse. It was a mark of how my power and skill had grown since those early days traveling with Sem that I could produce enough heat to warp the wooden shafts and roil the air, sending the arrows tumbling harmlessly away from the road.

They were closer now, and I could begin to see hints of the

pursuing army behind them. Another volley of arrows came and I released another flood of super-heated air. Some of the shafts burst into sparks in the heat, and none of them made their marks.

A ripple of fresh panic rolled through the galloping mass and several of the horses along the rear of Feren's troop crumpled and disappeared into the dust. I scanned quickly, trying to find some sign of the attack that had felled so many at once. My stomach became a ball of ice as I saw what was happening. A wide wave of earth rolled outwards from the pursuers, expanding like rings radiating across a pond from a thrown stone. More horses fell. There *was* a *nyssa* riding with the Fallians, directing their power against the Torfallin.

I saw the enemies' horses now, streaming through the dust and churn, some dozen lengths behind the last of Feren's men. They were closing fast, charging in disciplined lines. I braced myself against the parapet and turned my spyglass to one of the leaders across the front of the formation. I took a breath and pushed my mind into the charging animal's.

If not for my practice with the creatures of my wood over the years, I wouldn't be able to do what I did—the animal mind is so alien to ours, even those skilled in Mind Magic can rarely influence it. I could feel the conflict—the instincts of territoriality and aggression warring with fear of pain. Its training at war shored up the former and suppressed the latter, but the fear still simmered beneath the surface. I took its sense of fear—a visceral, vertiginous shock of movement and color and noise—and redoubled it, pushing and pressing it around the edges of the discipline imposed by training. At the same time, I drew away some of the animal's sense of aggression, turning it to confusion and anxiety.

As the balance tipped, the horse turned against its rider,

rearing and spinning and desperate to leave aside the charge, spooked by the herd around it. I moved to the next and next and next in turn along the front of the enemy line.

In seconds, the pursuing formation was in chaos and Feren's men were pulling away. I continued the intrusion into the horses' minds, bringing their lines to a confused and stumbling ruin. Their chase ended in a disordered milling mass just outside of the blackened remains of wooden structures that surrounded the walls.

The archers beside me were cheering now as I slumped against the parapet, spent and disoriented by my efforts in the animal minds. Feren led his men through the charred ruins of the Little Sister, across the bridge, and through the gate. As the last of them galloped across, I heard Joff's deep, froggy voice call the command to drop the gate.

We met in the war room. Feren and Mims, me and my two sergeants, Holder, the garrison commander of Fourth Sister: a man named Anjin, and a Lieutenant Callum who had taken over the remains of Pern's army that had fled west. All the newcomers still were dusty and unshaven from their hard ride to safety. Faces were uniformly grim around the table as Holder reported on the supply situation.

"You brought nothing from Fourth?" Holder asked Anjin.

"We were attacked on the road, and forced to leave our supply train behind," the dour man said defensively. "They had witches with them!" he said angrily, only then shooting me a wary sideways look, his face warring between hate, defiance, and fear of my reaction.

I sighed, and avoided meeting his eye. We had managed to

more than double our numbers within the walls, with no change in supply. If we didn't find a solution soon, we would be eating our horses before long. Callum and Mims were arguing over the supply lists, as if they could produce more grain if they only spoke louder. Joff and Holder argued over the opportune time to collapse the bridge. The tension around the table was building, and these men seemed on the verge of fracture. Feren glanced up and caught my eye, nodding his head to the side of the room. We moved a little away from the arguments at the table.

"I know it's an unfair expectation, but I sincerely hope you have some gambit in your mind to save us," Feren whispered grimly.

I looked over to the map once more without much hope. I had already spent days examining the maps, scanning the terrain from the tower, counting troops. There had been no way to break through the besiegers before. There were now four markers for our number stacked neatly atop the mark of Third Sister. Each wooden token counted for roughly eight-hundred soldiers—ten cohorts. Feren had doubled our numbers, yes, but also effectively halved our supply, and had also brought yet a third Fallian army on their heels.

I glanced around the war room, my eyes roaming the stones making up the walls. So little there was standing between us and them. Surrounding our position were *eight* tokens showing Savat's hawk and serpent. They were clustered mostly at the front gate, but had cohorts to spare to blockade the road in either direction and encircle the entire fortress. There was no way through them.

I hesitated. In truth, I *had* thought of an idea. But I knew none of these men—indeed, none of the Torfallin at all—would like it. Dane had sparked the notion some days ago, and the voices raised in argument crystalized it. We couldn't hope to win through by force of arms, and we couldn't survive a prolonged siege.

There was only one thing left for us to do: leave the field entirely.

I pulled him farther away from the table to speak privately. "If I had a way to bring us all out, every last soldier, citizen, and horse... Can you bring your people to trust me?"

Feren's eyes widened. "How?"

"You will not like it." I sighed. "You will *all* not like it."

Feren licked his lips and his eyes narrowed. He lowered his voice even further. "Magic?"

I nodded.

He closed his eyes, silent for a few moments. I was about to speak, to make my case, when he looked squarely at me and said, "Tell me."

Now at the moment, I hesitated, self-conscious of disclosing details of my power. I eyed the blue-gray stone of the walls of the Third Sister. Each block still carried its four-hundred-year-old history marked in its chisel-cut facing. My time with the stonemasons of Reft, and later in the tumbled ruins in my haunted wood had taught me: stone has an affinity for its past. It remembers.

"It is called a Bridge," I said. As the others argued, I outlined my plan.

Feren would have more luck convincing the others without me standing as a reminder of their fear, I reasoned. While he returned to the table to begin steering the conversation to what needed to be done, I left to find Dane.

Through the halls and stairs of the keep, I descended to the bailey where Winten and Dane had established a smaller field hospital under a broad tiled shelter attached to the side of the fortress. It was crowded with several of the soldiers who had been wounded in the chaotic dash to safety. Feren had lost almost two-hundred men in the retreat, but almost the same number had various injuries.

I found Dane splinting a cavalryman's broken forearm, wrapping it carefully but firmly against a piece of wood split from a turned table leg with a long strip of what looked like heavy winter curtains. The salvage from the Little Sister was being put to good use, I saw. I could tell they noted my arrival, but didn't look up at me until they were done and dismissed the soldier with strict admonitions to avoid use of the arm until further notice, and to return the following day.

"Walk with me," I said, turning. Dane followed, quirking an eyebrow in question, but said nothing.

I knew I could make a Bridge without aid. But what I could do alone—a portal the size of a door—would take ages to move all of us and all the horses. I worried that the longer the Torfallin had to consider the journey, the more would panic or refuse outright. I also had grander ambitions: I wanted a Bridge large enough that we could move the whole army of over three-thousand and all the horses and supplies in minutes. Move them and be ready to fight on the other side. Even a slight increase in the size of a Bridge demanded dramatically more power. To do what I envisioned, I would need the largest Circle I had ever joined.

"We have a plan," I started, looking at them squarely. I was done playing their game. "I will have your assistance."

I could see their shoulders tighten and their eyes narrow. "I've told you, I will not reveal another member of the Watch to pass messages for your war. You are not of Reft by your own choice, and—"

I interrupted them coldly. "That is not what I require. Our path forward no longer lies in knowledge of the enemy movements, but in taking the initiative. I don't care about the Watch network."

Their lips pressed into a thin line of disapproval. "What, then, are you asking of me?"

"I need a Circle. Sem and I alone will not be enough for the power I need. I want you to enter into a Circle with the *nyssén* of Reft, then give me access to it."

Dane's eyes went wide, and their mouth opened but they said nothing for a moment, struck by my audacity. "What... What do you intend to do with such power?" they said, finally.

My smile was grim. "We have successfully pinned our enemy here, though they see things differently. But the battle that matters is not here. If we leave this place, the soldiers out there," I gestured beyond the walls, "will stand for days before they try the walls. By then, even if they discover where we went and think to pursue us, the real battle will be well over before they reach it, and nearly seven thousand soldiers will have missed it."

I saw understanding begin to reach their face. "You mean to make a Bridge? I heard that you had done that before. You think you can control it? It is deemed an impractically difficult feat—"

"We will be a week's ride to the east by the time they breach the gate."

They looked at me with a flat stare, then lowered their voice to a whisper. "Beyond your life, what is this war to you? Why do you care who wins? Savat or the Torfallin lords, why should Reft care?"

"Because he can't win!" My voice roiled with fury. "I have seen the muster; the counts. Fall will lose this war—that is not in question. What matters now more than anything else is *how* it is fought. Do you not worry that his army has *nyssén* openly taking the field? Has Reft considered what new depths of hatred the people of Torfall will turn on us when this is all over and their soldiers return home bearing witness that witches waged their 'demonic power' in war against them?"

Dane stepped back in shock at my anger.

"This army," I said softly, "*here*, is the most important group of soldiers in this land to us. Some few of them have come to see *me*—a witch—as an ally, worthy of their trust and respect. Do you not see how vital that is? *They* are the seed that—if tended and allowed to grow—may be the only shield we have against a turn of sentiment that would plunge this whole nation into an existential war against Reft."

Dane thought this over for a time. Their voice promised little, but they said, "I will send word of your notion to the Watch."

It was the best I could hope for. I left them to commune with the Watch through their Pairing bond, and sought the privacy of my room for my own difficult conversation.

It was a small chamber, little more than an alcove, holding a bed and washstand. I left the small hearth cold in the warm nights, preferring the breeze that was sometimes caught by the only source of light: an arrow slit no wider than my hand. My cloak and satchel hanging on a peg were the only sign it was occupied. Both Joff and Bergin had protested when I chose it out, but it was not the worst lodgings I had ever suffered, by a wide margin.

I sat on the narrow bed and leaned my back against the cold stone, letting my breath and my heartbeat relax into a steady rhythm. I could sense Sem's presence in my mind and far to the east. I closed my eyes and pushed a thought to them.

What is the terrain like where you are?

In response, I smelled a ridge, rocky and broken, overlooking a sprawling complex of structures in crumbling blue-gray stone and rotting wood some miles away. Sunlight sparkled in sharp splinters from fine particles of quartz embedded in the rock. Figures in black moved here and there, visible only by their movement. Beyond and surrounding the once-abandoned town sprawled a sea of tents and soldiers, thousands of them. The individual camps were separated by picket lines tethering hundreds of horses. Banners fluttered over the largest tents and soldiers were everywhere like a swarm of ants churning after their hill is disturbed.

I've counted about nine-thousand Fallians, I felt them say.

The perspective shifted, showing the valley behind them, screened from the ruins of Old Quarry and the vast encampment beyond by the high ridge and full of a dense, low scrub that managed to grow in the rocky soil. I could taste the heady colors of the wide valley and cold silence.

Do you know where the Torfallin are camped? I asked. Through the Pairing, I knew Sem had been moving cautiously throughout the region scouting the terrain and the disposition of the armies.

There was a pause, then an answering thought: *They have made First Sister their headquarters, but are amassing only a few miles northwest of the army here, about ten-thousand strong. They've made no secret of their location, but as of yet neither side has the numbers or the position in the field to begin anything with any confidence.*

I sent another question: *If we bring our three-thousand to you, to that valley behind you, is there sufficient cover to hide us from the armies below?*

I could hear their silence and taste their surprise. *For a time,* they answered. *There are patrols through the valley, but not as often as there should be. The Fallians are overconfident of their position.*

Tell me when the next patrol passes through, I sent.

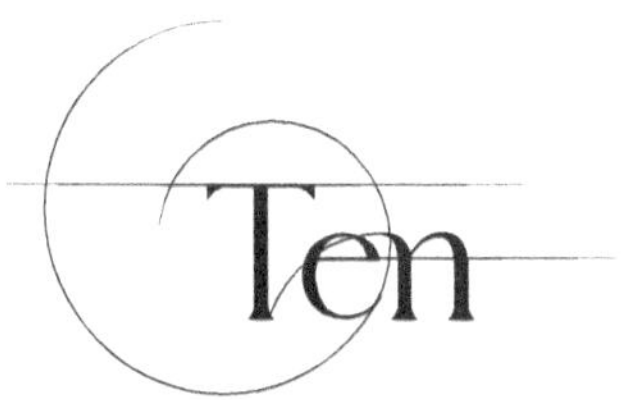

In the bailey, at the far end of the parade ground against the long inner wall, we gathered. I stood with Feren, Holder, and the other officers. Anjin's lips were twisted like he had bitten into a rotten apple, but he stood at attention and voiced no complaints.

Mims and the other sergeants were mustering the entire garrison into organized ranks in front of us. The stones echoed with the shouts and casual insults—uttered without any real heat, almost by habit—that I had become used to hearing from them when they addressed the men in their command. It was a wide open ground, but as the soldiers formed up it soon was crowded and close. Feren's instructions had those men most loyal to him in the front ranks, and those who were most comfortable with my powers towards the rear to put pressure on the files once the Bridge was opened. I had told them candidly what to expect, hoping that would help them avoid any show of fear or surprise. All the better if the soldiers unaccustomed to witchery saw veterans take it in their stride. It was the best we could do.

A low, shuddering rumble and series of sharp snaps echoed across the bailey and made several men jump in shock. It was like the monstrous roll of thunder that shakes the earth from a too-close lightning strike, though the sky was clear of any cloud. Whispers and murmurs tumbled through the gathered ranks, and heads turned to find the source of the sound.

"Hold, you sorry pinch of flea-infested jackdaws!" Mims' voice tore across the bailey, louder even still. "It's just the bridge-crew doing their work!"

The men snapped back into line, but I could see in their shoulders they were still filled with unease.

I looked to the left-most company to find Dane. They stood still beside Winten, who was busy organizing litters for those too wounded to walk. Dane refused to be near me in this endeavor—to protect their position they said, though I couldn't help but assume part of them thought I and everyone around me would be murdered by a mob of terrified soldiers when the Bridge opened.

They eventually looked up and caught my eyes for a moment. They spared a single nod for me. Now that I looked for it, I could see in their posture and restrained movements the tension that came with holding power. They were a conduit into a Circle in Reft, ready for me to tap. I hoped it would be enough.

One of Holder's corporals made his way through the muster to report to his commander. "We pulled the keystone and the bridge is down, sir. No one will be crossing the moat anytime soon."

"Good job, son. Take your place," Holder replied.

Scouts are riding out of the valley now, Sem sent to me. *It's time.*

I looked over to Feren, who was watching me. I nodded.

He took the reins of his horse from a private and mounted, turning the animal in a tight, controlled circle as it frisked. The horse wanted its head. It would have it soon enough.

He heeled the mount forward so that he was standing between me and the assembled army. Feren scanned the faces looking at him with expectation and apprehension. He pitched his voice to carry over the formations.

"By now, you've been up on the wall, or you've spoken to those who have. You know what awaits us in battle against the armies that have arrayed themselves against us."

Nods and murmurs chased themselves through the assembled men.

"You've also no doubt heard the rumors about our supply. Those rumors are true. You've been living on tight rations to try to extend our time before desperation sets in. But the men who rode in with me from Fourth Sister have doubled our numbers, and we brought no provisions with us. Now things are desperate indeed. We have days of food left. Days. Not weeks."

There was a restlessness in the ranks.

"So. We cannot survive within these walls. And we don't have the numbers to survive against the enemy who seeks to crush us. You've heard by now the rumors of what—of who is riding with the army beyond the walls. We can't stand against them. They know this."

The men were disciplined, I'll grant them. There were mutters and some fidgeting, but no one broke at Feren's words.

"The most important thing to understand is that whatever happens here, in this fortress and on that plain out there, is of almost no matter to the greater war. They seek to cut us off, to crush us here, because they fear what three-thousand of you can bring to the real battle."

Many of them stood up straighter at this.

"Two weeks' hard march to the east lies Old Quarry, where the Blackcoats have mustered an army that they hope will roll like breakers over the lands of Torfall. They mean to move north, killing and pillaging and subjugating our people."

The mutters from the men turned angry.

Feren's lips twisted into a grim, cold smile. "They won't. Captain Tomrin has an army of ten-thousand of your countrymen at First Sister: a hammer ready to strike. All they lack is an anvil against which to flatten the Blackcoats. We are that anvil."

I saw confusion now ripple through the men. Involuntarily, I felt my shoulders tensing. If they were to break, it would be now.

"*They* brought witches into this war, to assail us with their power. But *we* are not powerless. We have our own allies." I saw many eyes dart to me. I did my best to stand straight and keep emotion from my face, but my skin crawled with this rhetoric. Feren knew his men, though, and we both agreed his words were necessary. "Many of you know Arin. You have served under their command, and some of you owe your lives to their skills and power. After today, we all will.

"In a few moments they will open a gateway for us, a road to travel from the walls of this fortress to a valley high above the enemy fortifications at Old Quarry."

Gasps and rattled voices began objecting at this, but Feren raised his voice, talking over them.

"You will travel this road! You are men of Torfall! We fear neither death nor magic, and certainly not the power of our own allies! We will leave those Blackcoats out there standing in the dust, laying siege to an empty fortress! They will stand here like fools while we are crushing their vaunted armies, and when we are done, we will all march south and batter them back to the sea!"

If he was hoping for raucous cheers, he was disappointed. But at least the men settled into a stoic quiet. The murmuring still rippled through the formation, but the speech seemed to have stiffened their spines.

Feren turned to me and nodded. It was time.

I turned away from the assembled troops and reached out through the Pairing to Sem, drawing from them the pain that flared sharp and fierce across our arm. I drew on my own painful memories: Father and Ranji's deaths, my panic and gut-wrenching horror at what I had done to Cal, the pain I had caused my friends in Reft. The power raged within me, churning and frothing like an angry sea, but it was not enough.

I found Dane and reached out my senses, feeling the power that spilled from them. I embraced it and it flooded me, and I gasped with the force of it. It was all I could do not to be washed entirely away by the incredible power that flowed from them. There was no defense I could make, no barrier I could erect that could stem the tidal power. In a Circle, it was always the goal to hold oneself in as much control as one could achieve, but this... this was more than I—more than anyone— could possibly withstand.

I was myself and I had watched my family die. I had descended into horror and dissociation on the night I had murdered the man responsible. I had left my friends and lovers behind without a word and fled all that I knew.

I was Sem and my forearm throbbed with a deep well of angry, raw pain.

I was Dane and I had watched the love of my life die a withering, slow death of wasting sickness before I had found Reft and the healers there who might have saved him.

With a shock and a wave of sorrow, I was Turin and I remembered Arin arriving at Reft, helping them heal and develop their power, and my heart broke anew when I realized the sorrow of failing them; of not seeing their pain and crisis when it mattered and losing them to their own guilt.

I was Marki and Ciala and a dozen other members of the Watch. I was Ranji and Froley and I felt their sadness at the sudden departure and hushed whispers of disgrace of the teacher they had admired and loved.

I was sobbing as I remembered giving birth to two children, both stillborn. My shoulders were shaking and a cry started in the deepest well of my being, fighting its way to my throat as I felt the deaths of dozens of mothers and fathers and children and friends over and over again with myriad hearts.

And I shuddered with the overwhelming pain of finding Turin sitting in sorrow in our darkened rooms, of sitting numbly as they told me that Arin had gone—had felt so utterly lost and devastated at what they had been driven to do that they could no longer face me, could not bring themself even to say goodbye. And the crushing misery of loss, of grief and devastated love. Feeling it over again when Fanti returned to our rooms to learn the news.

I was on my knees on the dusty blue-gray cobbles, doubled over in the visceral pain of the enormous gift of power given me by the citizens of Reft. My mind was nearly lost in the swell and tide of emotion and pain. I was a husk with no self. I was all of them and none of them and the very pain and love that wove them together. My heart fractured anew at the loss of Kari and Fanti and Arin.

My fingers absently traced a weathered cobblestone, feeling

its texture and the life and history it had seen and endured. Stone has a memory... and it remembers its home.

I let the flood of pain pass through my fingers and into the stone. It rose in a great inevitable wash of power and I was wracked with cries of existential agony as the Bridge opened, stone to stone.

Hands were on my shoulders then, helping me to stand. I was still blinded by tears and shaking with the force of what I had done, but a voice I knew spoke to me—a voice out of my past and out of too many memories to encompass.

I cleared my eyes with a shaky hand and saw Sem standing before me, their eyes wide in concern and shock.

"Arin, what you have done..." they said. "I don't have words."

I looked beyond them then to the Bridge. It was as wide as the courtyard and tall enough that the bannermen could ride through with their pennants unfurled. I turned to take in the mass of soldiers behind me.

They stood still and full of awe at what they had witnessed. There was fear, yes. But there was something else, too. Not a few faces were fixed not on the angry coruscations of the Bridge, but on me. They looked on me with an odd mix of shock and honor and concern. They looked on me with empathy.

My eyes welled again with tears as the flood of pain continued to roil my being. I could not have remained standing without Sem's support. I heard Feren call the troops to order and begin their uneasy march through the wide Bridge. The columns passed through to either side of us. I can't say how long it took. They said nothing as they marched, but now and then I felt some reach out to touch me; a pat on my shoulder, or a brief clutch of my arm in solidarity and support.

I stood there leaning against Sem as the soldiers passed. After the foot soldiers came squadrons of cavalry and finally the wagons of the support personnel. At last the bailey was quiet save for Feren who still sat astride his horse, and Mims who led his own and Artem. Feren nodded to me in respect and shockingly, so did Mims. They moved through the Bridge.

Sem led me through, and as I released my hold on the power and I felt the Bridge collapse, so did I. The pain of the Circle dissipated, sublimating into nothingness and carrying me with it.

I woke to the splatter of rain on canvas. I was damp and uncomfortable as I sat up, trying to get my bearings and work my way out of the fog of sleep. A small iron camp stove radiated slight warmth beside me, but its handful of glowing coals gave little of the light and cheer a fire would have. A broad tarp had been tied down above me in a lean-to to provide cover from the drizzle.

I felt a wave of sadness and pain roll over me with the memories of Kari's pain. Tears began to fill my eyes and I forced my heart into hardness. I couldn't afford to lose myself now.

All around me, soldiers milled in various camp tasks or leaned on saddles to catch some rest. I scrubbed my eyes and was about to stand and explore the camp when I saw Feren coming towards me. I could see nerves and hesitation in his posture. He stopped two paces from me.

"You're awake," he said to me tentatively.

I nodded. "I am. What is our situation?"

My direct question seemed to comfort him. We could ignore the spectacle of emotion and pain that my feat of power had wrought. "You brought us out. Nearly all of us. Some few of the citizens of Little Sister opted to stay. All the better if the besieging army thinks the fortress occupied for a little longer."

He moved to squat down under the tarp. "I have two sweeps of riders scouting the surrounds and the enemy camp at Old Quarry. You put us right on target, and your friend's scouting was sound. We're secure here at least until they send another patrol. After that…" He shrugged. We both knew if they spotted us and attacked, we were doomed. They had near triple our numbers. "I sent twelve riders in two pairs of threes to make their way north and south around the enemy to reach Captain Tomrin's forces northwest of here and tell him of our position."

I gathered my wits as I took this in, the last muddle of exhaustion chased away by memories of maps and terrain. "So we wait," I said.

Feren nodded. "We wait."

Days of waiting passed. By my best guess, it would take at least three days for the messengers to reach the Torfallin army camped a few miles to the northwest, balancing stealth and speed. They had to go far out of their way to avoid Blackcoat patrols. If at least one carried their message safely, it might take as long for them to return with word.

Each day that passed brought a new knot of tension to my shoulders. Each day brought them closer to their goal. Each day brought us closer to battle. And each day made it more likely our camp would be discovered by the Fallians camped only two miles below our narrow mountain valley. Sem and I considered setting a Warding around the camp, but the terrain was too rough to make a clean circle, and I doubted it could be strong enough to turn aside alert soldiers on patrol.

Feren kept the men in constant activity, giving none the luxury of worry. Teams of scouts rotated through the surrounding mountains, intent on catching any enemy patrols before they could discover us.

On that first day, feeling recovered from my ordeal, I rode with Feren and Joff up the hill to the western crest above our camp to survey Old Quarry. It took a moment to make out the shape of the crumbling buildings, even with my spyglass. The bluish-gray stone faded in the distance and the haze of drizzle into a vague, muddy smear. The Blackcoats were easier to spot. We did our best to count, but they were using the abandoned structures for shelter, and so we could never get a clear sense of their numbers. I focused instead on the terrain, the approaches we might take in the coming battle. Looking past the town, I saw two ways the Torfallin army could engage.

Northwest a broad plain rolled out, an easy march from First Sister. At this distance, I couldn't make out the encamped army, but it was the obvious choice—with the enemy entrenched, the flat and smooth terrain would afford the attackers the best chance of keeping organized lines and arriving at the battle with the strength to fight.

Being the obvious approach, the Blackcoats had oriented their defenses most strongly in that direction.

The northern end of Old Quarry was warded by rocky, uneven hills and low scrub that would be death for the ankles of horse and man both. It would be mad to attack from that direction, and so, just as obviously, an attacker would try with at least a small force.

The three of us talked over what we saw and agreed that Tomrin would have the bulk of his army press the assault from the northwest, but was likely to send a small contingent through the rough northern ground to spoil the defenses. It could not be forceful enough to break through, but would be a distraction.

The path down the hill from our position to the enemy fortifications was relatively clear; a rough but manageable ride straight down into their backs.

The Fallians likely planned to retreat through the mountains if their defenses broke, trusting to the terrain and cover to give them opportunities to stage a series of turns, chipping away at the harrying forces. If we could begin the assault before they realized we were blocking that path, we could catch them in a devastating pincer. It would be a rout.

If. *If* our messengers made it in time. *If* Tomrin trusted and understood. *If* the Blackcoat scouts didn't find us. The days trickled on.

Sem and I took it in turns to range more widely in rambling arcs through the hills, exploring passes, looking for signs of enemy patrols, and planning escape routes should things go wrong. When they weren't scouting, they nevertheless stayed out of the camp, refusing to communicate with anyone but me.

Each day, I approached Dane, asking them to reach out through the Watch network, to pass our message directly to the Torfallin army or their command at First Sister. Each day, they refused. Reft would not reveal their spies embedded among the Torfallin. All they would agree to was that they would pass word to *me* if they learned anything of value from the Torfallin or the Fallians.

On the third day, one of our scouts rode recklessly down the valley slope from the east. Soldiers stood and we all tensed as he pulled up short in front of Mims. Feren and I both closed from opposite ends of the camp, arriving together in moments.

Mims repeated the report: "Blackcoat patrol, Captain. Four of 'em. Our boys took them all down."

"In, or away?" Feren asked the scout.

The rider only shook his head and shrugged.

Feren and I shared a grim look. It was not the worst possible news, but neither was it good. If the enemy patrol had been setting out from their camp, there was likely still a day or so before they were discovered missing. If they were on the return leg of their patrol, they would be missed sooner. The clock had now started in earnest, and we didn't know how long we had.

Feren doubled his scouting patrols and increased the standing watch we had on Old Quarry, and we waited. If they moved against us, we would know soon.

The men stripped down the camp to the bare minimum for survival and made ready to retreat or to engage at a moment's notice. Each cohort kept a rotating watch through the night, ready to rouse the squads at the first alarm.

I woke in the small hours of the night with a hand gripping my forearm. The tension I had been carrying wrung my muscles into instant action and I was sitting up with a drawn dagger before my mind was fully conscious. I saw Dane's eyes widen in the moonlight.

"Peace," they whispered. "I have word."

I put the dagger away and gathered my thoughts. "What news?"

"The riders have delivered their message. The Torfallin are mustering as we speak and will press their attack shortly before dawn. Their commander trusts that yours will see the right moment to strike."

That woke me fully, and I sprang to my feet. "You have this through the Watch?"

"Yes," they said. "I rely on you to maintain our secrecy." They gave me a hard look at that, and I nodded.

I jogged towards Feren's bedroll, not even bothering to put on my boots. I sent the news to Sem, calling them in. I got back only a vague impression that smelled like sour grumbling.

"Feren," I called sharply as I approached. "There is news."

He rose nearly as quickly as I had, rolling groggily to his feet. "You've communicated with your friend?" he asked.

I paused for a moment, inwardly amused and satisfied that I needn't lie. "I have. Our message got through. The attack will begin just before dawn." I looked up at the position of the moon and made a guess. "About two hours, I think."

Now his eyes were open wide. He called out to the nearest sentries, "Bell, Woten! Rouse the cohorts. Muster in half an hour."

After days of tense waiting, the soldiers were up and ready mere moments after waking. Bowls of cold stew and heels of bread were making their rounds by the time Feren's half hour was over. The men ate hearty, but their silence gave away the nerves. An hour later, we were moving in ranks up the hill out of the narrow valley.

Feren, his lieutenants, and I took the crest of the hill on foot, leaving our horses downslope a few paces. I could feel Sem moving, some distance to the southwest. The darkness gave us cover, but it meant the terrain was difficult to make out. I was glad for my previous scouting trips as I hunted out the approaches we had planned down into the rear and flanks of the enemy fortifications.

These were easy to see, as their sentries carried lanterns and their camps were lit in pockets by circles of glowing firelight. They knew that the Torfallin knew they were there and didn't feel the need to hide. But their lights blinded even the sentries who looked our way to our positions in the darkness.

We settled in to watch and wait, taking cover within the craggy stones topping the ridge. A faint glow was beginning to be visible in the east, and we had no desire to give the enemy silhouettes against the lightening sky. The men and horses down the hill behind were restive, stepping in place and swinging arms to keep muscles limber.

We waited.

A shrill horn pierced the night and the sentries below us began shouting, the command in their voices carrying, but the words were lost in echoes among the stones. Movement in the darkness, and a flight of arrows rattled among the forward entrenchments. Here and there a man called out weakly in pain.

A thrum like rolling thunder made the earth tremble beneath us, and then there was a wave of gray like ocean breakers flowing across the plains. Tomrin had moved his men quietly. Only now in an epic charge did they reveal themselves. The Blackcoats were scrambling now, manning their positions and preparing to take the charge. Their fortifications were solid, and the Torfallin would break against them. We could all see that.

Arrows sped now in great volleys from the entrenched soldiers, arcing out into the night to disappear in the dust and churn of the galloping cavalry. Each volley fell into the milling mass, surely killing hundreds. Any who fell wounded by arrows were likely just as dead, trampled by their own side.

Now the archers were trading volleys and screams reached us from both armies. A new shout arose as horns began to trill from the north and several squadrons of light cavalry poured down out of the hills, cutting amongst the Fallian defenses. They caused distractions, but it was clear enough that the enemy had expected a force to come down on them from the north.

The pressure of the main force pushed enough Blackcoats from their forward positions that they began to fall back in disciplined ranks to their secondary entrenchments. As their force contracted, it grew stronger, with more men defending less terrain. The Torfallin cavalry were forced to pull short and regroup as archers poured death into their vanguard.

Feren nodded to himself, then turned to us. "It is time for us," he said simply. He stood then and walked back to mount his horse. We followed. He rode at a walk back uphill, lit upon the ridge by the rising sun and turning in the saddle to face the soldiers arrayed below us. He raised his arm and held it, as the men noticed and silence settled among them. The lines firmed up.

He turned now to face down the hill to the battle raging below. He dropped his arm in a forward cutting motion and called out to the men behind him. "Advance for Torfall!"

We joined the fight.

Eleven

I let Artem set his own pace down the slope, trusting to his sure-footedness. We had descended only a hundred feet before the cavalry squadrons overtook us, charging down upon the enemy. I spared a glance to Feren who held his unsheathed sword forward and was yelling gleeful encouragement to his troops.

In the chaos and violence of the fighting, we were nearly upon the enemies' backs before they noticed us. At the last moment before our cavalry charged into the fortifications one of their captains turned his archers in time to draw and loose. Many of our horses went down under the assault, but enough remained to smash into the archers and soon we were fighting at close-quarters.

I had my sword out, but held myself back from the haphazard flailing I had employed in my last action. Artem picked his way through the melee, occasionally kicking out or charging here and there in brief lunges to keep us safe. I saved my strokes for when I could be decisive. This would be a long, drawn out battle, and I was still not fully recovered from my efforts to make the Bridge.

An officer in black with ribbons and a gold braid on his shoulder came at me with a spear from the side, trying to unseat me. Artem spun and tried to kick, but the Blackcoat leapt back, then lunged, catching me across the thigh with the spearhead. I hissed in pain and brought my sword down against the spear, batting it away.

He came at me again, meaning to take Artem in the belly and bring us both down. I pulled in the pain from my thigh wound, spinning it into my shoulder and arm and hardening my grip. This time when my sword met his spear, the wooden shaft shattered under my blow. He was left holding four feet of splintered wood and his eyes widened in shock. I pulled the reins to the right and nudged Artem's ribs with my knee, and the horse spun again, rearing and dropping both front hooves down upon the startled officer. He didn't even have time to scream.

I sensed Sem out there somewhere, taking one man after another out of the fight. They moved with their uncanny, augmented speed, virtually untouchable. Everywhere they went through the melee, pain and death followed. Our foot soldiers had caught up to us now and joined the fight, and the air came alive with clashing steel, calls for aid, cries of pain, and smell of blood and death. It all merged into a roar of violence and pain, and began to hang like a miasma over the battlefield. I could feel it in the air like the tension and clarity just before lightning strikes out of a storm.

Unwilling pain was a poor source of power, Sem had once told me, and I understood now. The field was full of agony and pain and hurt, but it was all held in check, suppressed and leashed in the desperation of survival. Any one injury those around me sustained in battle, dire as it might be, was of too little consequence to draw on because the wounded's every intention was focused on holding back the pain, on not feeling it.

But there were *so many wounds*.

Tentatively, I tapped the power and it flooded me from a thousand individual cuts, hundreds of men hurt and dying around me. Like a multitude of individual drops of water that can fill a pitcher, I poured the power into the cut on my thigh and it was fully healed before I thought to hold some back. I understood then how Sem did what they did.

When I looked up again, I saw Feren some dozens of yards away laying about himself with his sword, his horse kicking out to threaten a circle closing in around them. I heeled Artem to a gallop in his direction to lend aid, but before I reached them, I saw a spear take Feren's horse and they both disappeared into a press of black-clad soldiers.

I pulled in the ambient power of the battlefield once more, winding it through my muscles and body and leapt from Artem's saddle, sailing through the air and landing just behind the circle of Blackcoats in a low crouch. I struck out with the tip of my sword and the man in front of me fell, his legs turning to jelly as I severed the tendons behind his knees.

I sprang up through the space he left and landed with my feet to either side of Feren's chest. I had enough time to take in his horse, hemorrhaging from a vicious belly wound, and Feren's leg trapped under its weight. He looked up at me, dazed and eyes wide.

Around us was a ring of soldiers, only just beginning to see that I had joined the fight. They moved as if in a dream and I realized that I had instinctively enhanced my own reflexes and speed. I felt my lips twist into a grim smile. I swept my sword out in a wide arc to the right, cutting across one man's abdomen, and he crumpled.

A soldier to my left thrust his sword towards my chest and I twisted slightly, just enough that the sword point passed harmlessly past me. I reached up with my left hand and closed it over his hand on the hilt of the sword. A sharp twist of my hips and he was pulled off balance, falling into his companion and taking them both down.

I felt a sharp pain in the back of my right shoulder and turned away from it faster than thought. I bent forward and lifted my left foot, sweeping it upwards and around, kicking the spearman in the face. I dropped into a guard stance and swatted away the last man's sword with enough strength that he lost his grip, staring almost comically at his empty hand before retreating from me and disappearing into the melee.

I concentrated on slowing down my movements, feeling the speed of my limbs condense, solidify into strength. I pulled in more of the roiling pain from the men I had taken down and fed it into my body. With my left hand, I grabbed the saddle and lifted the dead horse's body high enough that Feren could pull his leg out from underneath.

He stared at me in shock; seeing what I was perhaps for the first time. Then he reached out and grasped my forearm. I pulled him to his feet. His leg was hurt and he was limping badly, so I put my shoulder under his arm to support his weight.

"Thanks," he said. He pointed to a squad of Torfallin pikes holding a short line against a sortie from the Blackcoats. "Let's regroup."

I nodded, and we hobbled in the direction of our troops. We reached them just as the enemy was retreating.

"Mims!" Feren called. He had recognized his sergeant rallying the pikemen.

Mims looked around and spotted us, rushing over to help Feren into the protection of the squad. "You've looked better, sir," he said. He nodded to me in silent respect.

"Not broken, I think," Feren replied. "Just bruised." He shrugged off my shoulder and settled roughly to the ground, massaging his knee.

I was still siphoning power from the death and hurt around me, and I spun some threads of it into him, finding the tears in muscle and cartilage, and mending them. I spread the power more widely, healing the handful of injuries the soldiers around us had taken. I heard more than one sharp gasps and saw a few furtive looks turn my way, but none of us said anything of it.

"Arin, you're bleeding, too," Mims said quietly beside me.

I looked up at him dumbly for a moment, then remembered the spear that had pierced my shoulder from behind. I was so full of power and focused on the fight, I hadn't noticed the back of my tunic drenched in blood, but now I felt light-headed. I closed the wound. "Thanks," I said.

We circled up and began to move the squad south to join a pair of cohorts that had pushed a salient deep into the Fallian line. They were close to breaking through to Tomrin's forces, cutting off a third of the enemy fortifications. Feren still limped, leaning on a spear he picked up from a fallen Black-coat. I had healed the gross injury, but didn't have the focus or peace of mind to smooth away the bruising and soreness. We kept him in the center of our formation and moved with weapons ready.

As we moved, I kept my eyes roving over the terrain, the pockets of fighting we passed, and all the fallen horses, looking for sign of Artem. I hoped he had found his way out of immediate harm.

The terrain became especially difficult, a loose scree of fine pebbles and fist-sized rocks. We pushed ahead as quickly as we could, but the footing was treacherous.

As we circled a larger boulder in our path, a shape in its moon-lit shadow resolved into a bearded figure in black crouched over a body in gray. One of the soldiers on my right cried out and lunged, driving the point of his pike towards the Blackcoat's chest. The enemy spun uncannily, casually grasping the pike shaft behind the point and pulling, turning again to cut across the soldier's throat with a dagger clutched in the other hand.

The pikeman turned slowly towards us, his eyes wide in confusion. His face went white as his blood spilled from his ruined neck and he fell limply to the ground. We all stood for a moment in shock. With the speed and power born of pain, the Blackcoat closed on a second soldier, gutting him in front of us before we could react.

He has recruited nyssén *to his cause*, I remembered numbly.

I drew on the power around us and moved, sliding forward on the loose stones and cutting my sword across their legs. They hopped back out of reach and drew their own sword, switching the dagger to their off-hand. We circled each other as the squad behind me spread out, moving slowly and dream-like in my enhanced perception.

A pike thrust out and the *nyssa* slid sideways, not even bothering to parry the strike. I swept in from the other side and they turned my sword casually with their dagger, bringing their sword in an upwards thrust towards my belly.

I braced myself for the wound, unable to shift my weight enough to dodge. Before their sword could touch me, a second sword blow hammered down from my left and battered it aside.

I pushed back with my forward foot and withdrew a pace, resetting my feet in a defensive stance, but Mims pressed his attack in my wake. I tried to move back into position for a strike. Mims closed the distance and was between us. I watched helplessly as he futilely tried blow after blow to counter the *nyssa*'s defense, but none landed.

With a sneer of contempt, they turned Mims's sword aside with their own and brought their dagger point up through his chin. The big sergeant's body went rigid for a moment, then he fell dead, his limp body forcing me to back up.

In a fury, I leapt over his corpse, my sword flashing in a wicked arc and forcing the Blackcoat out of their stance. They spun in a full circle and I saw their feet shift for a low strike, so I dropped my weight and planted my sword point down in the scree, the same move I had used on Eelie so many years ago.

Their sword struck the spine of mine and shattered, splinters of steel flying in every direction. Quicker than thought, they lashed out with their dagger and only my enhanced reflexes saved me. I felt the blade skate along my jaw and my tunic was awash in my own blood.

I rolled away to the side, and came up on one knee in a low guard. I drew more power and closed the wound on my face.

They pressed forward and I parried three successive dagger strikes. They drew back with one foot, shifting their weight only part-way and I could tell they were about to strike again. I tried to rise to a middle-guard stance but the gravel beneath my feet was suddenly flowing like water and I fell.

I saw their smirk as they moved in, but three of the pikemen pressed their reach, forcing the *nyssa* back. They turned away from me, throwing their hand out towards the Torfallin in a dismissive gesture and all three lost their feet as the ground rolled beneath them.

I spun my legs and used their momentum to spring to my feet. I dashed forward and forced them back with two low, arcing strikes. They dodged with ease but lost ground.

I saw them smile again, and this time I didn't wait. I pulled in as much power as I could draw from the battlefield and poured it into my bones and muscles and through the soles of my feet into the stones and the earth. The scree around me roiled with their power, but the ground directly beneath my feet held still and firm.

They tensed and moved towards me, but I pushed back, turning the waves of rolling earth back against them. They cried out in surprise, and as they lowered their hands to try to steady themself, I struck deep into their mind.

We were both drawing on the same ambient miasma of pain; we were nearly in a Circle together. They were strong, and well-practiced with the Dire Magic of combat. But I could feel at once they were lazy and had rarely drawn on their own pain since discovering they could use others'. And they knew nothing of Mind Magic.

I followed the flood of pain from the injured around us into their mind. I found the kernel of feeling that let them draw that pain from others and I flinched back, overwhelmed by their memories of self-inflicted pain. They could draw on the pain of others almost instinctively because they had *felt* every single one of those injuries themself at their own hand. It wasn't empathy so much as it was memory.

I pushed deeper into their mind and found something beneath even that. Belief. They would not be convinced to stand down, and they would not surrender, for they believed so strongly in their goal that they were willing to die that others could reach it. In that moment, I tried to see that goal, to find its shape, but it was mired in memory and emotion and sensation that would take time to unravel.

I turned instead to another place in their mind. That place *beneath* mind where pain was processed into feeling, where fear and lust and disgust and pleasure were born. It was a place so low—so far beneath consciousness—that all animals possessed it. It drove the basest behaviors of every living thing.

I found it and paced its boundaries and built a wall of bramble around it, thick and impenetrable. I turned the bramble in on itself and knotted it into a thicket that locked them away from their own feeling; away from their pain. Without it they could not draw on power—their own or anyone else's.

Having made the barrier, I was instantly repulsed by what I had done. It was necessary, but I shuddered at the thought of what I had made of this person's mind. Thought and reason and no emotion. I vowed to myself to undo it as soon as it was safe.

I came back to my own mind then, and saw the remaining pikemen rising to their feet, having slipped on the shifting ground only seconds before. Feren and two others were preparing to rush forward, but I called out to them.

"Stop!" I extended my sword at the *nyssa's* throat, and they wavered there, unmoving. "I have captured them. They can do no more witchery. Take their weapons and bind them. We'll bring them with us."

Feren looked to me and nodded to his men, who stepped forward cautiously to take charge of the prisoner. Feren moved over to Mims's supine form and knelt beside him. He placed his hand on his sergeant's shoulder and muttered a prayer under his breath.

"I'm sorry," I said to him. "He saved us. If I had taken that sword to the gut, I doubt I could have recovered in time."

Feren nodded numbly. He carefully removed Mims's knot of rank and his ring and pocketed the tokens. He unbuckled his sergeant's sword, and tucked it in his belt. "His family will want these," he said simply.

We stood then and checked on the others. The squad had seen to their own dead, and soon we were moving across the battlefield again. The pikes pushed the prisoner—who walked along passionlessly; an empty husk—ahead of them.

We joined up with our cohorts who were arrayed in a wide arc pressing against the enemy line. There was a hollow in the center of the salient. Bergin rallied two squadrons of cavalry there, holding ready to exploit any opening that appeared. When he spotted us, he immediately wheeled his mount around and closed the distance. As he rode, he called out to a private within the knot of horsemen.

The young soldier followed behind Bergin on his own mount, and was leading two other horses. As they neared, I felt a rush of relief. One of the two was Artem. The private helped Feren into the spare horse's saddle, and he looked to be in some relief at being off the leg. I would have to look it over again when we reached safety.

I vaguely heard Feren explaining our condition, and the nature of the prisoner, but my attention was on Artem. He was stepping lively and whuffed as I scratched his brow. He nosed my hand looking for an apple and gave me a sorrowful eye at finding it empty. I leaned against his neck and felt the warmth of his body against me for a moment, feeling my breathing slow and my shoulders relax.

Feren and I returned with Bergin and the private to the head of the cavalry squadron while the pike squad led the prisoner off. I realized I was feeling the exertion of my fight with the *nyssa* more than I expected... even days gone, I was still exhausted from making the Bridge. I let myself slump against Artem's neck and closed my eyes, trusting him to keep me with the others.

The battle still roiled somewhere in the distance. I could feel Sem moving across the broken ground. I could smell the splinters of color that flared in my mind every time they sprang into action and another enemy fell. But that was happening less and less often.

My memories of the fight with the *nyssa* and their capture, I sent to Sem through the Pairing. In response, I felt a wave of satisfaction and pride.

We will need to speak to them at length when this is done, Sem sent me. *Make sure these soldiers don't take petty revenge for their losses.*

I sighed, and straightened. "Feren," I called out.

He and Bergin both turned to me, pausing their discussion.

"The prisoner. We will want to speak to them when we're in a more secure position. There is much of value they can tell us, if they can still speak when that time comes."

Feren held still and looked back at me for a moment, saying nothing. His jaw tightened and his eyes narrowed.

I kept my face impassive, and simply looked back at him. I hoped he would understand. I knew that he and Mims had been close, and the foot soldiers had loved him well.

He closed his eyes for a moment, and then turned to one of the younger soldiers. "Go find the squad I came in with; they're escorting a prisoner. Tell them," his eyes flickered to mine and back. "Tell them they are to *make sure* no harm comes to the prisoner. He has important intelligence and must be whole and capable of giving it."

I relaxed and gave him a small, grateful smile, then closed my eyes again and leaned back against Artem's neck. I could hear the ambient shouts and cries of battle, and felt a tension rising around me. A part of me wanted to rise, to stand in my stirrups and scan the battle. It wanted to seek out the weaknesses I knew were there and to make the intuitive leaps and give the commands to exploit them. My fingers itched to draw my sword.

I resisted. It took every fiber of my will to keep my eyes closed, to relax my body against Artem's warmth, and let myself go. Feren and Bergin and all the others were capable soldiers, and this was their battle. They would see the moment. They would make the call. I could leave it to them.

A memory of floating, of drifting into sleep buoyed by the gentle current of the river came to my mind. I could feel myself losing my sense of stability; that anchor of self that I held to reflexively while awake. I lurched once, twice, thrice, feeling like I was nearly falling from the saddle though each time my consciousness reasserted itself, I was still, stable upon Artem.

Cries and a wave of tension and release swept over the battlefield—so pronounced that I felt it and bolted upright with enough force that Artem pranced. I shook my head to focus my attention, and looked around to find Feren. He was only a few yards away with Bergin, both scanning the lines.

I looked in the direction they were both fixed on, and saw it just as Feren raised his arm and pointed.

"There," he said, softly, almost to himself. The enemy line had buckled, and the slightest push would break it.

Bergin called out to the cavalry, and the whole mass heeled their mounts almost as one. Fifty horses broke into a thundering charge towards the weakness. Those in the lead lowered lances, and we behind them drew our swords. We covered the intervening ground in moments.

The foot soldiers pressing the line knew their business, and as if choreographed, their lines split and turned just as we came upon them, opening three lanes for the horses to charge through. Artem and I passed through the rightmost and before I could catch a breath to join my voice to the shouts of the Torfallin, we had broken through the Fallian defenses and they were scrambling for safety.

Their lines shattered and their defense collapsed into chaos. Men were throwing down their weapons and fleeing. Some dropped to their knees and raised their arms in surrender. Not all were fast enough to avoid being run through or trampled.

Then we were amongst hundreds of strangers in Torfallin colors. We had reached Tomrin's lines. It was over so fast, my blade remained unbloodied. We were all milling about in some confusion, but before long, I was able to spot Feren and Bergin, and I picked my way through to them.

The cohorts of foot were pressing the breakthrough along the flanks of the Fallians and the enemy lines were collapsing faster than I could follow. Cavalry circled in broad arcs, sweeping up stragglers and prisoners in wide pincers.

Having joined up with Feren, I followed behind as he led the way through the press of soldiers. We passed several cohorts of Blackcoats kneeling in the dust with hands bound and guarded by grim-faced Torfallin—captured or surrendered, I couldn't say.

Once we were moving again, it didn't take long for us to reach the center of the larger army's formation. It was odd to feel safe among so many strangers, but the sea of gray tunics around us lifted a weight of tension from my shoulders that I didn't know was there until it was gone.

We made our way deeper into the Torfallin lines and soon were among tents and pennants.

Twelve

It was a surprise to find General Hines in the great tent at the center of the camp. He and Captain Tomrin were leaning over a folding camp table that was covered in maps. More maps and reports littered the various chairs and benches nearby. The two aides waiting by the rear canvas panel were doing nothing to tidy the parchments. Hines looked up as we entered.

"Captain Feren," he said, smiling. "Well done. *Well* done!"

"Sir," Feren simply said, drawing up short and striking a hasty salute as his face reddened.

"And Arin, our wayward witch." He looked me up and down, assessing. After a few moments, he said only, "Astonishing, what you two have accomplished."

Feren found his voice. "Not only us, sir. The men of my company, of Third and Fourth Sisters, and Lieutenant Callum and the remains of the Winter Corps were instrumental."

"Yes, yes. Of course," he said absently, still looking at me. "Astonishing nonetheless." He turned his eyes away from me finally and looked to Feren. "How are your men? How many remain after breaking the backs of the Fallians?"

Feren looked chagrined. "I'm afraid I'm not certain, sir. We rode in with a mixed company that broke through the enemy lines—about two squadrons of horse and two cohorts of foot—but in truth we were separated from my command structure early on in the charge."

Bergin spoke up from behind us. "They had dedicated squads seeking out and unhorsing commanders. It's a miracle Captain Feren made it through."

Tomrin grimaced. "A nasty business, that. We saw some of it from our skirmishes."

Hines nodded. "Yet you made it through. Excellent. We got word just before you came in—their lines have collapsed across the field. It's only mopping up now. Old Quarry is as good as ours. We're looking to our next steps." His eyes danced between us, but I don't think I imagined that they lingered on me. "Care to inspect our position? Perhaps you can lend us some strategic intelligence."

I waited for Feren to move first, and I followed behind. The map was much as I remembered. Only the tokens were newly arranged. The bulk of the blue tokens were now arranged in three clusters: in the plain just west of Old Quarry, around First Sister, and north of the narrow northward chevron of the Danin. The black tokens around Old Quarry had been thinned considerably, and I noted a stack of black tokens casually pushed to the edge of the map, discarded.

Feren reached out and shifted several of the black tokens from the west, bringing them east towards where we had last seen them at Third Sister. "We left them guarding the fortress," he said, explaining, "It's empty, but for stragglers from Little Sister. We dropped the bridge before leaving, so they'll all have a time crossing the moat, in or out."

Hines and Tomrin shared a look. "Indeed," said the general. "I would be very interested in how you managed that."

To his credit, Feren did not look at me, though he fidgeted with the effort. "Sir, I will be happy to tell you the how, but it is not a maneuver that will avail us here."

Hines seemed to accept this for now. "Well then, what are your thoughts on this?" he asked, nodding his chin at the map.

Feren said nothing, only studying the dispositions of the armies.

"Is there," I asked, "any intelligence on S—the Duke's whereabouts?"

They all looked at me.

"His people began this, so I've heard," I said simply, shrugging. "Perhaps it can be stopped with him as suddenly."

Tomrin replied, "The last reports we received have him holed up in his ancestral holdings at Sind. It's an ancient castle, but the fortifications are sound."

I traced the distance on the map. Due south of the camp, along the sinuous line of the Balnin mountains and on the southern bank of the Folnin river, Sind was marked as both a town and a fortress. It was perhaps a two-week march from where we stood.

There was a tight cluster of black tokens around the marks on the map. I counted their numbers and came up with nearly twenty thousand soldiers. Pressing the war there was possible, but would not be as easy as the victory here had been. The Torfallin could afford to send perhaps twenty-two thousand south, while holding this position against the armies to the west. The armies in Sind would have time and warning to entrench their defenses.

Once again, I sent my impression of the map to Sem. This

time, I was surprised to receive an immediate response.

I'm coming in. Kindly see to it that your friends don't try to stick me full of holes.

I sensed Sem nearing before I saw them winding their way through the camp. They were riding the gray once more, and trailing Beatrice on a long tether. They gave off no sense of unease at riding between so many soldiers. Indeed, it was the men they passed who seemed skittish.

I had told Feren and Hines to expect them, and Bergin had spread the word among the cohorts to make sure no one got over-eager with their pikes. Still, stares followed Sem in. I was used to their scars by now, but even the most grizzled of soldiers seemed to look on in a sort of respect mixed with horror.

They looked small riding in. Having spent so much time lately riding with soldiers, it appeared I had grown accustomed to the height and broad shoulders that Torfallin men tended towards. Sitting a mule and riding by warhorses only amplified the effect. They were small, aged, dark, and of indeterminate gender, against a multitude of tall, muscular, pale young men.

They drew every eye and still seemed to dominate the camp, riding on a weathered gray mule. It was the way they sat, I thought. Their posture was no different riding between ranks of armed soldiers than it would be were they riding among pines on a lonely hillside.

I stood my ground at the entry to the general's tent, waiting for Sem's stately progress through the camp. I watched the soldiers watching them. Their eyes darted from their swords to the pair of mules to their long braid to their distinctive, if threadbare clothing. Invariably the eyes flinched at their scarred face, arms, hands. A silence fell along the line of men as the gray stepped calmly down the path to me.

Sem patted the gray's neck and straightened their back as they reached me, and the mule stopped. Beatrice continued a few more steps to nose my hand, taking the half carrot I held out for her. The gray turned jealously for her share, and I held my other hand out to her with the other half.

"Where's your prisoner?" Sem asked.

"In time," I replied. "We must speak to the general first."

I saw their lips compress into a tight line, but they dismounted and followed me into the tent.

Hines had sent his aides away for the meeting. Sem and I stood facing General Hines and Feren across the map table under the shaded canopy. For a time, no one spoke. Hines and Sem eyed each other warily, each taking the other's measure.

Feren was the first to break the silence. "Thank you, for helping us. We owe you a great deal."

Sem said nothing, their face utterly blank.

"*Ai me guentéde!*" I threw up my hands, swearing.

Sem turned to me in surprise, their lips quirking into a tight smile. Hines wore a look of shock and... humor? It was good to know that he understood some Somiri.

I shook my head and sighed. "Will you stand there staring each other down until Savat's reserves come marching through the camp? Does it really matter who is the more stoic or the more stubborn? We just fought a battle together! Can we move on to the talking now?"

Hines grinned at me, then turned back to Sem. "Was it you who taught this one? They have an astonishing strategic mind for one so young."

Sem shrugged. "I found them at thirteen. I taught them what I could. What they have made of themself since is more their own doing than any of mine," they said grudgingly.

I looked over to Feren who was struggling to suppress a smile. I rolled my eyes. First they stared each other down, then they discussed me like a child.

"They're both right though." Hines nodded first to one of us, then the other. "We do owe you a great deal," he said to Sem and I, "and time is short. The prisoner has said nothing to my men. If he—they speak to you, will you share what they say?"

Sem hesitated, and I could sense their stubbornness asserting itself. "Yes," I said. "I will share whatever military intelligence we learn."

The general's eyes darted to me and his lips twitched into a small, knowing smile at my words. "Well enough. Feren, take them to see the prisoner."

We left the tent and Feren led us through the camp. The Torfallin were still coming in from the wider battlefield, cohorts separated by the chaos of battle reforming, tending their wounded and dead, setting up tents. Here and there, I was comforted to see a face I recognized. A squad of archers who had ridden with us from Third Sister, a cohort of pikes from Quarry East that I remembered by their captain's colors. Further on, we passed Joff assembling a mixed cohort that included some of my men who gave us small salutes.

Just beyond the assembly ground, we reached an open tent with a guard facing out from each corner, and two at the sides facing in at the prisoner, who sat placidly in the center. I recognized one of the guards from the squad that had fought with me to capture the *nyssa*.

Feren addressed the guard lieutenant. "We're to interrogate the prisoner. Please give us some space and privacy."

The lieutenant saluted, and gave orders for the other guards to untie canvas sides that were rolled up into the canopy of the tent. These dropped down one by one, turning the open canopy into a dark, closed space. The front panel was split down the middle to form a door, and one guard held this open for us to enter.

Through all of this, the *nyssa* remained seated, eyes staring blandly into nothingness. They didn't react to the guards' activity and departure, or to our entry. Feren stood quietly in the corner as Sem and I sat down on the ground an arm's length away from the *nyssa*. For a time, we simply sat in silence.

"What is your name?" Sem asked.

"Penarth," they answered simply. There was no emotion in it; just a statement of fact.

"To whom do you owe allegiance, Penarth?"

"The Duke of Fall, Tamar Savat." Again, the voice was flat, as if they read the words written by another hand.

"What is your goal in this war?" I asked.

Penarth turned to me and answered mildly, "To win."

Sem closed their eyes in frustration. *Perhaps you should see what you can find?* they sent me.

I replied through the link in the affirmative, pulling on my well of pain—freshly churned by my experience in the Circle— to delve into Penarth's mind.

"You're doing a poor job, then," Sem answered mildly. "Was capture part of your plan?"

"No."

Seeking memory in another's mind is far more difficult than finding it in one's own. There's a natural affinity a person holds in their own memories, an intuitive familiarity for the shape of experience that guides you through your own history. It's something like the comfort and sense of presence that helps you move through your childhood home even in the dark.

Delving a foreign mind for memory is an alienating thing. Every turn and movement is a chance to break upon the unknown, to drive headlong into pain or to find your path interrupted by a chasm of loss or flood of acute pleasure.

It is not a thing to be attempted lightly.

Finding your way requires a map. Something like enough to that innate affinity that the individual holds in their own mind. A way to translate their self-experience to your own. The most effective is a shared memory, but finding even that can be a challenge.

Fortunately, I had left myself a trail back to it.

The tendrils of briar that I had woven around Penarth's mind still held. I winced once more as I felt the pricks of thorn and constricting vine that held their emotion and pain strictly in check. I would release them from this the soonest I could.

But for now, the bramble was rooted deep in their mind, and those roots were anchored in the moment of memory where I had planted them, coaxing them to grow and strangle the *nyssa's* self.

I could feel the loose scree shifting under my feet, the rough grip of my sword against my calloused fingers. The cold, crisp air of night caught the tip of my nose and my ears, and I felt a chill breeze ruffle my short hair.

I also felt the warmth of my beard; the echo of nerves in my hand from the impact that had shattered my sword. I felt the comfort of the soft leather-wrapped hilt of my dagger and saw the jeweled glint of my enemy's blood along its cold steel.

The certainty of my belief warmed me against the chill of the early hours. What we did here was *right*. Whether this young *nyssa* killed me or I them, I would win, for the Vision would be achieved.

...the Vision...

I sat at a campfire in the cold night, all too aware of the milling mass of black-coated soldiers around me. They were crass, offensive, ugly men. Laughing and joking, disrespectful and lewd. Some were drunk.

A pair of them lurched through the camp, arm in arm raising their tin mugs in toasts at the prospect of the coming battle and the chance to kill Torfallin. Nonetheless, they skirted carefully around my fire, keeping their distance. That they thought I fought for *them* was the perfect joke. It proved why what we did was necessary.

They're incapable of justice, immune to reason, I thought. All they did was breathe and eat and shit and fuck and make noise. They were unworthy of such joy, unworthy of their rule, unworthy of *life*. What gave *them* the right to rule over *us* who were beyond such boorish pursuits?

I stared into my fire, imagining the coming battle, thinking happily of all the grays I could kill. The sooner they died, the sooner we could be rid of the Blackcoats as well; the sooner we'd be done with this… messiness. I thought of the night *they* had revealed the plan to me… their grand Vision. That night had changed everything for me.

…that night…

I shifted nervously in the cold chill of the southern air. The common room bustled with drink and dice and camaraderie, but I stood apart. Always there was a palpable air of distance between me and others. I had never quite understood it, how people—even other *nyssén*—could smile and be close and *share feelings* and seem utterly sincere with each other. It had to be an act, but I could never fathom why they bothered.

Deeper into the room, the warmth of the fire took the edge off the damp sea air and I could see that the people here seemed relaxed and were enjoying themselves. My shoulders tensed further and I held myself more tightly at guard.

A hand touched my arm, and I turned to see a tall, slender form—Torfallin by their coloring—with a tight, muscular body, a sharp angular face, and long hair, nearly white. Their lips quirked into a knowing half-smile.

...I recoiled in shock and nearly lost my connection...

—I couldn't understand why they were so far away. The room swayed as I leaned to reach them—

...lost...lost in memory...

—a fine single thread of clarity in the fog like a ray of sun cutting through heavy storm clouds—Eelie grasped both sides of my face, leaning close, their eyes fixed on mine and desperate. Their face held concentration and anger and fear—

...no... that night... back to that night...

"Why do you think they hold power in this world?" Eelie asked me.

The answer seemed simple to me, as all things seemed simple. "Because they took it. There are more of them," I said, shrugging. "What can't they do, with their endless armies?"

The slender, pale *nyssa* with the feral, fox-like features shook their head. "No, Penarth. Try again. I didn't ask you to meet me to hear you whine about why they're crawling over the land like ants. I am gathering those who can see the truth; who can understand what needs to be done, and what we can make of this world when the power over justice and reason is in *our* hands."

They leaned close, wrapping their arm around my shoulder. "Look at them," they said, waving their free hand before us at the drunken mass in the common room. "Can any of them best you? Could any of them take from you what you don't allow them to take?"

"No," I said, realizing it in full now. I could always take

what I wanted. Who of these could stand against me? "But..."

"But what?" Eelie asked.

"But... they *do* hold power."

Eelie nodded.

"And... there's no reason we couldn't take it from them..."

Eelie smiled.

It dawned on me, finally. "They hold power over us because we allow it." As I said it, I realized it was true.

"And what," they asked quietly, "would happen when we stopped allowing it?"

It was my turn to smile.

Having seen all that I thought could be of use, I withdrew, lurching to my feet more suddenly than I meant to.

Sem looked at me mildly and then caught the look in my eyes. I sent them the experiences I had just drawn from the captive and watched as their face turned grim. They stood also, and we gestured Feren to follow as we left the tent.

Far from oblivious, Feren must have seen our expressions. "You've learned something," he said. "From your faces, it isn't good."

I shook my head, still trying to put into words what I had remembered. I felt Sem press a thought to me and felt a sense of aversion at telling Feren the truth.

Do you really expect him to take well the news that his nation is at war with witches and not with Fall? they asked.

They deserve to know. And honesty will serve better than silence here. I replied. I hoped I was right.

"I don't know what pretense was given to the Fallians for this war," I said slowly, "but the *nyssén* they're fielding are fighting their own war, and *both* Torfall and Fall are their pawns."

Feren stopped short and turned to me sharply. "Say that again."

"This one," I said slowly, gesturing to the tent, "has a memory of being recruited by another *nyssa,* one I know. They are rotten to the core." I paused to let my mind put pieces together. "They are in service to Savat... have been for years, since long before he rose to Duke. I... I don't know what their relationship is, but I know this: Their goal is to tear down the systems of power in both nations, and wrest that power for themselves. I don't know how many—that one didn't—but I suspect that every *nyssa* in black is biding their time before they turn on their own armies."

The three of us stood there, taking this in.

Sem wore such a look of distaste that I was genuinely surprised when they spoke. "There is still something in this that doesn't smell right."

Feren looked to them, a question in their eyes.

"How many *nyssén* can there be involved in this? A few dozens? All of Reft is less than two thousand and many of those are families and children. Suppose they win and achieve everything they wish. Suppose they uproot the Lords of Torfall and the Dukes of Fall and between them they hold all Seven Keys and the Three Diadems and the Scales? What then?"

I realized what they were saying. "Rule is held with the hearts of the people, or the will of the armies, or both. No one can stand long without either," I said, paraphrasing the philosopher *Brene.*

Sem nodded.

Feren was nodding also. "They can't hope to win over either, in either nation. They operate now in secret, but if they topple the leadership, they will have to show their hand at some point, even if only to make their own lives happier."

"Forcing their way into power will only turn the common sentiments harder against us," I said.

"And the hatreds of the people already turn to the murder of *nyssa* children now and then," Feren said, grimly. "This will be worse. It will be open massacre."

"It will be worse than that," Sem said grudgingly to Feren. "Reft will not stand for the wholesale slaughter of *nyssén*. You can not fathom the destruction we could unleash if provoked to that degree."

Feren eyed them warily.

"The world will burn," I said softly. "None of us will escape the catastrophe."

"This Eelie is not so mad by all accounts," Sem said thoughtfully. "Are they strong enough in Mind Magic to think they could control a nation?"

I shook my head. "I am stronger by some measure and I know I could not. They are arrogant, and willful, and... ruthless, but mad? No. I fear that we still don't have the whole of the picture. There *must* be something more at play."

"There's one place we can find out," Feren said. "This—Eelie?—has long been close in Duke Savat's counsel, yes? Then whether he is conspirator or dupe, there may be something to be learned with him."

I turned to face south. "And the Duke is at Sind, last we knew. So. Whether through the defeat of his armies, or... whatever else is happening, it seems we will meet him there. I suppose it was inevitable."

"How will you go?"

I looked over the cohorts forming up behind us. "Southeast along the mountains. The mules can handle any terrain, and I trust Artem's footing well enough. We should be able to avoid any troops that way, though it will lengthen our journey."

"Even so, we'll be slower than you two can manage alone," Feren admitted. "But I'd feel better with you riding with us."

I nodded. "I don't relish our facing Savat's armies alone, believe me. But we cannot afford the time. If this war is to end, it will take more than armies battering each other to end it."

Feren looked to the side and his jaw worked as if sorting through some memory, trying to find particular words. Finally, he turned to me and said simply, "For my part, I'm sorry for things I've said about your kind in the past. I hope... I hope you can think of me now as an ally."

It was my turn to turn away. I struggled to suppress a laugh—I can't say where it came from. It was not humor; perhaps it was pathos.

"Feren... we've been allies since the woods south of Balifere. Since the morning I raced Artem through the hills to warn your company of the ambush, we were allies. We've marched and stood and fought as allies throughout this war."

I reached out and grasped his shoulder. "'Ally' isn't enough anymore. What we've done here—you, me, Mims, Bergin and Joff, *our* men; all the soldiers we brought out from Third Sister—We can be *something else*. Something more than just foreigners who either recoil in hate and fear or vie for advantage or make tenuous, doubtful truce with each other."

I looked north to the horizon, shimmering and indistinct in the morning haze.

"Remember Balifere. Remember the fear and hate that drove people to murder a child from their own village! As much as Savat began this war with you, your people *allowed* him to turn the power of the *nyssén* against you, and it's only by Sem's power and mine that his forces are on the run now. I am not of Torfall. Neither is Sem."

I turned to look him in the eyes. "How many *nyssén* are chased out of Torfall to take refuge in Reft every year? How many of those you face now were taken in and given succor by Savat? Do you wonder why they fight in his army? How many Torfallin *nyssén* have been killed by their neighbors over the years, who might have fought for *you*?"

I shook him by the shoulder. "Your allegiance is not enough! You cannot call me ally while you stand by and allow such injustice to thrive across your own lands. You have come to know me and what *I* stand for. What *I* fight for. Now, *you* have an opportunity to become something *more* than an ally. You have a chance to change the way people like me are treated in your world." I released his shoulder then and softened my voice. "I hope that you take it."

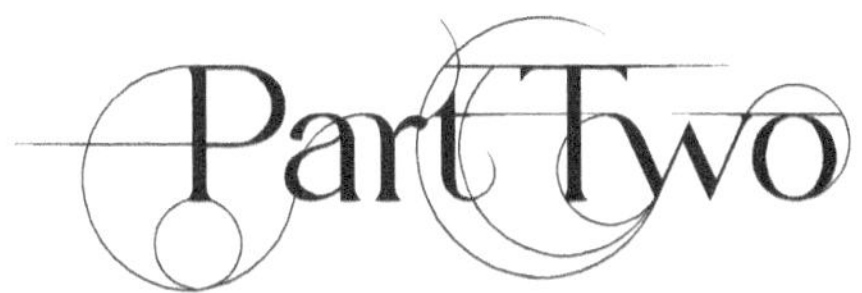

SOMETIMES, LIFE CAN lead you in circles. You set out believing that with each step you take—first one then the next—you're moving towards something meaningful. Or moving away from something painful.

There are times, though, when you can find the briefest glimmer of truth: That meaning is found in revisiting the past, not in discovering the future. That the pain that drives us to escape our own history is the very thing that shapes our lives. That it's those moments that break us that can lead us to feel the most whole.

When I lost my family to violence and horror on the trail to Anbress, I wished that I had been killed along with them. I was numbed at least as much by that pain as by the drugs that Cal's men used to keep me subdued.

When I left the family I had grown to care for in Ma'am's house after the ferocity of Sem's assault, walking voluntarily away from luxury into the unknown deprivations of the wild that awaited me on that journey, I had no idea that I would find a life even more fulfilling.

When I abandoned the family I had made for myself in Reft, in that tumult of grief I had wondered aloud at the whims of chance that bent my life into circles. *Was* there some hand at work? Some inescapable pattern that has shaped my life? I never thought that I would find an answer.

Now I sat Artem's saddle on the rough peak of dark stone that overlooked the broad descent west into Sind, and I wondered. Somewhere beneath us waited an army. Beyond the army waited the ancient fortifications raised by the Duke's ancestors. Within those walls, waited Savat himself, and beside him more likely than not, waited Eelie.

I suppose it is only right that it should eventually come to this.

Thirteen

As Sem and I descended, letting our mounts pick their own way down through the rocky scrub of the hillside, my mind was full of half-formed questions. Now and then, one found shape enough to be voiced.

"Did you know, when you fetched me from that house all those years ago? Did you have any idea where you were taking me?"

Sem didn't answer for some time. When they finally did, they reached to the heart of the question. "No one knows," they said. "No one ever knows where they are taking themselves. How can we know where we're taking others?"

"You took me out of my life as a keeper of the house. That was my path then. Bringing me to Reft was the least of the change you wrought in me. You were the first to tell me that I could be... that I could be what I am."

I knew I was ruminating. Our quiet journey through the broken mountains under the cold gray sky seemed to make hopeful thoughts harder to find. Each mile we traveled south brought the chill deeper and deeper into my bones. My mind was turning maudlin and introspective.

"Do you thank me for that?" they asked, catching my mood.

It was a good question. It took me some time to find an answer.

"When I was five, I wanted nothing more than to grow up farming with my family. When I was ten, I was scared of what I didn't know about myself. When I was twelve, I thought I could be happy caring for the girls of the house. When you took me from that place, I *hated* you."

Sem rode on in silence, waiting for me to find more words. Part of me thought of the place in my mind where they still resided, wondering if I could find their thoughts.

"I really hated you. You destroyed my world, just as Cal had done. How could I feel anything else? You tore the house apart, hurt people who cared for me, ripped me from my family. Then you broke my veneer, tore away my mask and made me confront what I was, without even the balm of anesthetic to numb the pain of it."

My forearms itched in memory. "You taught me to cause myself pain, to ravage my own body for a power that I didn't even want."

Sem said nothing, taking my rebuke with a stoicism that I doubted I could have held to, were it directed at me.

"Did you know then what you were doing? Did you know that the pain of the scars was nothing compared to the pain of knowing that I had it within me to save my family even as they died, if I could have only controlled it?"

"We all have those regrets," Sem said quietly. "No one lives through this life and doesn't accumulate an overwhelming mountain of 'what if.' What if I had tried this? What if I had done that? What if had left the moment I received word? What if I had never let them leave without me? What if I had been faster on the road—not taken that detour—and gotten there before…" They shook their head. "Do you regret your life then? Did I do you so much harm?"

It was my turn for silence. Thoughts chased themselves through my mind.

"When we reached Reft, all I wanted was to keep riding with you. There was no future I could envision better than the life you had shown me."

"And did you still hate me?"

Right to the quick. "I did." We reached the bottom of the descent and started up the opposing rise. I took a deep breath and squinted up at the ridge, trying to find a path, though I knew I could trust Artem. "I loved you, too." I let that settle in my ears and my mind, feeling the truth of it. "How could I not? You had become my life by then. In the weeks we traveled together, you were mother, father, teacher, tormentor—you were everything."

Sem's voice was soft, almost sad when they spoke. "And did you need those things?"

We were nearly at the top of the ridge and the sun was dipping now towards dusk. The cold sky bloomed into a tapestry of purple and orange, striped with the iron clouds rolling in from the south.

"I did," I said. "I did."

"Then I can live with what I have done," they said, almost coldly. "I have seen too often the results of letting the lies we tell ourselves fester: Children who take their own lives out of pain too deep and devastating to endure, or who grow into adults who hate themselves—who hate the world around them. If there is need to hate, then better it falls on me. You deserve none."

We reached the crest of the ridge and found it the last, the land falling away in smaller and smaller hills rolling westward to the horizon. A broad river curved southwest just to the north, and at the far edge of what we could see unaided, a squat fortress perched over a low expanse of a town. Sind.

Sem and I looked grimly over the army camped in a sprawling horde that spanned the plain surrounding the walls of the fortress and spread north to the river. Almost twenty-thousand Blackcoats were between us and our goal.

It was the fourth such vista we had found over the last three days, seeking the best approach. We had finally come to the realization that there was no way to Savat but through his army.

North of the river, the first signs of the approaching Torfallin were just visible, rising in dust and haze on the horizon. They would be days yet before they could be a threat to Savat's army, but their presence meant the soldiers below us would be alert and wary of any attempts to infiltrate their perimeter.

We looked at each other, and without a word—not even one passed along our Pairing connection—we both heeled our mounts forward.

"There's little chance the army below lacks at least one Grim," Sem said. "When that army crosses the river, this will be death, bloodbath, and devastation, far beyond what your friends in gray have seen before."

Just below the last hilltop before the plain, Sem dismounted, leaving Beatrice and the gray un-hobbled. I dismounted also, giving Artem an affectionate pat. We climbed the hill and surveyed the plain rolling out before us. We were perhaps a mile from the nearest edge of the Blackcoat army.

Without looking back to me, Sem said quietly, sadly, "If you hated me after Anbress for the violence and pain I caused... I am sorry for what we are about to do. But you need to gain the castle if there is to be a chance at stopping this. Do not think too badly of me... after."

I stepped up beside them and touched their arm as Sem closed their eyes. I could feel them shudder, and through the Pairing bond I felt a slow wave of pain rise, becoming a nearly unendurable mountain of hurt and power. I gasped with the strength of it and nearly lost my footing on the hill. I had never felt a power so strong outside of a Circle, and the ferocity and singularity of it was overwhelming. My eyes filled with tears at the magnitude of pain that I felt—and yet it was only the smallest trickle that perfused involuntarily through the bond. I could not imagine what fully tapping that well of pain would feel like.

"Follow behind me," they said, their voice strong as stone despite the sound of grief it carried. "Not too close, but don't stray far." They drew their swords from the scabbards.

First one.

And then two.

They moved steadily out into the plain between me and the waiting army, the short sword in a backhand grip along their forearm and the long held downward and to the side. Both blades gleamed wickedly in the dwindling sun. Their pace quickened from a walk to a run to something more than human.

I followed behind, drawing on my power to speed my legs, but Sem was moving at a pace I could not match. They soon pulled ahead of me despite my best effort to keep up.

I kept my eyes fixed on their back as they closed the distance to the line of soldiers. Despite their speed, Sem was still a hundred paces away when they were noticed by the sentries and a call went up. Moments later, the call to arms turned to panicked alarm as they realized what was falling down upon them.

Soldiers are trained to face a charge of cavalry, to stand firm in the face of overwhelming force. They train to meet naked blades without flinching away—to know that they risk pain and injury and death every moment of battle—for the only way to survive such conditions is to match strike for strike, to push aside the fear and horror and embrace the violence.

There was no training they could have possibly had for what they faced this night. Sem's swords flashed and spun, at once striking out, parrying, and deflecting in the space of a single breath. They moved unhindered through the lines in an unswerving path and men fell to either side like mown barley stalks.

With the fresh violence came an overpowering storm of pain and I drew on it hungrily, feeding my muscles and pushing myself to catch up to the whirlwind of death that drove onward to the castle. As I closed the distance, I could see a shift in the defenders, like the gathering fabric that concentrates on a pulled thread. The lines condensed and hardened ahead of Sem's assault as soldiers tried to form interlocking defenses.

No defense could avail them. Sem's pace didn't even slow as they carved through the waves of soldiers. Spears were deflected, blades turned. Blood was spilled. And soldiers fell.

With my enhanced senses, I could pick out the individual, almost delicate movements as they stepped relentlessly through the ranks. A step forward with their right foot; the wooden plank of their sandal planted firmly as they swept their short sword low under one man's spear haft to cut into his belly, even while the longsword flashed out in the other hand to cut a precise line through the gap between helm and gorget of another. They shifted their weight forward then from left to right, pivoting the short sword into a defensive guard to deflect an incoming thrust of spear while the long cut through the leather boot of a fourth man. A forward step with the left and their short sword came down squarely against an attempted parry, the soldier's blade shattered under Sem's enhanced strength. The man fell back in shock, pierced by shards of his own sword even as the uncanny force of destruction pressed on.

In four strides and the flicker of an eye-blink, nine more men were broken and bleeding, littering the ground to either side of an alley cleared of defenders in a line pointed directly at the stone keep ahead. The awe and terror inspired by such impossible devastation is undoubtedly what has given rise to tales of the Grim. Though surely more myth than truth, still, no one can witness such power without a sense of dread that permeates the bones. Even I felt it.

But even with all the power they held from their own life of pain and the dire miasma of suffering they wrought, Sem was still human, and the whims and chance of battle fall eventually to favor no one.

I noticed first an arrow, loosed perhaps in panic from a soldier far enough from the melee that he had time to nock and shoot. It took Sem in the thigh, slowing them for the briefest moment. Only long enough for them to pull the shaft free and close the wound, but slowing them nonetheless.

Hundreds of soldiers had fallen to either side of their assault, and it was still shock I felt when I saw they had taken an errant cut to the shoulder. They closed the wound as quick as thought, but the bloodstain on their jacket showed like a flag. Uncanny as they were, one against thousands was not a calculus that could hold indefinitely. Sem was slowing.

I closed behind them, working now to keep the defenders

from drawing in on our flanks. My sword turned more than one strike that might have landed, and both of us were taking minor wounds, but we didn't dare let up on the pressure of our assault. We were still pushing forward, and the walls of the castle were looming ahead.

Keep going, Sem sent me.

In my mind, I nodded back to them.

I took a moment to draw a thread from the power that roiled around us and drove it into the two of us, changing our clothes, our skin, our eyes to a uniform black—we were shadows that swallowed the fading light. Eyes flinched back in horror at the sight of us and I smiled.

We pressed the attack.

Men continued to fall before us under Sem's flashing blades as mine took down men left and right. We kept moving and kept striking. Our steps were losing some of their lightning speed and becoming more measured and deliberate, but we still cut our way forward through the mass of soldiers. The stone walls of the fortress seemed nearly close enough to touch.

But then something changed in the texture of the lines to our right. The defensive line was falling away now faster than we could account for and suddenly there was an opening on our flank.

Standing there within a ring of empty ground was a wiry figure dressed all in sleek black silk striped with lavender and orange. A brush of short black hair stood upright and stiff on their head, stark against alabaster skin. They smiled at us and raised two curved daggers, one held lightly between thumb and forefinger, the other in a reverse grip along their right forearm. They spun the dagger in their left hand, and the blade flashed silver and made an audible hum as it sliced the air at an impossible speed.

Sem felled the soldier closest to us and then without pause or breath, they pivoted smoothly and closed with the *nyssa*, the four blades ringing together in an almost musical clangor.

I turned to face the soldiers at their back who thought to press forward, and they retreated a step. A quick glance behind showed me Sem and the *nyssa* turning and trading strikes, locked in a deadly dance of inhuman speed. I could barely track the play of cut and deflection and counter, and my perceptions were enhanced well beyond normal and I realized why none of the Blackcoats were pressing forward to bring Sem down.

Go! Sem sent me fiercely. I could smell the acrid color of it, so intense were their thoughts. *Keep moving forward and get inside! You cannot afford to be held here while more* nyssén *close on us.*

Indecision froze me for several moments. I felt Sem take a wound from the spinning daggers, and then another. I turned to join them in the duel.

GO!

With a groan of frustration and anger, I turned away, leaving them to their fight and pressed into the wall of soldiers, carving my way towards the castle. It was agonizing. It felt like I was fleeing, leaving them alone in that press of violence and death.

But they were right: If I stayed to help, we would soon be overwhelmed and our whole endeavor would fail. I had to get inside and confront Savat and Eelie.

I cut and turned and killed and maimed, and step by inexorable step, I came closer to the walls of the fortress. Above me I could see the shadows of crenelations atop the wall, about fifty feet high. There were no openings I could see, and I didn't have the time or the strength to fight around the perimeter of the wall searching for a gate.

I drew a flood of pain from the swath I had cut through the soldiers behind me and wound it into my legs, building a concentration of power there in my muscles. I kept pouring in more and more power, winding it down like the crank that twists the bundle of ropes that powers a catapult.

I knelt down and released the force all at once, springing high into the air and vaulting over the wall.

On the other side of the wall, the silence was palpable—it made the violence of our incursion feel like the din and fury of a vast battle, instead of what it was: two people with three swords between them. I made my way along a narrow stone walk that circled the parapet until I found a winding stair downwards and emerged in an open courtyard.

Word of our assault didn't seem to have reached the garrison yet. I noted guards patrolling the wall above me, and some few stationed at gates and doors of the inner keep, but none appeared especially concerned for the security of the castle. Nonetheless, I held myself to shadows and spun more of my power into my skin and clothing. I ran my hand over the rough wall and shifted from pure blackness of deepest shadow to a more mottled shade, picking up a little of the gray and purple that tinted the stone.

Booted steps rang above me as a soldier paced off his rounds along the wall. There was a pause, then a call of alarm. There was no urgency of fear... only the interest of unexpected action on a cold, dark watch. He had spotted the battle occurring outside the wall.

Even though I could feel them through the Pair bond, it still gave me heart: Sem was still fighting, and well enough to draw an audience.

I stepped back into the darkened corner of the stairwell, pressing myself against the wall as two soldiers came running through the arch from the courtyard and up the stairs, only inches from me. I could have touched them as they passed.

After a count of five, I stepped out into the court and moved silently along the wall, picking my way carefully to avoid making any noise. Twice more, I paused as a squad of soldiers jogged past me. They were confident in their walls. It didn't even occur to them that the deep shadows of the castle could hold any sinister surprise for them. I thought of Sem's warning to Feren: *You can not fathom the destruction we could unleash if provoked.* Indeed, I realized with a start, there was no camp or capital that could keep out the likes of me if I intended dire ends.

The main door of the central keep was a little further along, guarded by two pikemen to either side. I stood in my shadow and watched for a few moments. They didn't seem inclined to move, but there was no real need for them to. Some ways further on was a cluster of barrels stacked neatly against the wall, and some twenty feet above, the keep's stonework flared outward a pace, cantilevered on great stone buttresses and penetrated at intervals with arrow slits that angled downwards.

From behind those walls, a squad of archers could rain death down upon any army who breached the outer wall before they could possibly batter down the gate. Faint light spilled from some of these, but others were dark—they were not all manned. I found one just beyond the stacked barrels that was dark, and made my way around until I was across from it.

My eyes still tracked the two guards at the main door, and

when they turned towards the men clustered atop the wall, watching Sem's uncanny melee, I moved swiftly across to stand against the inner wall, screened now by the barrels.

Gauging the height of the arrow slit, I pulled on my memory of loss, of death, and of pain. I filled my limbs with it and held some in reserve, ready to pour into the stone above me.

I leapt, catching the narrow sill with my power-strengthened fingers and softening the stones to either side of the arrow slit with my power, remembering the way the Reft stonemasons grew new tunnels deep into the mountain. The hand-wide opening flowed open to either side like an eyelid turned on its side and I pulled myself lightly over the sill and into the darkened room.

I returned the stone of the wall to its original shape and peeked down out of the restored arrow slit, confirming that I had gone unnoticed.

The room was a narrow chamber, little more than a watch-post, stocked with arrows and a small heating grate waist-high in the inner wall that sat cold. A wooden door under a low lintel—barely more than a plank on iron hinges—led deeper into the keep. I peered through the finger-width gap between the door and the stone to find a narrow hallway, empty and lit with oil sconces on the wall. I watched for several moments before stepping out.

The walls of the keep were cut from the same purple-tinted gray stone used in the outside wall, though the interior walls were more finely dressed with smooth faces and tight joints. Under the flickering light of the lamps, I could see small flecks of quartz inclusions in the stone. They caught the lights from some angles and glittered subtly.

The hallway to the left ran to two more narrow doors on the outside, and one other to the right. At the end of the hall on the right, an alcove opened into a tight spiral stair up and down, and opposite this, a normal-sized wooden door, stout and bound with iron. This, I guessed, led from the guard rooms into the living areas of the keep.

I drew on my power and Delved through the nearby chambers. I felt the reverberations of living minds to the left, perhaps in both watch posts. I felt more above and below me. To the right, there was no one behind the small door there, and no one beyond the heavy door.

I moved towards that door, tracing my fingers over the latch and lock of iron. I let my power run through the metal, finding the shape of its inner workings and the tension that held the latch fast. Working metal was similar to stone, though subtlety was much more difficult to achieve. Metal was like stone that had been distilled, purified, hardened. It had been forced far from its natural state and locked away from whatever affinities it might once have held.

But subtlety wasn't necessary here. There was a bolt that kept the latch closed. That bolt was strong iron, but as strong as it might be, metal was also brittle. I poured heat into it and just as fiercely drew it out. I repeated this process several times, as quickly as I could. There was an audible snap as the metal cooled for the fourth time. I lifted the latch and pushed open the door just wide enough to peer through.

Here was another hall, wider and more finely appointed. A lush woolen carpet ran down the center, and the dark stone walls were layered with rich panels of polished wood and tapestries that had a feel of time upon them. The lamps were larger here, hung in filigreed brass mountings.

As I closed the door softly behind me and stepped out, I heard a door open further down to the right, beyond a turning. I held still, listening for footsteps that would tell how many I had to deal with.

There were none. I breathed deeply and tried to slow my heartbeat, but on hearing the voice that called out, it set to racing again. It was a voice I hadn't heard in many years.

"Enough with the skulking. I know you're there; I watched your entry through a Delving." There was a lightness and humor in the voice, and a sharp edge of mockery. I could hear the knowing smirk that I knew was on their lips and could swear I smelled lilac and spice. "Come, let's see what you are and what you expect to accomplish here."

I took a deep breath, calming my nerves as well as I could, and walked around the corner to confront Eelie.

Fourteen

Eelie stood on a large formal landing at the top of a wide staircase. They wore the same sleeveless black tunic slashed with Savat's colors and slender flowing trousers. A wide belt sat low on their hips and held a longsword in a black-lacquered scabbard. Their face was exactly as I remembered. Sharp, vulpine features in cream-colored skin. Hair so light it was almost white, falling in a straight, fine line past their shoulders.

They were still beautiful.

Some distance behind them stood the other *nyssa* I had last seen when Savat had come to Reft and I had helped him find Cal. When I had murdered Cal. I cast back in my thoughts, trying to remember their name. They were broader of shoulder and darker of hair than Eelie, but had the same pale skin—almost alabaster—and wore a similar uniform. Their build ran more to muscle and brawn than Eelie's lithe elegance. Tanith, I thought suddenly, remembering the name.

I shifted my stance slightly, right foot back and turned so

my weight was on the ball of my foot, ready to spring. My muscles were already primed to move quickly.

"Arin, you've got something on your face..." Eelie said with feigned concern. "Sort of... here," they said, touching their nose.

Reflexively, I raised my hand to wipe at the tip of my nose, and noticed I was still carrying the shadows I had spun about myself on my incursion into the castle. I felt my face go hot, and was glad I didn't show the blush on my skin.

I took five slow breaths, letting the tension in my shoulders relax, and willing the flush in my face to recede. I twisted *something* within me, and the deep purple-gray of twilight evaporated from my skin, my clothes. From one breath to the next, I looked like myself again.

"That's so much better," Eelie said. A satisfied half-smile quirked on their lips. "You're looking good Arin. It's been a while." They turned to their companion. "You remember Arin, Tanith, yes? Arin of *Reft*?"

Eelie took a small step forward towards me, their face open and bland with mild concern. "What have you been doing with yourself all these years, Arin? Murder anyone else lately?" they asked sweetly.

I kept my face as blank as I could manage, though I grimaced inwardly. They were trying to put me off balance; get under my skin. The kernel of disgust and shame that resided ever at my center warmed at their words.

They were succeeding.

"What is this war, Eelie?" I asked, finding my voice at last. "How many have you killed for whatever aims you drive at?"

"Me?" they replied, their eyes wide and face innocent. "Me? I've killed no one." They turned and stepped casually across the wide landing, tracing an arc through the space as if walking a large circle around me. "I'd guess, of the two of us, you've killed more men. How does it feel, Arin, to take a life?"

I flinched, but held my ground. "Tell me, do you truly do Savat's will? Or does he do yours? Whose war is this, really?" My eyes now danced between Eelie and Tanith, trying to keep them both in my vision.

"What war?" Tanith said, their voice gravelly and low. "My lord Duke is only bringing justice to the nation of Torfall. Long overdue justice."

I kept myself focused on Eelie; only glancing at Tanith every few seconds. "You can't believe that, truly." I said, speaking to Eelie. "You *know* the world won't long stand for *nyssén* seizing control of the affairs of nations."

They laughed, a low, throaty chuckle that set my teeth on edge, but also made my heart skip. "Oh Arin, you never were too quick to figure things out. Strong, yes. Brilliant, absolutely." They took a sudden step towards me, closing the distance. "Tempting..." Their eyes danced up and down my body, "Oh, yes. But always just a bit too slow to catch on."

My cheeks warmed again, and my hand was on my sword before I could control my movements.

They turned their back on me, and spoke calmly as they walked back to stand beside Tanith. They didn't seem to care that I was primed for attack.

"The world is broken," they said fiercely. Somehow, it seemed the first words they had spoken with any real feeling of truth. "It is broken! And we mean to heal it."

I struck out at their mind with all the power I could draw on, striving to learn what I could. These words, full of emotion, were an anchor into their memory. I poured my power into the space between our minds and bridged that divide.

It is broken...

I was standing on the edge of a wood, thick and dark with densely-packed trunks and interlaced branches. The treeline ran to the horizon in either direction, and under-foot, the ground shifted suddenly from an indeterminate mix of gravel and dry, gray-green stubble of grass to thick leaf litter in damp, spongey piles underneath that darkening canopy.

I pushed my way between the trees, threads of my cloak catching on scratchy bark and grasping fingers of low branches. Before long it was caught fast in a snarl of branch and I was forced to shrug it off and continue without it. The chill crept into my bones as I moved deeper into the wood. The light faded from dusk to twilight to the deepest oppressive night.

I found my path blocked by a thicket of bramble, dense and matted with interlocked tendrils of needle-sharp thorns. At first, I tried to pick the wall of briar apart, but no matter how careful I was, my hands were soon torn and bleeding, and the vines grew back faster and thicker and sharper than I could tear them away.

I knew I had to press on. What I sought was deep in the heart of this wood. I stepped back and focused my thoughts on fire. An angry inferno, a blistering wave of bright blue fire that blackened the tendrils and spread as the charred remnants of the vines became coals glowing fiercely with their own shimmering heat. New growth tried to fill that space, but it soon began to catch and feed the conflagration.

...I felt their mind lurch...

I stood before a wall of stone. Its color was a sickly mauve shot with rust. Starlight filtered sullenly through the leaves above and picked out flecks of mica in the stones, sparkling in dull silver.

The wall ran to either side of me through the wood, seeming

to curve gently away in both directions so that I lost sight of it as it diminished. It was no taller than my waist, but I couldn't see anything past that wall. It wasn't darkness it enclosed. It wasn't mist or fog or foliage. It was simply nothing. There was nothing there to see.

I knew I couldn't climb over that wall because until I breached it, there was no *over*.

I began to walk, choosing at random to follow it to the right. The stones were sharply cut and finely dressed, interlocking in neat staggered rows. The joints were so tight that I thought not even a sheet of paper could be slid between.

As I rounded the endless perimeter of the wall, a twist of thorned creeper occasionally reached out from the woods to my right, lying across my path or catching at my boot. I fed them to the fire that I carried within me, the same fire I had left behind to burn down the bramble wall.

The wall ran on and on, still curving gently away to my left. I realized that I was getting nowhere. I had the deepest belief that I could walk the entire circle and never know when I came back upon my own path. Perhaps I never would.

I thought back over what they had said. "A bit slow to catch on," they had said of me. "The world is broken."

...the world is broken...

I stopped and turned slowly in place, letting my eyes wander the wood and get lost in its depths.

A green tendril was wrapped around the toe of my boot. I burned it away.

...the world is broken...

I knelt down in front of the wall, leaning my left hand in the soft leaf litter and running the fingers of my right over the stone. The blocks were finely cut. The edges were sharp and tightly joined. But my fingers found a stone that bore cracks.

They were fine, barely perceptible even as I looked at them, but cracks. The stone was on the second row from the ground, just to my left. I had almost walked past it.

...the world is broken...

I moved to stand and found my fingers caught in a twirl of bramble. I pulled, shaking drops of blood from my pricked fingers. I almost burnt the creeper away, but changed my mind.

When I was a child, one of the monthly chores that fell to me was tearing out weeds and briar that had established itself near the goat pen or along the walls of the house, or among the river stone walls of the spring house. Father's voice came to me, the memory bringing fresh tears to my eyes.

"Gotta root them out, Pips. If you let the creepers get a hold, they can tear down a wall in time. Yes, Pips, even stone."

I wiped tears from my cheeks and gently, delicately laid my hand on the thorn-covered vine. I squeezed slowly, feeling each thorn pierce my flesh, feeling the warmth of blood run through the creases in my clenched fingers. I drew on the pain and fed it back to the briar encouraging its growth, leading it to the wall, showing it the fine cracks.

It flared to life, sprawling along the face of the stone, fine points of budding tendril finding the spaces between those cracks. The cracks were wider now, still fine as a hair, but several shoots had found purchase in the surface of the block. They were spreading along its face, finding its edges.

A flood of bramble coursed over me, wrapping my neck and face, lashing my arms, pulling me back and trying to drag me away from the wall into the wood. I let the fire in me rage and the tendrils fell to ash around me. I urged on the little shoot climbing the wall, pushing all my urgency into it.

A *snap* rang out as a small flake of stone fell to the forest floor.

The vine was twisting now, curling inward on itself as it hungered to bring down the wall. A grinding sound, and the cracks widened further. The block crumbled before my eyes, and soon the briar was a lush thicket of thorn and white flowers and spiraled green.

...the world is broken...

The stones of the wall collapsed inside and out, and a staggered "V" opened in its forbidding boundary. The stone blocks extended beyond the wall; a narrow, dark alley. I stepped over the low tumble of stone, hoping to find some hint as to Eelie's plans.

The sky was visible high above only as a thin strip of dim gray, scudded with iron clouds. The walls of the alley were dingy, stained with years of soot and muck and filth, and the rough cobbled ground was slimy with moss and mold and unidentifiable refuse. Here and there, small windows above were shuttered tight, and beneath each were the spreading stains of emptied chamber pots and washing tubs.

The smell was overpowering.

Ahead, just where the alley opened into some wider space, I saw movement—two children crouching in the shadows. The younger was perhaps ten years old. The older only a few years more. They had the same pale hair. It would be nearly white except for the muck and dirt that covered them head to toe. They looked as if they had rolled in the alley.

I watched the older child push the little one further back into the alley and then dash out. As I neared, I could see the opening spilled out into a broad street full of hawkers and pedestrians. Carriages rolled by on the street, the horses and the drivers both seemingly unconcerned about the people who milled about beneath the hooves and wheels. The street ran north and south with multiple large intersections visible from where I stood. Far to the north, large buildings rose to crenelate the sky, their roofs flashing in gleaming tile and copper.

I leaned against the opposite wall, and looked down at the child. They were rail-thin, all baby fat burned away so their face had the narrow, sharp features of a fox. Hunger was evident in every line of their body. I turned out to scan the street, looking for the older of the two.

There was a shout some ways down the street, and calls of anger rose above the clatter of the city. Then I spotted the older urchin, dodging recklessly between the wheels of a cart to escape the grasping hands of the pursuing stallkeeper.

The child made it to the alley, flashing past me and grasping the younger by the arm to flee deeper into the shadows.

This was not what I had expected to find. I followed them, trying to understand what I was seeing.

The two children squatted down in a shallow alcove along the wall—a former doorway, long-ago sealed up with mismatching bricks. The older of the two pulled two loaves of steaming bread from under their filthy tunic, passing the smaller to the young child.

"Eat fast, Medi. We need to move quick now."

The child didn't need a second prompt, and they both were soon tearing into the stolen bread with a kind of steady desperation, wasting no time or energy on further talk.

With them both now sitting side-by-side, I could see the same vulpine faces, the same lithe frames, the same coloring. They were siblings.

Footsteps sounded near the opening to the street. With each loaf half-eaten, the two rose from their niche and scrambled deeper down the alley to emerge on another street. I followed, my curiosity urging me on. The sky darkened above, and a sense of foreboding filled me.

"El, where are we going?" the little one said.

El's lips quirked into a half smile. "We'll find a place, Medi."

I saw it now. Their narrow fox-like face. White hair, hacked short and stained with dirt, but gleaming nonetheless. Their cold eyes scanning the street for threat or mark.

Eelie.

...the world is broken...

I felt their body close to mine, the heat of it warmed me and drove me on with a pressure I couldn't stand. My face was hot and my heart was racing. Their left hand rose to touch my face, their thumb tracing the scar from my temple to my chin. I could feel their breath against my lips.

I wanted to turn away. I wanted to lean closer.

Then their lips were on mine and I was powerless to break away.

...the world is broken...

My mind lurched.

...the world is broken...

Medi seemed to shiver, to flicker slightly sideways—there and not there at once. I felt my heart wrench in that moment, and the sky was black and cold.

We stood now by a door as the rain sheeted down. There was a boy standing in the doorway. In the memory, I was uncomfortably sure he was a boy, though I was taller than he. The rain was loud, drowning out the rest of the world. Almost drowning out Medi's whimpers.

"El, I'd love to let you stay. Both of you. But you know I can't do it for nothing."

"But she's sick, Jame, please," I begged. "Just the night so she can dry off and warm up a bit."

"If I give you beds for nothin' then everyone will know it, and they'll be beating my door down. Now, if you got something for me? That's another thing."

Medi coughed; a deep, wracking cough that almost doubled her over. I bent to help her, to try to pull her up, but weak as she was, the labor of her breath kept her folded nearly to her knees.

I looked up at Jame, the rain streaming down my face hiding my tears from him, but not from me. "Only one bed—for her—and food and a fire. Only, let us in."

"Well now, seems like I can make that happen," Jame said as he put his arm around my shoulders. The cold of the night was in my stomach now, turned to ice. I was numb as he guided us both inside and shut the door.

...the world is broken...

I slipped from the bed, as quietly as I could to avoid waking him, and pulled a robe on. Down the dark hall was a narrow door into a small dingy room. It was little more than a closet, but it had a small iron stove for burning coal. There was still a bit of heat radiating from the embers. I picked up a lump of coal from the nearly empty bin and nestled it in the glowing pile.

Medi was curled up on the narrow cot, asleep. Her coughs had subsided at last, though she still shivered and sweated with fever. Her helpless form flickered and danced like a guttering candle even as I stroked her hair.

...the world is broken...

This was not right, a part of me thought. I didn't need to see this. This wasn't what I was looking for. I tried to back away, to leave—

I tried to...

...the world is broken...

Each morning when he woke and climbed out of bed, I sobbed quietly, disgusted with myself. Each time he left the room, I railed silently to myself and planned how to hurt him. Then I swallowed the rage and hatred and self-loathing and went to check on Medi.

She was getting better, I thought. The coughs came less often now, and seemed less severe. She was still warm to the touch, but no longer sweated through the night. She even ate a bite now and then.

She's not getting better, I knew.

I wanted to go out during the day. Maybe I could steal some coin or jewelry or food. Something I could use to pay our keep, instead of—

But I didn't want to leave her. I didn't trust Jame or the others in the house.

Each night—

Each night I hated myself a little more.

...the world is broken...

I woke this morning to find that her coughing fits were finally over. Her fever was gone and she no longer shivered.

Her body was cold and stiff.

...the world is broken it is broken it is broken it is broken it is broken...

I stood numbly as I watched Eelie pull themself up to their knees from beside the narrow cot. They didn't look down at their sister. They didn't see anything. There was nothing left. A cry of animal rage began deep in the back of their throat and rose gradually until the tin walls of the coal bin rattled with it.

Jame tore open the narrow door, his friends behind him. He shouted for Eelie to stop, to shut up.

Eelie didn't even see him. Their face was suffused with guilt and hatred and devastation, contorted into something unrecognizable. And then they broke, and the air itself erupted into a conflagration that would burn the world down to ashes.

They didn't look back as they walked away from the burning pyre. There was nothing left of the building behind them, and the fire was spreading to nearby tenements. They couldn't even remember why they had come. Couldn't remember who they were. Couldn't remember what they walked to. Fin-Torfall held nothing of value. There was nothing ahead either.

There was nothing. The world was broken.

"I told you," a gravelly voice said from over my right shoulder. I turned, trying to place the voice, and found Tanith standing beside me. "It's only justice, and long overdue."

Fire and pain and darkness consumed me, and everything I knew dwindled into nothingness.

There is a kind of peace that can be found in defeat. The oppressive certainty that nothing can be done can lead to utter despair, or it can settle like a thick comfort that deadens the senses. Having felt before the weight of a drug-induced torpor, I recognized it now each time I woke.

My thoughts were slow. My bones were sluggish and my pain was distant and out of reach. For a time I plucked futility at it, trying to grasp some shred of power but it was like picking out a pebble through a down-filled blanket.

I was in a cell.

It was little more than an alcove with the open side covered in a grid of heavy iron straps. That much I could see before the weight of my own head made me drowsy.

There are other things I remember, though I can put no time or sense of order to them.

I remember tracing the ridges of rough stone with my fingertips. It was inches from my face as I lay upon the floor. No motivation to move, no reason to lift my gaze. The stone was fascinating so close. Whorls and subtle variegations of purple and gray that ran through it like the veins of some vast dragon out of myth or memory. Flakes and curls of quartz that shone a dull silver here and there made me think of scales.

I remember being carried to a bucket by an indifferent guard, to void myself in complete disregard of any sense of dignity.

I remember the taste of someone else's worry, the color of argument, and the smell of accord. A person I should know: dark and scarred and grim, and another: young and pale and gray; they shared an intensity and a purpose that made me weary. *We are coming*, their determination said. I couldn't understand why it mattered or why I should care.

I remember being fed a thin, tasteless gruel and the blissful weight of sleep that pushed me back down into dark depths of vague dreams each time I swallowed it.

Most of all, I remember Eelie. I can't say how many times they came—the visits all run together. It seemed vitally important to them that I know that they had beaten me.

"You are such a fool, Arin. You came all the way here thinking you would stop me, as if I was the one who stood in your way."

I said nothing.

"I told him from the start that you would never accept his ideals. I told him that you were too in love with the peace and surrender of Reft. You bought into their beliefs so *quickly*."

I was following a delicate spiral of bright purple through a maze of gray.

"You don't even know how wrong everything they taught

you is, do you? You still think you're somehow whole and healthy and as you should be. As if we were meant to live like *this*."

I felt myself roll on waves of stone as the room tipped and wobbled. In some corner of my vision I could see their lithe form pacing, the glow of their pale hair interrupted by the rhythm of the cell bars.

"He's played you all from the beginning. You, he was playing like a fiddle from the moment we met."

I slept for some unknowable number of years or seconds.

"*He* told me to try to seduce you away from your friends. *He* wanted to see if you would join us. I told him it wouldn't work. I knew what a simpering fool you were."

My finger traced a ridge of silver that wound through the stone, shimmering like a river through the world.

"He wanted you so badly—as if *I* wasn't enough—but it was *my* plan that finally worked. He thought if we pushed you hard enough, if you lost your place in Reft, you would come to us. I think he still thinks that."

I paused, the line of dull silver ended at the edge of a stone, and I couldn't understand how to connect it to the next stone, where there was no silver inclusion.

"But *I'm* the one who told him to find that man. To hire him to rob his own manor. To go to Reft for the Finding. You are all so predictable. *Of course* they would pull you into their Circle. I *told you* they would use you up!"

I couldn't remember why I was hesitating... the line of purple was so bright in this stone; easy to follow.

"And you. So powerful. So strong. So predictable. From the moment we met you, *I* knew how to break you."

My heart was racing and my stomach clenched on itself; my mind was wandering and confused. Why were they so angry?

Why so adamant? There was nothing to fear; nothing to fuel such passion; nothing to be done.

The stone beneath my fingers was far too interesting. Far too intricate. There was so much identity and memory embedded within its infinite variation. The colors had a heartbeat and a life. There was a yearning here, just beneath my eyes, if only I could find it.

The mists of smothering sleep took me once again.

Fifteen

There were endless brief moments of awareness scattered like seeds in the field to disappear in the dark rich soil. I was sometimes more lucid than others, but rarely better than half-dreaming.

The world was a little clearer when they finally came to bring me out. The guard riffled his keys to find the one that fit the lock on my cell. The clinking sound was both distant and familiar by this point.

With the door unlocked, Tanith came in and pulled me roughly to my feet. The world pitched and swayed around me. They wrinkled their nose as if I stank. I likely did.

They pulled me out and the guard locked the door behind me as was his habit.

"We need to wash this stink off them before we take them up," Tanith said to Eelie.

Eelie turned to the guard indifferently. "See them washed and clothed, then bring them out to the main guardroom."

Tanith shoved me towards the guard who caught me and guided my hand to the grate of my cell door. I wasn't steady enough to stand, but I could hold on enough to lean against the cold metal.

I felt the chill, damp air hit my body as the guard cut away the filthy tunic and trousers I wore. Then the icy violence of a bucket of water indifferently poured over me. A rough cloth and a hard lump of acrid-smelling soap was shoved into my hand.

"I ain't going to wash you. You want clean, you do it your own self."

I did what I could, but the room was still wobbling about too much. I suppose I scrubbed myself to his satisfaction when I felt another deluge of water hit me, then he grabbed my arm and led me naked and dripping down the hall to a larger room, with tables and chairs.

He pointed me to the table where there was folded a tunic and trousers in rough wool, a faded and dingy black, but clean enough. There was no towel or underwear, so I shrugged and pulled the clothes on. The thin wool stuck to my damp legs and back as I pulled them on, and I nearly fell. I had to sit on the chair to get the trousers all the way on.

I stayed there for a time, feeling the room spin.

Eelie and Tanith returned and they both looked me over. Eelie's lips twisted into their half smile.

"Not so comfortable as you're used to, I suppose. Well, that's what you get for choosing the wrong side."

Tanith hauled me up once more and I staggered between them through a winding maze of hallways and stairs and doors. My mind was still too clouded to keep track of the turnings or the distance. All I knew was the rough, cold stone on my bare feet. I imagined I could feel the whorls and threads of purple and veins of quartz that wound through it.

We are coming, I felt. *Hold on*. I heard the pulse of an image: Sem and Feren, moving together upon a steel-gray ocean. The colors of it tasted sharp and bright.

They brought me through a final door of heavy, coarse wood, and then I was walking on lush carpet beneath the warm light of oil lamps behind glittering cut-glass bulbs.

The hall ended at two large doors, polished and oiled to a dull luster. They opened these and we stepped into a grand sitting room.

It was nearly as large as one of the eating halls in Reft. It was a rectangle, with the doors we entered by along one long wall. Two mammoth fireplaces on either short wall roared with fire set on logs as thick as my leg. I thought I could have stood up within them. The ceiling far above was spanned by great beams of oak, each as wide as a whole trunk.

The other long wall was pierced at intervals with sprawling windows made of myriad fragments of cut glass in as many colors as I could imagine. They were cunningly set in narrow frames of lead so that they formed glittering mosaics in dizzying color. They must be astonishing in the sunlight, I thought.

I was lost in them, feeling the room swirl around me, when Tanith pushed me forward and I stumbled to the floor, catching myself on the thick carpet.

"Tanith," said a soft, firm voice. "That is no way to treat our guest."

I looked up to find Savat leaning over me, his hand extended to help me up.

"Come Arin, let us talk. It has been some years since we last spoke. I'm so very glad to see you alive and well."

He led me to the near hearth, where a series of plump chairs and couches were set in a half circle around the crackling fire.

The edge of the carpet stood well back from the blaze, I noted idly. The quartz inclusions here and there in the gray and purple stones reflected the flickering orange of the firelight.

He sat me upon one of the chairs and took the one beside it for himself.

My mind was still fogged, my head still dizzy, and a softness like a layer of thick gauze still kept me from my power, but between the heat and the comfort and the threat all around me, I was beginning to find my wits. I tried to focus on Savat and ignore Eelie and Tanith.

"What do you want of me?" I asked.

"What I've always wanted," he said. "I want your help in my great work."

I shook my head. "I don't understand. I've tried at every turn to defeat your armies and undermine your victory. What makes you think I would help you now?"

"Because, Arin, you don't know what it is I have worked for all these years." He leaned towards me and placed his fingers lightly on the arm of my chair. His eyes were wide, honest and reasonable. "I followed your story from the first word I received from my man in Anbress. I tried to seek you there, but you had already left. I knew that *you*—what you have experienced, what you have endured—*You* would understand."

A horn sounded out in the night. More echoed its call.

"Don't worry about that. It is beginning. Everything I have planned is nearly in place."

I shook my head, trying to find the threads of rational thought through the haze of the drugs. "Eelie told me what you did. What the two of you planned. What you did to me. How can you think I would help you after that?"

Savat turned and gave Eelie a level stare, then looked back to me and shook his head. "I'm sorry you had to find out that way, Arin. I truly am. And I'm sorry for how it played out. You'll remember I apologized to you even then. But... I needed you to see what they really were there in Reft. What they really care about. They used your power, and when you no longer fit their image of the good little *nyssa*—once they found you didn't match their tracings of the life they had planned for you—they cast you out."

I blinked. He didn't know. For all their planning and Eelie's pulling of strings. They didn't know that I had left of my own choice. I felt a warmth and a rising comfort, as if an old friend were drawing near.

Alarms began ringing through the castle. None of the three with me in the room seemed concerned.

"Then tell me. What is this great work?" I asked.

Savat smiled gently. He opened his mouth to speak, but Eelie broke in.

"No, Tamar. They are not with us."

He turned to them again. "Eelie, we've spoken of this. Their power will be a great addition to the Circle, and their skill with Mind Magic surpasses everyone's here, even—even yours."

"They are *not* with us. They *will* betray you." Eelie looked at me coldly. "Even now, I can see it in them, biding their time, hoping for an advantage to turn the knife."

"The time is nearly upon us. If it is to work, let us have the best chance. I know you believe in your own skills. Can you honestly tell me that your power of the mind is enough to do what we need to do?"

Eelie looked at him, their jaw set. They took a deep breath, wanting to claim that assurance. I could see it. I also saw the moment when their eyes flickered to me, and their shoulders slumped.

"I don't know. Yes, they are stronger than me. Are they

stronger than all of us?" They shook their head, "I don't know. But, Tamar—"

"Enough, Eelie," he said coldly. "The time for these doubts is past. We need their skill, and we need them on our side. Willingly or not, I will have them."

I was tired of the argument and wanted an answer. I raised my voice over them and stood. "Surely, you cannot believe that you can raise your *nyssén* to power over the world through force and hope to hold that power. You have to know what the result will be. You cannot both be so foolish. So what *is* your plan?" The room wobbled and I was forced to steady myself on the arm of the chair, moving me closer to Savat.

As quick as a breath, Tanith was standing beside their lord, sword drawn and at my throat. I tried to wave them off, to gesture that I was no threat but only succeeded in tumbling sideways to the carpet. Eelie stepped forward and Tanith's sword point followed me, even as Savat raised his voice.

"Stop, Tanith! Stand down, both of you," Savat shouted.

I looked up at the three of them, wondering how I had wound up beneath them. I took a deep breath, willing the room to stop spinning. There was a tension in me that felt like a rope pulled to the breaking point.

It was then that the great window of colored glass exploded.

Sem followed the expanding cloud of bright splintered shards like a hurled stone. They landed with both feet planted firmly, the slaps of their wooden sandals muffled on the lush carpet.

Their face was bloodied and grim. Their arms and chest dripped red from a thousand wounds to stain the ruin of their clothes and rain upon the carpet. But their hands held their two swords at the ready, and they scanned the room looking for me.

Eelie stood in front of Savat, shielding him from the worst of the glass with their own body—their face and arms covered with fine cuts. Tanith roared in pain as they plucked finger-sized shards of glass and leading from their body, and turned to face the new threat.

Tanith closed with Sem, swords clashing in a whirlwind of inhuman speed. I couldn't track their movements. They struck and spun and parried so fast that the blades hummed in the air.

Eelie pushed Savat to the carpet behind his chair and vaulted over it, drawing their own sword to join the melee.

I cried out a warning, but the sound was hardly free of my throat before their sword was in the fray, their own movements accelerated with their power. I tried to rise, still shaky and unstable, and found crushed glass under my knees, my feet, my hands. The lacerations burned and the flare of pain nearly broke through the fog that dulled my mind.

I tried to pull on that pain, but was not strong enough. I still couldn't reach it. I tried to find the doorway in my mind into the Pairing with Sem, to draw on their pain, but couldn't find its edges in the dark shadows. I was still wrapped in gauze and floating at the edge of a sea of drugged limbo. I screamed in frustration watching the three of them spin and flash, dancing across the carpet of shattered glass in a flurry of deadly steel.

Even slow as my perception was relative to their movements, I could see the shape the battle was taking. Eelie and Tanith were gradually widening their attacks, drawing Sem first here, then there to defend against two fronts. Soon, Sem would be forced to turn their back to one of them.

Sem was good. Even astonishing. But Eelie was at most half their age, and even if I couldn't draw on it I could feel the shadow of the pain of Sem's injuries through the Pairing bond.

They were slowing. They had already fought an army, and now their storming of the castle had used much of their last strength. There was a limit, even for one of us.

I looked around desperately for some way I could help. There was nothing. I could barely stand, I had no weapon, and I had no power to enhance my speed or strength. I clenched my fists in the debris of glass and metal on the carpet, feeling the shards cut into my skin, feeling the pain rise.

I focused on the pain. Centered it. I let it flow like the blood that seeped from my body with each heartbeat. I rode the pain with each swell, a tide that pulled me ever forward, pulled me up. The pain was everything. I ground my fists through the broken glass and let it fill me.

And at last, I felt the finest thread of that pain sharp and precise, a needle pierced deep into my mind. I drew it in, the merest trickle of power, and let it fill my arms until they were near to flying apart. With a shout, I threw two fist-fulls of shattered glass and lead at Tanith and the missiles flashed through the air in a whip-crack. They struck them in the face and chest, and the *nyssa* howled in pain and fury as blood bloomed on their face.

Sem took advantage of the moment of confusion, stepping forward to deflect Eelie's strike with their short sword and then pivoting cleanly, driving the long sword deep into Tanith's chest. The *nyssa* fell wordlessly even as Eelie pressed forward in a rage.

I collapsed on my side, the little effort I had managed bringing me nearly to unconsciousness as the room began to spin again.

Eelie passed Tanith's body and took up their sword in their off hand. Now it was Sem's turn to fall back under their relentless attack. I tried desperately to find the Pairing bond, to feed some of my pain to Sem but I was flailing in the dark. I could sense it was there, but couldn't touch it.

Eelie drove them back and back and back. Sem was flagging now, their strength waning. Each move was a little slower, a little more clumsy. They were bleeding from too many wounds to count, and I realized that the wounds were old, already drawn upon and of no use to them now.

Eelie had understood as well, and was avoiding injuring them anew until they could land a killing blow. They pressed their attacks methodically, each stroke a play for position, for control of the fight. They held their line and moved it step by deliberate step.

I watched helplessly, knowing the inevitable outcome and watching it play out before me.

Sem turned a low strike from Eelie's sword and drove them back a step, raising their longsword for an overhead strike. Eelie raised their sword overhead to block it, but even as I watched them raise their guard, I realized the feint. Sem's stance was widening. Their feet were too wide to support the overhead strike.

They dropped suddenly into a low strike that would have taken Eelie in the gut with their short sword.

But Eelie had seen it too. I had taught them the move, after all. They still held one sword in an overhand guard, but the second was thrust out low and straight, taking Sem in the heart.

I cried out in agony and disbelief as I felt the Pairing fade from my mind.

I scrambled to my hands and knees, shoving past Eelie and crawling over the broken glass to reach their body. The room still spun, and now the tears flooded my vision so that I made the last few feet blind, reaching them and cradling their small form.

I hadn't ever held them, but I did now, rocking with them clutched to my chest as the pain of their loss came crashing down upon me. They had followed me across half the world, taken me out of obscure servitude and brought me to where I could learn all the things that I could become.

They had found me again when I had thought myself lost beyond any finding, and followed my lead without question when the world began its perilous slide towards chaos and madness. They had spent themself utterly in the effort to get me through Savat's defenses and into this keep, and then found the strength somewhere to regroup with Feren and press the attack again to bring me out of bondage. Only to fall here.

Sobs wracked my body as the waves of pain and guilt washed over me. Sem was dead because I had pushed them to aid me. Because I thought I could right the world. Because...

Sem was dead.

The agony of that truth filled me and pushed every other thought from my mind. There was no room for anything else because the pain was everything.

And then I remembered the lessons that Sem had taught me.

First one:

Relax. Don't fight the pain, don't flee from it. Embrace it. Feel it.

I found every tension in my body and let it go. My shoulders sagged. My arms fell, releasing Sem's body to my knees.The pain of their loss flared and I felt it, tears flooding my eyes anew.

Relax.

I slowed my breathing, the short gasps relaxing to deep breaths.

Feel it.

It hurt. Their death was real; my grief was real. I let it fill me and the power suffused every particle of my being.

I wound it into myself and wiped my blood clean of every trace of the drugs. I let it fill me and bring clarity to my mind and strength to my limbs. I let it heal me and my myriad cuts and abrasions flowed with fresh blood, forcing out fragments of broken glass and closing cleanly.

I gently lowered Sem's body to the floor, brushing stray shards of glass from their clothes and skin. Their face was calm and at rest; at odds with the violence of their death. I leaned forward and kissed their forehead.

Then two:

From now on, you go nowhere *without a blade.*

I wiped my eyes dry. As I stood, my hands closed around the hilts of their swords. I held the short reversed in my left hand, blade tucked along my forearm. The long, I lifted in my right as I turned to face Eelie.

The cold, endless pain of Sem's loss filled me like water from the deepest well. I overflowed with it. As I walked slowly towards Eelie, it ran in rivulets from my body with every movement. Glass shards shifted before me with each step, avoiding my bare feet.

Eelie's eyes widened and they stepped backwards, their boots crunching on the ruins of the great window. Savat had regained his feet while I held Sem, and now he backed away, trying to placate me, but I couldn't hear him. He moved as if in a dream, and I realized I had sped my reflexes unconsciously.

I held the longsword out, pointing at Eelie, and moved lightly towards them. I extended my foot and slid to the right, a sparkling wave of broken glass rippling away from my path as I moved. They turned, expecting a low strike as I stepped fast across with my left foot, turning my body and catching and lifting their blocking sword with the short. I completed my turn before they could bring their other sword down, and my longsword cut upwards across their forearm. Their sword clattered to the floor and they flinched back in pain.

Eelie took two steps back, backing off the carpet onto the polished stones before the roaring fireplace. They reached back and picked up the fire poker that rested in its holder upon the hearth, resetting their stance.

I kicked their fallen sword away and closed again, step by deliberate step. The cut on their arm closed as they drew on its pain. I paused my advance. They shouldn't have been able to heal the wound entirely from its own pain.

I reached out then, and I felt it. There was a great wash of pain rolling from outside the wall. It was like the endless crashing of the sea, breaking upon the fortress with relentless pressure. I remembered then the horn calls I had heard. There was a battle happening outside the walls. The Torfallin army had arrived, and was locked in furious warfare with Savat's Blackcoats.

Eelie smiled, and we were dancing once again. The air rang with the clash of metal as I turned their sword cuts with delicate twists of my blades and they battered away mine with the heavy poker.

The ground was mine—I still cleared each step without thought while the window fragments crunched and rolled beneath their boots. But they were more practiced with dual weapons. I had studied the technique in the Watch many years ago, but hadn't kept up my skill.

With us both suffused with seemingly endless power, it came to a nearly perfect balance. Neither of us could gain the advantage no matter how we turned and twisted, seeking it.

"Why?" I asked. "Is it worth all this death, whatever your aims?"

"All this and more," Eelie said softly. "You will never understand. I keep telling him that."

"Eelie," I said, trying to reach them with words. "It wasn't your fault. What you went through... you did all you could. Medi's death—"

At the mention of their dead sister, Eelie flew into a rage and I was ill prepared for it. A desperate, animal cry of agony ripped from their throat, and then I was turning blow after blow, backing away, trying to find enough of a pause to reset my stance.

Eelie battered my swords left and right with such a fury that I couldn't stand my ground, even with the power from Sem's death filling me. A wild strike to my left with the poker, and I lost my grip on the short sword. I tried to cross the long to defend, shifting to a two-hand grip but my left hand was still stinging and numb from the blow.

Eelie struck overhand with their sword and left to right with the poker and I turned both with little more than luck. As they spun away from me, I reset my guard, drawing my weight back over my left foot, expecting another sword blow.

Their sword flashed before me, but instead of striking, they lowered their weight to the left and brought the poker down on my right knee.

I screamed as I felt bone and sinew shatter and tear, and I collapsed, my vision going white with pain. My breath was gone and I thought I would suffocate. I couldn't pull air into my lungs and with every heartbeat, fresh agony shot like fire through my body. I was shaking and even though I lay inches from the broiling hearth, I felt cold as ice.

A quiet, calm compartment of my mind, built up of books

and learning and reason kept a running diagnosis as if I were tending a patient. *Shock. Severe crushing trauma to right leg. Multiple complex fractures to the lower thigh and knee joint. Probably torn collateral ligaments.* The litany continued in my mind.

I lay face down against the stone, both swords lost. I couldn't stand... couldn't move... couldn't breathe. My ears were ringing and my vision was beginning to go black around the edges. All I knew was the heat of the fire on my left, the chill of shock creeping over me, the hard stones beneath my face, and the roiling fury of pain that was consuming me.

I saw Eelie's boots step up just inches from my face. I could tilt my head just enough to see them raising the poker over their head to strike the death blow. Their face was twisted in a visceral, primal rage.

I looked down again, waiting for the end. Defeat holds its own kind of peace. My eyes found the subtle, twisting whorls of purple within the stones and I traced them. It was difficult... my vision was growing hazy and dark, and the dancing orange firelight reflected off the polished stone and obscured the lines. But I ran my finger along that path, trying to trace it to its end. The fine threads of purple that spiraled and flowed like veins in the stone and held my focus.

Stone has an affinity for itself. It remembers.

I pulled on the storm of pain that ravaged my body, let it wash like a cleansing white heat through my chest and down my arm to my fingertips tracing that vein. I wove it in and out of the spaces in-between like a running stitch, and with a smile of satisfaction, pulled it tight.

A ring of angry coruscations a pace across erupted beneath Eelie's feet, and they dropped through the Bridge, falling dizzyingly up out of the floor of the cell far below in the dungeons of Sind. Their eyes were wide with shock as they fell past me. As I watched them reach the peak of their fall beneath me, I released the Bridge and let it close them away even as gravity reasserted itself and they fell back down towards the stone floor.

Sixteen

I poured what was left of the pain back into my leg. It wasn't enough to heal the damage, but I was able to pull the larger pieces of my bones roughly into alignment and dull the pain enough that I could catch my breath and pull myself up to sitting. Still, it took me several minutes to get upright.

Every breath, every slightest shift of muscle, sent new shocks of pain radiating from my leg. I slid backwards until I could rest my back against the stone wall beside the fireplace. The pain was almost more than I could stand. I reached out my senses to the battle raging outside the wall.

I had no idea how long Eelie might remain contained in the cell. The guard had locked it behind me, and I had rarely seen him except when he came with food or to help me to the bucket. But Eelie could easily break out of the cell with their power. I siphoned off a trickle of power and Delved downwards to try to find their mind.

I found them unconscious, at least for now, likely knocked

out by their fall. With any luck, no one would visit that cell for some time.

"Arin," Savat said.

I looked up and he was bending over me, concern in his face. I pulled on the pain and suffering that raged outside and gasped with the first flash of fresh pain that came from piecing my leg back together.

Savat said something to me, but I lost his words in the intense spikes of agony as I pushed and pulled with my power, trying to fit the various bone fragments into place. If I could align everything, I could coax them to knit back together. I had done the same for several soldiers, but the flares of white-hot pain with each adjustment I made was too distracting to continue except in small moves. My face was beaded with icy sweat. I knew that I was in danger of slipping deep into shock and passing out. I focused on doing what I could, my breath hissing through my teeth with each movement.

"Arin, I'm sorry. This was never my goal. All this... anger. This destruction. It should not have happened this way. I'm sorry for your friend."

"How should it have happened?" I gasped, tears coming fresh to my eyes. "What of all the dead soldiers? What of all of them out there now, dead and dying and maimed?"

Savat's eyes widened. He shook his head. "What do you care for them? They are not of your kind..."

I laughed desolately, and immediately regretted it as new torture stabbed from my leg. "Not of my kind? Are they not people? Or—ah," I gasped, "do you mean that I am not a person?"

"No... I—" he shook his head again. "I meant only that they would kill you readily enough given the chance. Why care for their wellbeing?"

"Some would," I said quietly, "except for the ones that wouldn't." I took a slow fortifying breath and shifted again, trying to find a position where the pain was less. "Is that your great work then? To fuel an endless war until everyone who might challenge you is dead?"

Savat sighed, and stood, pacing slowly before me as if trying to find the words. "The war was never the purpose. It is necessary, but not for the usual kind of power that drives people to such means."

"None of them know what it's really for, do they, your armies or your *nyssén*?" I asked.

"Some do," Savat said softly. "Tanith did. Eelie..." He turned to me suddenly, not meeting my eyes. "Is—Does Eelie live? Did you kill them?" He sounded like he wasn't sure he wanted to know the answer.

"They live. They are safe; Unconscious and contained for now."

I saw him relax then.

"Eelie knows. They—It was always my plan. But they were the first to see the truth of it, and to join me. They helped me build my real army."

"And what is the truth," I asked finally. "I know you will tell me. You want my help, yes? You need me, now that Eelie and Tanith are lost to you."

He sighed. "I only ever wanted to bring healing and set the world right. There is something fundamentally wrong with the world. You must have felt it. It needn't be that way. We can repair things. We can make things right, not just for—not just for Eelie and you. For everyone. For every *nyssa* in the world. We can make you all whole."

"Make... us whole," I repeated. I didn't understand.

His voice took on an absence, as if he were suddenly far

away. "What was it like, when you first knew what you were? How did it feel, to understand that you could never fit into the framework of this world? Were you confused? Were you lost? Did you grieve for the girl that might have been?"

"I was never a girl," I said fiercely. "I might have looked like one to some. But I never was."

"Yes. I'm sorry, that's right. That's the truth you accept." He turned now to face me. "What if there was another truth waiting for you? Harder to find; more painful. But when you found it—when you dug it out from the depths of yourself with your fingers torn and bloodied—you knew at once that it was more true than what you knew?"

"*Maita je teminénen,*" I temporized, quoting Mallier. "Truth is absolute. It either is or is not. It does not have degrees." My leg flared, interrupting my thoughts, making it difficult to concentrate. I still didn't quite understand, but I was starting to feel a certain unease at his words. A vague shape was forming in my mind, a pattern that I knew I didn't like, though I couldn't see it yet.

"They call it breaking when your powers manifest, yes? Your powers lash out in destruction and rage and violence, and your mind flees. Does that sound like something that we should accept? Something that is meant to be? Don't you see, Arin? They call it 'breaking' in Reft and they're right about that, at least. The *nyssén* are broken!"

I flinched back from his sudden vehemence and the implications of his words. "And... you mean to... heal us." The pieces were slowly coming together. His drive to make the *nyssén* "whole." His need for someone strong in Mind Magic. And his sparking of the greatest war the continent had seen since the Mad King's armies ravaged the land, to rage across Torfall. Tens of thousands of soldiers brought together just beyond the walls of Sind to slaughter each other in violence and misery. All that pain roiling the air, within reach of a powerful *nyssa*.

"You can't," I whispered in horror.

"We can *heal them all*, together, Arin. You and me, together. We can change all the *nyssén*: Make them men and women as they should have been, healed of mind and body. No longer this... this 'in-between.' All of—all of you."

I nodded slowly. I thought I understood it all now. But there was a last piece missing. Something still itched at my mind. It all made a horrifying kind of sense from one point of view. All that I lacked was the *why*.

I looked Savat in the eyes and pulled on the power that raged outside—drew it into myself. And I lashed out with it and dove into his mind.

...Eelie knows...they helped me build my real army...

The room was dark but for the fire that flickered in the corner. Eyes caught and reflected the glowing embers. There were no lamps to light the room, only the meager glow of the flames.

Eelie stood in the center of the room, their white-blond hair shimmering and tinged by the orange light. My mind spun and I felt the memory of pain—fire burning my body from my knee into my heart. Their face flashed in animal rage and was still once more. I couldn't breathe for a moment. I couldn't remember why I was here. Then I noticed him standing beside me.

Savat.

I focused on him instead, turning with some difficulty away from Eelie. He was dressed in a dark coat over pale lavender, and the enameled hawk pin on his lapel glittered in the firelight. He watched Eelie speak; watched them hold the eyes of all those gathered. I saw a smile on his face, a smile of appreciation and pride and... something else.

We stood in the shadowed corner opposite the fire, watching them capture the minds of the three *nyssén*. The eyes darted towards his corner and at each other now and then, suspicious. But they stayed. They listened.

I let my awareness shift, no longer holding myself back; letting go of my anger and pain, and I saw the room through his eyes now. Saw the eyes and the glow of embers reflected in Eelie's silver hair.

They gave the details as we had planned, leading them along the path until the cause was the obvious choice. Delicately nudging here, diverting there, until there could be no reasonable dissent.

Eelie had their attention now; they were magnificent. These new ones didn't trust yet, not completely. I was still keenly aware that they worried over my presence, my influence.

But they listened. They watched and now and then, they nodded. They didn't trust fully yet, but they would follow.

...I had my anchor. Now...further back...

I stood over a table, intricately carved into a model of the continent. Mountains rose in rough peaks and rivers gleamed in a rippling mosaic of blue glass. I knew where I needed to draw the armies, and so I started there. Dozens of delicate ceramic troop markers were arrayed around Sind, black and gray circles flying miniature flags.

I stroked my short beard for a moment, thinking. Then I began working backwards, moving pieces here and there, bringing armies apart from battles that played out in my mind. I saw each move and each counter.

The Bluecaps would rally *there*. The Winter Corps would hold the Sisters Road *here*. Defeat by defeat, I wound the little world back in time, relieving the pressure that Torfall would bring against my armies. The black markers radiated outward now to take positions won in victories to come.

Sometimes, I made a mistake and saw it only three moves later. I reset the board and tried again. Again and again the model played out the war that would reshape the world.

There were questions; unknowns, to be sure. But those could be wrapped in contingencies and fall-backs and redundancies, so that whichever way some of the more questionable battles went, the result would still play to my plans.

The door to my chamber opened, and Eelie came in. They wore their arrogance and prickliness as a defense as usual. It was an armor they wrapped themself in whenever they thought someone was looking. Even me.

"When do we start?" they asked. They leaned against the table, and the ceramic markers rattled.

"Please don't do that," I said. "And we start once I've figured out all the variables. When we know how it will play out."

"Really? Is that how it works? So it was the *plan* to get Arin thrown out of Reft but to let them disappear into the world without a clue to their whereabouts?"

I grimaced. That hadn't gone as well as I had hoped. Yes, Eelie had been right. Bringing them face to face with the man who had killed their family had triggered the child. They had spiraled into rage and despair in every way I had hoped.

But then they had declined my offer. Declined flatly and disappeared. In the two months since, I had exhausted every effort to find them and gotten nowhere.

"You were right," I said. "Is that what you want me to say? You were right, they were never going to join us."

"Thank you for saying it," Eelie said, pleased.

...further back...

"My lord," he said, bowing to me. He was gray now, gray and wrinkled and old. He had served my father and now he served me. I was determined to be a different sort of master.

"Demen, how many times have I said, 'no bowing?'"

"Sorry mi'lord. My agents have found him."

I sat upright in my chair. Finally.

"You're sure it's him this time?"

"Certain, mi'lord. There's no doubt. We questioned him discreetly, while he was drunk. There was no chance for clever lies, and the man knew too much in too much detail. It is him."

"Good. Make the deal as we planned. Pass on the instructions, the floor plans for the manor, the coin. You know what to do."

"Very well mi'lord." He hesitated. "Are you certain, sir, that you want to do this? Entangling yourself with such as he... it is... unseemly."

"Make sure he understands that he is to be witnessed," I said, ignoring his protest. "If he tries to abscond with the money or with the spoils without meeting the very letter of the bargain, he must know that he will not survive. If he does what he is told, then promise him triple value for anything he manages to steal."

"Of course, mi'lord."

Demen turned to leave.

"Demen, send Eelie in will you?"

His lips twisted in a grimace, but he bowed. "Yes mi'lord."

A moment after the door closed behind him, it opened again and Eelie entered.

"We've found him," I said, satisfied.

"Finally." They slumped in a free chair.

"You're sure you can do it?"

"This man—he is everything to them," Eelie said. "Arin's whole life circles him in endless spirals, and he occupies a space deep in their soul. They will never let him go from their mind until one of them is dead."

"I don't want Arin dead. I want them broken free of that place, so that they will join us."

"They're never going to join us, Tamar. They *believe*."

"Perhaps," I said.

"They won't work for you, and even if they did, they will never accept what you plan. They are too sure of themself by half."

"You accepted it," I pointed out. "Why do you think that is?"

Eelie turned away, their gaze going vague and distant. "Because I was already broken—broken and bleeding—when you found me. You didn't need to sell me your vision. You didn't need to convince me that your path was right. I already knew it for truth."

...further back...

They stood out, even here. Even among so many others who were so broken. Not just physically. Yes, their white-blond hair was striking, almost silver. Yes, their features, even young as they were, were sharp and focused in a way that all the others around them couldn't match. But they carried themself with a tension, a vibrancy that was almost violent and couldn't be ignored. There was a discordant note of rage and self-loathing that undercut every gesture, every move, every breath.

They walked the halls of the mountain arm-in-arm with the Somiri child. I had listened and observed in the past few days. I knew the plump, dark-skinned one was a caravaner's child, newly arrived. They were already fast friends with this pale creature. I had watched as this ghost of a child deftly manipulated the newcomer into a relationship, separating them from others, isolating them. Making them utterly dependent.

I wasn't sure even they understood what they were doing,

but I could see it, and I understood where it came from.

They were broken.

They had a desperate need for the unconditional love that they had once had. However it had been lost, they sought to replace it. This latest target of their affection was not the first, and likely would not be the last. I was certain they had played out this pattern over and over again, pushing and pushing until what they tried to shape into love collapsed under their frantic manipulation like overworked clay.

"This way, lord Savat, if you will."

I nodded gracious thanks to the *nyssa* who guided me to the Council chambers. As we walked, I made a mental note to re-visit this child, to continue to watch them while I was here. I could sense they wouldn't last long under the oppressive rules of Reft. They would chafe. They would balk.

They would fall.

And I would be waiting to catch them.

...Further back...

The rain sheeted down around me. It didn't touch me though. A servant stood behind, holding a parasol over my head to keep me dry—the world was not allowed to touch me. It was not allowed to leave any mark upon me.

No one was, anymore.

The cleric intoned his empty words over the grave. There was no reason for me to listen. I was beyond caring. It had been years since Father had spoken at all, and years more since he had spoken to me. Not since—well, those last words didn't bear remembering.

I stood still and placid, pretending to listen, pretending to be somber and to mourn, because it was my duty. I was Vis-count now.

Finally.

There was no one to check me; to hold me back from what needed to be done.

Demen stood beside me, his elegant cloak—purest white for mourning—shedding the rain well enough from his shoulders, but doing nothing for his head and face. His black hair was limp, his mustaches sodden.

"He loved you, you know," Demen said in his gentle voice.

"He did," I said. *He hated me. He hated Mother for making me.* It was easier to agree.

"I know he didn't show it much. After your mother died—" Demen wiped his eyes futilely, "he never really knew how to show it. But he loved you. When the—when the stonework collapsed and he pushed you out to safety, he showed how much he loved you. He used to tell me, before the accident; he used to say how proud he was to have a son to carry on the legacy."

Father did love his legacy.

Demen fell silent again. The cleric continued his pointless drone.

Father's last words to me nearly surfaced again to roil my mind and stir my anger and shame. Always thus, when I was forced to think of Father. But I was well practiced at this by now. I could let them drag me down into the icy depths of the dark sea of my guilt. Sometimes I wallowed in them, when I felt I deserved the pain.

Today, though, I was feeling good. Feeling free for the first time in a very long time. I thought of a dark, ancient well, its stones crumbling, the well cap long since rotted away. I let the thoughts and feelings come one by one, and as they came I plucked them from my thoughts, releasing them to the pull of the earth and imagining them tumble down, down into the dark depths to disappear in the void and trouble me no more.

The shame and anger dissipated, lost to the mist that clung

to the wet cemetery soil.

Well. The house was mine now. It was my legacy to shape; to fulfill it how *I* wished. Damn him and his history and his visions of the past.

There was a secret I knew. There was a truth deeper than his prattle of family and legacy and power. There was something broken at the core of the world. Something twisted. It shouldn't be this way. Children shouldn't suffer.

The Savat legacy had history, it had fame, it had pride. But it had money most of all. Centuries of money. Money would beget power and power would beget change. With enough leverage, enough power, the world *would* change.

The cleric finished his liturgy, and the somber mourners broke away into small clusters, commiserating. None of them approached me. I held an intangible barrier between me and the world.

I stared into the haze of rain and mist. "Come, Demen. We have work to do."

...those last words...

I was walking through a fog. It shifted and swirled around me forming vague shadows. It made the world around me indistinct, impossible to navigate. There was no visible path.

I was on a wide lawn, its green barely discernible through the mist. A manor house broke through like a pale ghost in the distance. Four tall chimneys rose from the slate roof, and the fog spilled endlessly from their tops, draping the land in undefined shadow.

I walked forward in a daze, unable to focus. To my left was a regiment of tall shapes in rank and file, looming and threatening and shapeless. Smaller shapes in black moved between them like crows picking at the bone field after a battle.

I moved towards the house as if in a nightmare, unsure of

what I would find, not wanting to see. A tension was rising in my shoulders and my stomach was tight with unnamed worry.

There was a feeling of time in the sky. I can't say what exactly I felt, or how I knew, but it seemed like what I saw here had happened long ago, and like it was happening over and over forever.

I neared the manor and saw that it was wrapped in a low platform of paving stones that formed a kind of floor, though they were cracked as if from a hammer blow. The mist held back from these, afraid to trespass upon them. Tendrils spun delicate fingers from the wall of fog only to evaporate against the stones. A great ragged opening was torn into the house—a gaping maw of dark shadows, ready to devour an unwary intruder.

I stepped upon the paving stones, looking down at a smear of dried blood that stained two of the broken pavers. My stomach lurched at the memory. The bloodstain thrust like a spearpoint from the opening in the wall; a straight line of dark red starting a full pace from the doorway and radiating a foot outwards toward the mist behind me.

A voice ranted endlessly from inside that room, deep and terrible.

I hesitated, standing now on the threshold, I couldn't understand the words, but the tone was fierce and angry. Full of rage and hate and odium. I didn't want to enter. I didn't want to understand the words.

I stared down at that line of blood. It was a stain on the house.

Without thought or intent, the mist swallowed me again, and the house was gone.

Seventeen

I tried to reach back through the mist, but the memory was gone. I pushed past the fog. Further and further back. Deeper into his history I delved.

There was a kernel here, somewhere. A seed to explain the madness of his plan. There was some key I needed to find to unlock all the secrets. Some clue to help me to understand why something so inherently evil felt to him so much like a kindness that he would sacrifice so many lives to his plan.

The closer I got, the surer I was. I circled it now, stalking it like a cat. I was so close...

...a stain on the house...

I watched from the darkness of my room, crouched in fear and my gaze fixed on the door of their room across the gallery. I needed to see; couldn't stand to hear. I covered my ears to block them out, but it was no use. I *felt* the anger and rage like a blow with each word.

"You will not lecture *me*, woman! He is my son and he will learn to be a man or he will die trying! Either is acceptable."

Mother pleaded, her voice more filled with tears than with words.

"Speak no more! Keep your mouth shut, or I will shut it."

"But Tammen," she pleaded, "he is only *nine*. He is ill-suited to the sword! Why must you push him so?"

There was a crack like the sound of a whip, and Mother was whimpering. I cringed at it.

"You have done your job. You birthed him; you swaddled and weaned him. He is my son now—no longer a child. How I push him and how I punish his failings are no longer any of your concern. He *will* learn the sword and he will be blooded or he will fall. There is no middle ground, and I will hear no more of this womanly nonsense."

Father strode from the room now, and I flinched back, though I was deep in shadow. He rounded the gallery and reached the top of the stairs directly across from my door. I sighed in relief: He was not coming for me.

Mother followed him from the room, the right side of her face was aflame from the slap. It was a sharp contrast against the pale cream of her skin; against the deep purple bruise she carried from last time. Her lip was already puffing on that side. She was sobbing and her speech was thick with it.

"Tammen, please. Let him be. Let him become what *he* chooses. He is so clever, he can carry the family forward without a sword in his hand."

She reached him and tugged at his sleeve, trying to circle around to face him. He flung her off his arm, lashing out again and catching her backhanded on the left cheek. The force of the blow spun her, and she tripped over her skirts.

I watched in silent horror as she tumbled down the grand staircase to slide in a crumpled heap of pink and lavender silk upon the marble floor. Her face was turned towards me, and for a moment I thought she wore a smile for me. But she didn't move. Didn't breathe.

I bit down on my hand, looking to my father, waiting for his cry of despair.

He looked down on her pale body and sighed, shaking his head.

He called out then. "Demen! Demen!"

Father's man came from the servants' entry below, striding quickly. He froze in shock, seeing Mother on the floor.

"My lady!" He ran to her.

Father descended the stairs calmly to stand above them. "She fell, Demen." He looked at her for a moment, dissatisfied. "Please see to arrangements."

He walked out of view.

...why must you push him...

"No!" Father roared. "Higher!" He grabbed the blade and pulled my arm up into place. When he released it, it fell a few inches again. The sword was too heavy.

Nonetheless, he reset his stance and moved against me, striking with his training blade. I tried to shift my feet and bring my sword into position but I was too slow. Father's dulled blade battered mine aside and struck my shoulder, knocking me to the ground.

My blade hit the dirt and I clutched at my bruised arm. I bit down on my tongue, trying to fight the pain.

"You need more strength, boy. This will never work if you can't lift the blade. Again!"

I gritted my teeth and picked up the sword, pushing myself

to my feet and setting my stance.

Pain flashed and my ears rang as Father's hand struck me. I kept my feet and I held back the tears. That was the important part.

"Not that way, boy! Left foot further back! Gods above."

That was most important, that I not fall down and that I not cry.

If I could stay standing, then he could see me as a man. If I could keep my eyes dry, I could still pretend.

He wouldn't know how I'd failed him.

I fixed my stance and raised my sword into position as best I could. My arm still hurt. My sword still wavered. But I stayed standing.

...further back, there's...

"Don't let him see you cry, dear one. You mustn't. Always hold back the tears, the fear, the pain. Pain is nothing to you, you hear me? It doesn't exist." She stroked my hair and held me close. "Don't ever let him know you hurt."

"Why doesn't Father like crying?" I asked through tears.

"He doesn't care about crying in most people. But you..." She pulled me close and squeezed me for the length of a breath. "You, Tamar, are his *son*."

I flinched.

"That means everything to him. He will burn down the world for his son." She seemed inordinately sad when she said it.

I felt cold suddenly, despite the warmth of her embrace. Could she know? She couldn't see my guilt, though I was sure it was written on my face. I said nothing. I held it inside as she taught me. The tears wouldn't come and the fear wouldn't show and the pain wouldn't hurt.

I could live with the pain inside, I thought. I could live with the uncertainty and the fear. As long as I had Mother to hold me. As long as Mother was there to console me and give me the comfort that Father never would. That I couldn't give myself without—

That I couldn't give myself.

I held her and hoped that she would never discover my secret. That I could hide my guilt forever.

...*something there, something*...

"Kindi! Wait!" I chased her down, dodging the halfhearted swats that the women doled out as we passed, weaving in and out of the trunks of the pear orchard.

An army of apron-clad women dressed in black house livery worked up and down in the lanes between the trees, each bearing a pair of baskets front and back on a leather yoke. Fruit by fruit, they filled the baskets with the pear harvest. Father's men would press the pears to make cider and wine, and his distillery master in Sind would pick the choicest casks for the secretive and magical process that produced brandy.

I was five and already knew the principle sources of income of my house, the house names of our vassals, and was learning the towns and villages that owed us allegiance. Child as I was, even I knew I had little enough time left of chasing my friends through the grounds. Mother had told me so.

Soon enough, Father would have me step up and learn the workings of the house.

A wet jolt burst upon my back and I felt the soft, sticky slime of overripe pear on my neck. I spun and saw Kindi and her friend June sprinting away in a joyful panic. I pursued, calling out again.

"Not fair!" I wailed. All I heard in response was frantic giggles.

I kept on their heels through the last rank of pear trees and out into the meadow beyond. They were running towards the blackberry thicket that overgrew the stone fence along our eastern fields.

Kindi was a year older than me and June a year older than her, and their legs had the advantage of those years. They pulled ahead of me, gamine limbs flashing through the grass as they ran. They rounded the thicket and disappeared.

I wiped the smear of sticky pear off my neck and out of my hair as best I could and smiled to myself.

I guessed they were both just around the edge of the thicket, ready to spring upon me as I rounded behind them. I turned my path further south, where a stone coping over a wellhead crouched below the line of the fence.

I pushed myself into a sprint, leaping to the top of the wellhead and then onto the wall, landing atop the narrow edge on all fours. My hands were pricked and scratched by the bramble, but I stuck the landing and trotted along the wall as quietly as I could.

They were just ahead of me, crouched down and facing the end of the fence, watching for me to emerge. I smiled to myself. As I crept closer, I plucked ripe blackberries, stuffing the first few in my mouth.

I perched above them now. With a warbling war-cry, I pounced upon them, landing with enough force to smash a handful of blackberries into each girl's hair. They wailed in satisfying fury as my weight carried them both down into the grass.

"That's taught you to throw—" I began to say, but Kindi launched herself at me with all the rage of a mortally offended six-year-old. We tumbled to the ground and there was a fierce struggle for position, for control, for dignity. We rolled over and over more than once and came finally to a stop with me straddling her midriff. She lay pinned supine beneath me, our hands each struggling to control the other.

"Do you yield?" I asked, victorious.

Kindi only smiled. I felt a blow of another body slamming into me and I was thrown sideways off of Kindi. June stood over me and helped her friend up.

"You can't wrestle girls like that. You're a boy!" she cried, her voice full of scandal and affront.

I looked up at them, confused and ashamed. My head felt suddenly light and my stomach leaden.

"Why do I have to be a boy?" I asked quietly.

They both looked at me, confused. Kindi's expression showed concern and worry. June only looked amused.

"Because you a..." June's voice trailed off into a buzz. The memory faded into a haze of discomfort and a roiling of my gut. A gray blur skewed the world and then I was standing, watching the two of them running off again, giggling.

...important, something... crucial...

I stood still, trying to find that moment, trying to understand the pain and confusion and unease that I felt.

...something...

I was running again, chasing them around the perimeter of the house. I lost them both each time they rounded a corner or climbed over a low fence, and each time I spotted them again, they were further away. Soon I was chasing the faint sound of their laughter, unable to see them at all.

I came around the far corner of the house and skidded to a stop, pressing myself behind a rose-laden trellis that decorated the stone. I peeked around to see Mother seated at one of the tables on the paved terrace outside Father's study.

Her back was to me, and she was bent over her needlework, enjoying the placid autumn afternoon. Beyond her, I could see my quarry chasing each other within the orchard again. I debated my next move. If I followed them out, Mother was sure to see me; to scold me for ignoble behavior. There was even the risk *Father* might notice, and that would be disastrous.

Indeed, I could see that the study doors were open to the afternoon air, and I could hear voices within. Mother seemed to ignore them, but I couldn't help but listen. Too many times I had been punished for failing to attend Father's lectures, so his voice now took my attention immediately.

"And what of the northern territories?"

"Panar's harvest is on track, mi'lord." I thought the voice belonged to Father's seneschal, Anders. "They have had a good year and should be over their quotas. Unfortunately, Sinderan Springs will be well under. They had a nestworm infestation during the summer, and lost a quarter of their harvest."

"Damned nuisance," Father said with little heat. "I suppose there's no one to hold to blame for that, but see that they're on notice for next year. I won't accept another shortfall."

"Yes, mi'lord. Er, my lord, the worst news is out of Jumai's Grove. There is... unrest... among the tenants, and the harvest has been delayed."

"Unrest?" Father's voice was raised, and I flinched back involuntarily. "What by gods do they have to agitate about?"

"My lord, the word I have—and I don't know for sure yet—but the word I have is that the mayor is under pressure from the council to disown his child, and he has refused. It has caused an uproar in the village."

"Disown? Why should he?"

"By the accounts I've received, mi'lord, the child is a *mixie*."

There was a chill silence, and even Mother froze in her needlework. When Father spoke again, his voice was low and strained. Cold and impassioned and frightening.

"Gods-damned mixie filth. A slip or a dunt? No, it doesn't matter. Fucking filthy mixie witches. Last thing we gods-damned need. Who's mayor there... Danda? I want a squad of house guard up there by day-after-tomorrow. Either he drives that filth out of the village and gets the harvest underway, or they're to drive the whole gods-be-damned family out and let the council choose a new mayor. They can flee or drown themselves in the Folnin for all I care, but Danda will not harbor that filth on my lands."

"At once mi'lord."

"Fucking filth. I'll not have it, not in my..." the voice became a drone; a low buzz and a high ringing that pierced my mind like a spike. The memory dissolved into a gray wash of fog as the pain roiled in my gut and head and the muscles of my shoulders. The world twisted and spun, tumbling in a dizzying whirl.

...have to hold... this is the key... can't let it slip away...

I held on, holding myself up, holding the memory in place, desperate to keep the reality from sliding away into mist.

I felt Father's words like a knife in my gut. His sheer hatred of... I barely knew the words: *mixie, slip, dunt.* I had heard them muttered before, thrown about by other children as grave insults of unknown provenance.

The pain I felt at his heat confused me. It churned in my belly and his words landed one after another like punches that doubled me over. The weight of the grief and confusion were upon my shoulders, pressing down, forcing me to my knees.

"But why," the question echoed plaintively in my memory, "Why do I have to be..."

...Ah...

Eelie always said I was slow to catch on.

The world washed away in a blaze of gray, like ashes smeared across a fine painting, and then I was swallowed in a mist of memory.

I pushed through the fog, sure now of the shape of the path that I walked. It opened before me. I emerged into a wide lawn that spread lush and green over rich earth. A manor house in pale stone and covered in silvered wooden filigree loomed in the distance. Four tall chimneys rose from the slate roof, spilling billows of white smoke high into the bright blue sky.

I walked forward in a daze, sure of what I would see. To my left was row upon row of short pear trees in regimented order. A dozen women dressed in rough homespun dresses, dyed black for livery, moved up and down the rows carrying baskets and plucking pears from the branches.

I continued walking towards the house, certain of what I would find. A tension was rising in my shoulders and my stomach was tight.

There was a feeling of time in the sky. What I saw here had happened long ago. Was happening forever.

I neared the manor, and saw that it was wrapped in a low platform of paving stones that formed a kind of floor. Large doors intricately set with panes of glass stood open from the house, looking out onto the paved yard.

I crossed those paving stones, looking down. There was something there, I thought. A stain? But the stones were clean; pale and neat. He would accept nothing less.

Just inside the doors was a rich room, all golden wood and leather and wine-colored wool.

A voice ranted from inside that room.

I hesitated, standing now on the threshold. I couldn't understand the words, but the tone was fierce and angry. Full of rage and hate and odium. I didn't want to enter. I didn't want to understand the words.

I was turning, wanting to walk back the way I had come; to stand under the eaves of the pear orchard. There was peace there. Peace and joy and comfort.

I was facing into the doorway and my foot lifted, crossing that threshold.

I was standing in Father's study. Father rarely let me in his study. My arm hurt where his fingers had crushed, dragging me in through the doors.

"*What* did you say?" Father was angry, but he was often angry. This went beyond anger. His voice was cold and emotionless. It sounded like death.

I'm sorry, I thought.

"I—I'm sorry, Father."

"I don't care that you're sorry! I asked you what you *said*." The rage was boiling. His face was flushed, his nose and forehead turning red against the white of his skin like a streak of blood on pale stone.

...This feels wrong...

"I feel... I feel wro—" Pain burst upon me like an explosion of fire and sound. A roar of heat washed over my left cheek and the sharp sting hurt all the more for the soft cushion of wool against my right. I opened my eyes and saw his shoes.

"Get up!" Father roared.

...I can feel my shoulders clenching... Can't find my breath... My stomach hurting...

"Hurts," I whimpered as I climbed back to my feet.

"Do you know how long this family has stood on this land? Don't you remember what it *means* to be a Savat? We *made* this land! Our name is listed on the rolls of the First Ships! The Savats have held *four* of the Seven Keys! Our family have held the Scales *twice* since the Landing, and even—once—the Three Diadems of Torfall! You do not get to discard that legacy!"

"Father, I—"

"Father? Who is 'Father?'" he screamed, inches from my face. I felt drops of spittle fall on my skin.

...I wanted to wipe tears from my eyes...

He turned his back on me and took three deep breaths. When he spoke again, his voice was measured, calm—

...the calm is pretense... he is still furious...

—but I was not fooled. I knew that coldness.

"Tell it to me again. Say the words you spoke."

It felt like a dare; like a threat. But *not* saying them wasn't enough anymore. Hiding and pretending wasn't fooling him or anyone else anymore.

...I know what is coming. I feel it as surely as I know my name...

"I... It feels..." I flinched away, expecting another blow. "It feels *wrong*, when you call me 'son.' It feels as wrong as if you named me daughter. It is *wrong*. I don't know why, but it is not who I am," I finished, my voice stronger than I expected.

I waited. Waited for the blow. For the rage. For the anger and the violence and the vitriol.

Father's shoulders slumped. I watched him take a deep slow breath in and then release it. When he spoke again, his voice was soft and far warmer than I could have imagined.

"The days of this house have been long. They stretch back to royalty across the sea. We hold to the old ways—always have, and ever will we."

He turned to face me, though I didn't look up at him. "I'm glad you were finally able to tell me this, son, while you are still only eleven years old. Children are the future of any house... But *we* are *Fall*, Tamar. We are Savats. The future of *our* house is in its *sons*." The warmth was entirely gone now from his voice. "It's a good thing that I am still young enough to find a new wife and to make another."

I looked up at him then, and his strong hands were at my arms once more, lifting me up. He was entirely cold, and he moved with a deliberate, measured step. There was no rage in his voice anymore—no anger in his actions. Pain radiated from where his fingertips held me.

"Well and so," he said. "Your mother failed you with her softness. You have failed me as a son. You are broken. I will not allow you to break my house, also." I felt the world lurch and the room tumbled in my vision as I fell through the open door to sprawl across the pale stone paving. I felt bile rising in my throat and only the new pain flaring from my face and chin held my sudden nausea in check.

I touched my face and felt warm wetness. My eyes finally focused and I saw my own blood staining the stones in a line beneath me where I had slid across them. I was shaking.

His voice called out to me calmly from inside the study. "You are not my son. You are a stranger. If you still trespass on my lands by sunset, I will tell Demen to release the dogs." He turned back to his desk and sat down, getting back to his ledgers and correspondence.

I stood by numbly as I watched the child pull themself up to their knees—slow and awkward in pain. They were shaking, vibrating with unchecked emotion.

He had killed the child's mother years ago. Now he tried to murder the child's spirit.

I saw the very moment their power broke. They didn't understand what they did, but I could see it. I could feel the memory of their mind crumbling under the pain. Their life was falling down around them—their very self collapsing in an avalanche of misery and turmoil.

The ground trembled. The paving stones cracked, fracturing into a spiderweb of sharp lines radiating from their toes towards the foundations of the manor. Tears were sheeting down their face as the cracks climbed the walls and the dust of ancient stones shivered and rained down.

A voice cried out in terror from within that room, and the lamps guttered and crashed. Timbers shifted and the masonry that had stood for hundreds of years—generation after generation—came tumbling down like a body thrown casually down the stairs, discarded with little care.

The lintel collapsed and stones fell from the open doorway, leaving it a jagged maw of teeth, ready to devour anyone foolish enough to venture within. He tried to escape it, running out from behind his desk to the light outside, but the stones kept falling, torn down in dissociated fury. He was struck once, twice; his limbs broken, his body bleeding. He made it as far as the threshold, and a final stone came down on his back.

The shifting subsided. The earth settled. The child slumped forward onto their hands, numb and silent.

The only sound left was the sifting of dust falling through the broken stones, and the labored wheezing of the broken man, crushed beneath the weight of his own house.

Eighteen

I looked up at Savat through the tears welling in my eyes. The pain of the breaking was real. Witnessing it in memory was no less terrible than the memory itself. "You're one of us," I said. "And you—You think *you* are broken."

Savat looked at me—eyes wide; jaw open. "Don't—don't! I don't want it. I don't want—Never wanted it. We have to be free of it, Arin! The pain and the rage and everything that surrounds us!"

"You can't make that choice for all of us!" I raged. "How *dare* you! You think you are the only one to face confusion? To face pain? To wonder if you are to blame for the terrible things that befall those around you?"

"You *do* understand."

I closed my eyes. "I understand that you've suffered. I understand that you are weighed down by pain and guilt and shame for what you are."

Savat flinched away from my words.

"For what you *are*! You are *nyssa*! You are exactly who you were supposed to be, only you believed the ugliness your father hammered into you, and so you hide it from the world and from yourself. If you are broken, it was your father and *his* beliefs that broke you. Well and good! Reject yourself and hide what you are forever, if you like. That is *your* choice." I slapped the stone floor with my hand. "But you do *not* get to reject it for me!"

"I wanted your help," Savat said sadly, quietly, turning away. "I did want your help, Arin, but maybe Eelie was right. Maybe I didn't *need* it."

My eyes widened as their words sank in.

Their gaze went vague, lost in something like ecstasy as they drew on the power that flooded the land beyond the walls. I reached for that power too, desperately; clawed at it as if my life depended on it. My life as I had lived it did.

We grappled, both reaching the flood of pain at the same time, both drawing on it as the drowning draw desperate breath. As we embraced the pain, as we drew it into ourselves, we found each other. We joined in a maelstrom of pain, the power entangling us, encircling our minds and binding us together in something like a Circle.

I tried to push my way back into their mind, but they were pushing too. They weren't as strong as me, but they were stronger than Eelie. I had never had to guard my own mind against such strength.

...Stop that, Arin...

Mother held me by the shoulders, shaking me. Her eyes were wide, filled with fear. "Stop that, Arin!" she cried.

The fear filling her face was overwhelming in my memory. My skin, my face, my hair, my clothes, were red. The red of ripe peppers.

I remembered this day—it was my Red Day. I stood beside myself and watched as Mother shook my seven-year-old self, trying to catch my attention, to draw me out of whatever spiral of witchery and horror she imagined I had descended into.

"She's afraid of you," Savat said from beside my shoulder. "Don't you see that?"

I turned, finding them standing at my side, both of us watching my memory unfold. I glanced back and saw the color drain from my skin, clothes, and hair in a blink of an eye. Mother shook me for a moment longer, then pulled back, hesitating for only a moment before taking the knife from my hand; pouring water over my wound.

"She's afraid," I agreed. "What is that supposed to prove? She had never seen the like before."

"And should a mother be afraid of her own child?" Savat asked, reasonably. "How could you be loved as you should have been when your mother was afraid of you?"

I shook my head. "She was afraid. Afraid of the magic. Afraid *for* me, not *of* me."

...Why did you do it, Pips? Why did you cut your hair...

Mother was sobbing in the house, and I was pacing outside the yard. I shivered in the cold winter night air as I moved, the chill ruffling the short uneven hair on my scalp. Father stood at the door, watching me pace. I didn't know how to answer him. Didn't know how to describe what I felt. I didn't have the words. I said nothing.

"You hurt her," said Savat.

"I didn't mean to," I replied. My eyes were wet, I realized. I hadn't meant to hurt her. I missed my mother. She was dead, and I didn't want to cause her pain, even in my memory.

"What she wanted of me, I couldn't give. I wasn't the daughter she wanted me to be."

"And what if you could have been?"

...but I couldn't be...

...What are you, Arin? Really? Are you a girl, or a boy? Or...

Ranji turned away from me, hiding his tears. He leaned against the fence of the horse paddock, hunched in pain around his bruises.

I looked over the bar of the fence, past the frolicking horses, past the haggling men and the spectators. My eyes reached over the horizon to the distant sky, drawn out beyond the edges of my memory, trying to find the words that I wish I had been able to speak to him in that moment.

"He wouldn't have fought, you know, except for you. Despite his questions, he knew what you were, long before you knew the words; before you had the courage to speak them."

"Stop," I said, my eyes welling with tears. "Please stop."

"He wouldn't have been hurt that day, or the days to come. You could have been his sister. You could have been a daughter. You could have been..."

...please stop...

...You ought to know, I came down through Meers this morning...

Bran's gravelly voice ground out of the deep recesses of memory. I had forgotten its rough tenor. Its low rumble. "There's a right fuss brewing," he said.

There was silence for a time. I trembled.

"Geoffs," Father said.

...I can tell if you're a girl...I felt his hand at the ties of my trousers. His calloused fingers slipped underneath, against my skin...

"A man's family is his family...but a thing comes out, and there's no penning it back up," Bran continued. "I been farming these hills damn near fifty years. Seen a lot to come and go…"

I was crouching in the house, under the window. I was standing in the yard, watching Father and Bran.

Savat put their hand on my shoulder. "Your breaking tore your family apart, didn't it? Your father had no plan to leave the smallholding he and your mother had spent years eking out."

I shook my head.

"They left it because of you. Even you know it."

…*"We're leaving the farm?" Ranji asked again, still puzzled. He lifted a forkful of chicken to his mouth, and his eyes darted to me for a moment, then looked away…If I hadn't been a mixie, if I'd died in birthing, if I'd never come about…*

We trudged through the wilderness: Milly pulling the cart and the four of us walking ahead, behind, and to either side. We made our way back to the spring, the place we had camped more than one night after failing to find our way through the mountainous terrain. I watched us make camp on the flat rocks, still warm from the afternoon sun.

"Not this again, please," I begged. I had seen this play out in my mind so many times—I didn't need to be dragged through it again. I thought I had come to peace with their deaths.

They came up the trail despite my denials. Despite my begging, they came.

I watched Cal and Beaty approach my family's fire.

"Please," I whispered.

"Would you have been here—any of you?" Savat asked me. "Would you have been in Cal's path, to be surrounded by his men?"

I shook my head, my eyes closed.

"Would your bother have died? Would your father have

died? Would your mother have died?"

"No," I said finally. Quietly. "No, they wouldn't have."

..."In my house everyone works their share"...

I was in the room I shared with Ardenne, seeing it for the first time again. Beaty left with Elyse to find her own room. I watched myself turn slowly, taking in the small, windowless chamber before pouring out water into the washstand bowl and washing my face and hands.

We stood above me as I knelt on the wooden floor in the small chamber. I was folded over double, weeping silent tears, forehead almost touching the floor. We both stood watching, hearing my gasping as I took ragged breaths between each sob.

"You know the truth here," Savat said quietly. "It was your power, your identity that brought you to this."

I felt the irony. If I had really been a girl, I wouldn't have ended up pretending to be one in Ma'am's house of pleasure.

In my memory, I cried myself out and stood once more, washing my face again and finding my way down to the kitchens. We followed.

I continued to watch, feeling utterly detached from myself as I chopped onions for Cook with the overlarge knife. She watched me critically, now and then pointing to this bit of onion or that with some comment or correction. I took the criticism stoically, too afraid to bristle.

"How can growing up like this—as a scullery in a brothel— be anything but a tragedy, Arin?" Savat asked. "Can't you see? The very degradation of being a *nyssa* is what brought you to this. And even this—even this life in this brothel serving the ugly whims of others' pleasure for coin—was brought lower into indignity and devastation because of what you are..."

...a tremendous crash and an explosion of purple splinters spilled down the hallway...

I watched from above, peeking over the edge of the gallery and also watching from the railing. The height, the dual perspective, the unreality of memory—it all combined into a dizzying impression. I grasped the railing with white-clenched fingers.

I watched Sem step casually through the ruined hall and my heart lurched. They were smaller than I remembered. They were younger than I remembered.

Two toughs charged Sem's diminutive form and were ruthlessly brought down and immobilized just as I remembered.

I saw my younger self gripping the balusters, watching Sem's movement. I realized I would never see them again but for memories, and tears came fresh to my eyes. I knew they would speak next. I knew they would speak, and I felt a pain rising from deep within me, knowing I would hear their voice.

"Is this all worth it to you? All I want is the child."

I watched myself cringe back from the balustrade; watched the tension in my shoulders driving my whole body to shake.

"Can *you* teach them what they are and how to reach their potential?" Sem called out. Their reedy voice echoed off the scarred walls. "Can *you* teach them to survive the blades and the hate and the violence that the world will hurl at them when they stop pretending to be what they are not?"

"Look at it," Savat said from beside me. "Look at the destruction wrought upon this house. All of this pain, devastation, and violence. All over you. They fought over you *because* you're a *nyssa*."

I shook my head. I was desperate to deny it.

"Violence begets violence begets violence," they whispered to me.

"Please don't—" I gasped.

...no. no... please don't take me there...

I could feel them taking hold of my memories that I had hidden years ago. They grasped them and pulled violently, forcing them into some semblance of order. They were still dream-tinged; still vertiginous, but there was a path through them now.

...“Alright, lovelies, time enough.” I said to myself in a whisper...

I passed through the doorway into my rooms, aware of the hollow emptiness as the slap of my sandals echoed off the stone. The room felt long abandoned, full of ghostly echoes of memory and absence. I watched a version of myself watching myself stride through with purpose. My mind reeled at the stacked visions and I had no ability to untangle my past and my present and my future. I watched myself stride to the wardrobe. I watched myself watching myself reach out and take the sword.

I pleaded in my mind with my memory, with my reality.

...no...

I stood aside and watched myself watching myself watching myself crumple to the floor in pain while I ran towards the balcony and leapt into the rain. My reality shattered into endless fragments and my dissociation was complete. I had no self. There was no me. There was only the truth. The pain.

Arin tore open the Bridge with ruthless violence, forcing a thought upon the universe, forcing it to bend to their will. The path was open and Arin marched through with purpose. They couldn’t feel—they couldn’t feel anything except pain.

Arin’s body was wracked with pain and the twisting of guilt and shame. I can’t say which one of us it was. A sword flashed and blood spilled. There was a soft sigh, a release of life and pain and breath that seemed to flow from a place of impossible tension to formless peace. There was also a rising, urgent gasping and a pain so acute that nothing—no part of any mind could possibly stand up to it.

"This hurt you so much, Arin," Savat said, their voice full of regret and compassion. "I'm sorry—I'm truly sorry that we put you through this. I didn't realize..."

I said nothing. There was no me, only those shattered fragments of memory and pain.

"But, how can you not see that all of this—the pain, the guilt, the shame—none of it would have happened without that curse that you carry. That we all carry. Can we not be free of it? Why is it too much to ask to let go of the pain and the burden of that which sets us apart?"

I tried to push myself out of the memory. Tried to take back some control.

...The pain was too much, and the pain was just enough...

"I've come to ask you to talk to me," Turin said. "Please, Arin, tell me what happened. Why won't you explain yourself?"

I stood at the open balcony of my rooms and stared out to the distant horizon where hazy blue-gray mountains touched the clear blue sky. For a moment, I felt like I was tumbling helplessly away into that endless blue.

"And then, after the pain of your fall, after all the pain and trauma you were subjected to," Savat said beside me, undaunted by the shift in memory, "then, they cast you out!"

I shook my head. That was wrong.

"This Turin, who you looked up to all those years... What did their compassion amount to in the end? Did it stop the Council from discarding you like refuse when you broke their precious oaths?"

...You don't know...

...Marki and Ciala say that if anyone can find a way out of this, it's you...

...My heart broke anew when I realized the sorrow of failing Arin; of not seeing their pain and crisis when it mattered and losing them to their own guilt...

In my memory, I turned to face Turin. "I made a new family here, and I love them dearly. I always will. But I can't live here among you."

...The pain was too much, and the pain was just enough...

"I don't understand," Savat said, less certain now than they had been moments before.

...The pain was too much, and the pain was just enough...

"Arin?" Turin's voice came from the sitting room.

Tears flowed down my cheeks as I wove the pain back and forth between my rooms in Reft and the distant clearing near Branmoor and opened the Bridge.

"Arin!" I heard Turin shout from beyond the door.

...The pain was too much, and the pain was just enough...

"I... I don't understand," Savat repeated softly, beside me. "—*you* left?"

...The pain was too much, and the pain was just enough...

In their moment of confusion; in the betrayal of their expectations, I struck, seizing the power and taking control of our small Circle.

...Why did you do it, Pips? Why did you cut your hair...

"You're wrong," I said. "You've been wrong from the start."

We stood in a wood, some distance from Arin, who sat with their back against a wide tree. They wiped tears from their eyes and slowly, inexorably raised their knife and unfolded it with practiced hands.

Savat looked on in confusion, trying to understand.

"This wasn't a moment of pain," I told them. "Those tears, they're tears of relief. Because I finally understood why I felt so lost."

We both watched as Arin began to cut tufts of their long, tangled hair away, letting the breeze carry them away to disappear into the woods.

"I wasn't lost because I was a *nyssa*—it was because everyone kept telling me I was a girl. I couldn't understand why the people I loved would tell me such blatant lies."

As the locks of hair were diminished one by one, as Arin cut them away and felt the weight of those expectations float away on the wind, a look of peace and lightness spread across their face. Savat stared, trying to understand.

"This is the first moment I had an inkling of what it felt like to be me. When I began to find the path to myself." I turned to look Savat in the eyes. "This is a moment of *joy*."

...What are you, Arin? Really? Are you a girl, or a boy? Or...

We were standing well back, behind the two children leaning on the fence to the horse paddock.

"This too, you've entirely misunderstood," I said. "This isn't a memory of pain and sorrow."

"What is it then?" Savat asked quietly. Their voice had a hint of pleading.

"It is pride. And unity. And strength. It is the love my brother had for me and that I had for him."

...Old Bran sighed, long and sorrowful...

We were watching Father and Bran leaning on the edge of the goat pen. Savat and I watched as Father waited. Old Bran looked away down the road and into the distance. He was dissatisfied and pensive. There was so much he wanted to say to Father.

"I been farming these hills damn near fifty years," he said

instead. "Seen a lot to come and go, and time was, something like this would quietly fade away. There's no shame to put to it, exactly."

I touched Savat's arm and pointed. "This is a community coming together to show protectiveness and concern. Never mind that they didn't understand. Never mind that some people are bent on trouble. There's more good than bad in these people."

Bran was still speaking, "The trouble they're stirring up right now isn't the kind that'll leave your little one alone."

"My family chose to leave everything to protect me," I continued. "That was an act of love. That was them showing that their will and their love was stronger than the hate of the Geoffs; that it didn't matter what I was. They were my family." I wiped a tear from my cheek. "No matter what came after, this was an act of *strength*."

Savat shook their head, trying to deny my words.

...*"Most girls groan and complain of the drudgery of housework"*...

We followed as Arin carried the tub, heavy and sloshing with sodden clothes, up the narrow stair from the Laundry to the roof. Their step was measured and unfaltering, with hardly a pause to shift the weight of the laundry tub from one hip to another to open the roof door.

"This wasn't a house of shame and degradation. It was a place of healing. This is where I found peace and solace enough to heal the open wounds of the loss of my family. Where the strength of those around me buoyed me up; made me whole enough so that I could choose to protect them."

...*a tremendous crash and an explosion of purple splinters spilled down the hallway*...

We watched together from the shadowed doorway of the

linens room as Arin peered over the edge of the gallery. I could hear Sem's flat sandals crunching on the broken glass and porcelains in the hall below. Their voice carried and echoed as they shouted their challenge. Ma'am emerged from her rooms, and Arin looked on in agony.

"You failed to see the most important part of this memory," I chided. "Watch."

It was clear once the decision was made. We watched together as Arin shifted their fists deliberately up the balusters and pulled themself up from prone to standing. Their hands braced on the polished wooden railing and they looked for a long moment at Ma'am. Their eyes traced around the perimeter of the house, taking in the closed doors around the gallery, then looking up at the ceiling.

"*Stop!*" Arin called. "No more. I will go with you."

I faced Savat. "I claimed my own agency here. I was empowered to make my own choice, and I made it. *I* made it." I held their eyes. "That is *strength* that cannot be diminished or denied. *I chose* my path, and it wasn't because 'I am a *nyssa*' or because 'I was in such pain.' Every moment of my life, up to these very words I speak to you, traces back to that choice."

They tried to pull away from me, but I grasped their coat and drew them forward through my memories. Places and people spun and shifted in disorienting flashes of vision that spiraled rapidly into a frenzy of moments, one after another.

...Neme giving me what was to be my first lesson in Somiri medicine...

...Lane's face looking down on me in care and worry as I bled all over her carpet...

...Beaty tying the first braid into my hair with a twist of ivy...

...Benjin's doting...

...Cook's stern approval...

...Ma'am's flinty judgement...

...Sem's teachings, in power and in movement as we jour-neyed north...

...First one, then two...

...Turin...

...Kari...

...Migs, Chan, Deme...

...Fanti...

...Atua, Marki, Ciala...

...Froley, Berin, Ranji...

...Feren...

...Bergin, Joff, and the other men who had followed me...

...Mims...

...Dane...

Sem.

The pain of Sem's death exploded anew against my mind. I could hear wailing, and I realized it was not my own voice but Savat's. I rode that pain, tearing them out of my own mind and bringing us firmly into theirs.

Nineteen

...You can't wrestle girls like that. You're a boy!...

We stood beside the wall, watching the three children scramble and roll, finding their feet. Two had blackberries smashed indelicately into their hair, dripping down their backs and cheeks.

The smallest of the three looked confused and ashamed, but not contrite. The young Tamar withdrew into themself as we watched, voicing their thought despite knowing it was a mistake.

"Why do I have to be a boy?"

Kindi's expression showed concern and worry for a moment.

"Because you are a boy, stupid," June said, amused. "You're not a girl." She giggled.

Tamar looked pleadingly at Kindi, but she had already dismissed the deviant question. She leaned in and whispered something to her friend, and the two ran off together giggling.

"Even now," I said, "you knew what you were. Was it so terrible and shameful a secret?"

"Of course it was," Savat answered angrily. "You saw them, how they responded. I knew not to push the feelings I had. I knew that there would be nothing but pain at the end of that path."

"And yet, you were still just as clever; still the strategist you would become. Your flanking maneuver with the wall and the berries was inspired. Did you need to feel like a boy to get the better of them?"

"No," Savat answered quietly. It was almost a whisper. "But I needed to be one to survive."

...Disown? Why should he...

...By the accounts I've received, mi'lord, the child is a mixie...

Tamar's father's voice was low and strained. Full of icy passion and frightening.

"Gods-damned mixie filth. A slip or a dunt? No, it doesn't matter. Fucking filthy mixie witches. Last thing we gods-damned need."

"You see," Savat said, gesturing to the open doorway off the terrace. "*That* is what I faced. *That* is what waited for me if I voiced such feelings!"

From our vantage, we could see young Tamar crouched by the corner of the house, keeping out of sight, but not keeping the pain and confusion and the disgust from their face.

I grasped Savat by the arm and forced them to turn to me.

"Yes. Exactly that. That is what you faced."

I pushed through, pushed their mind, and a dense fog coursed across the lawn. It engulfed the paved terrace, swallowed the house. It enveloped us and the world melted away. Savat's eyes were clenched shut and sweat beaded on their forehead.

The power still raged within me and I swept my free hand out before us, brushing the fog away. The mist cleared and retreated from the house, but it took power to hold it at bay. It wanted to shroud the memory again and hide it forever.

Tamar stood on the paving stones, hesitating. The table and chairs were gone, wiped away along with every remnant of Mother's presence after her death. His father sat quietly in his office, marking ledgers and comparing figures to large parchments and scrolls that were half unfurled on the wide desk.

Tamar looked longingly out over the lawn towards the pear orchards. It was six years since the blackberries. Five since Kindi and her mother had been sent to work a different estate. Tamar's body wanted to turn, to walk under the trees or out into the woods north of the house. Anything but enter Father's office.

Instead the child squared their shoulders and lifted their head, stepping slowly and determinedly across the threshold.

"Do you not see how much strength it took for you to confront him?" I asked Savat beside me.

They shook their head. Their breathing was strained, rapid.

I siphoned off some of the power that raged within me and very delicately wiped some of their fear and hurt away. It was like smearing a drop of dark, fresh ink to lighten its mark on parchment.

"Father," the child said.

Tamar's father sighed, a great huff of annoyance. He finished the notations he was making in the ledger before looking up. "Yes?"

Tears were freed from the corners of Savat's clenched eyes. Young Tamar's cheeks were also damp as their words spilled out.

"You confronted him," I whispered harshly, close to Savat's

ear. I was pressing my case, yes. I was also distracting them from their fear of what was to come. "You said the words that had been boiling in your mind and weighing down your heart for years. You feared his response, but you knew what you were and you claimed your identity. Can you not see the power in that? The strength and honesty to yourself that you revealed by your actions?"

"My actions!" Savat roared. In a fury of raw emotion, they asserted control of their mind, tearing it from me and the memory whirled in a violent spiral. I thought they would cast me out—it felt as if I would fly from my feet. But the sensation lasted only a heartbeat, and we were standing on the far edge of the same terrace.

Young Tamar pushed themself up shakily from the stones, their face bleeding freely from a great abrasion that ran from lips to chin. They pressed fingers to their face and saw the stain of red, only then understanding that their father had thrown them bodily out onto the stone. Tamar was shaking with the pain of betrayal and all its rage.

Tamar's father's words came calmly from within the room, but the sound was drowned out by the fury and the pain. The words were still clear. Rejection and abandonment and be-trayal.

Savat spoke quietly beside me, shaking with anger. "My actions... Watch them."

We stood still, somberly watching as the eleven-year-old Tamar pulled the Savat house apart stone by stone. We watched as the foundations fractured and the walls crumbled. We stood silent witness to the end of the elder Savat's lordship. We watched until the grinding stone and sifting dust fell into an eerie silence.

Young Tamar was on their knees, head bowed and hands

shaking. There was a soft, labored wheezing sound coming from the wreckage. Tamar's father's body was broken, and though he would live on for some years, he would never again lead the house.

Savat was standing beside me, watching, breathing in heavy gasps and eyes wild. Their hands were clenched into fists.

I put my hand on their shoulder, pressing with more than a little force to make them feel my touch. The pain of loss was still raw in my mind and I recalled the words that Sem had spoken to me not so long ago.

"Do you think," I asked softly, "that you're the first person to lash out in rage and violence at someone who caused you such pain?"

It took some moments, but finally I saw their eyes focus and return from the infinity of pain and settle upon mine.

"But he was my *father*," he cried, pleading.

"And so? Is it fitting or fair that your life be shaped by a man who can so casually cast aside his child? His wife? A man whose heart is so full of bile and hate that he cannot accept the very existence of someone like me, like you, like Eelie?"

"But—what I did..."

I tried again, more softly. "You responded to violence and abuse with a power that you had no way of understanding or controlling. So. Is it this child's fault that their father chose hatred and cruelty over love and acceptance? The pain you carry, the self-hate and the fear... You've been haunted by it your whole life, but *it doesn't belong to you*. It. Is. Not. Yours." I leaned close, whispering, "Let it go. I can help you."

They looked into my eyes, their expression was wild and desperate. They felt too much, too fiercely and it took several moments for my words to penetrate. Still, they stared into me, barely comprehending. I felt their hands on my arms, clinging desperately for support.

Savat's head dropped: the slightest sketch of a nod.

I placed my hands on their forehead and pushed them out of the memory. Then I set to work.

Tamar was still kneeling at the center of a ring of cracked stones. I stepped close and knelt beside them. As I reached out to touch their shoulder, it was like pushing through a caul and like trying to pass through a wall of brick—the very reality of the memory resisted my attempt to interact.

Tamar was shaking, their skin had gone white with rage and pain and shock. I pulled on the power, drawing the pain and fury of the raging battle between armies into myself and funneled it into that contact between my hand and their shoulder. I could feel the wall thinning, but it took every bit of my concentration. It was like threading a needle.

I touched them, and they flinched involuntarily. They still didn't see me, but they had felt my touch. There was a small, wounded keening sound coming from deep within their throat. I moved around so that I could face the child and took their other shoulder.

"Tamar."

The keening stopped. Their breathing was ragged and their eyes wild.

"Tamar," I said softly.

Their eyes flickered to mine, then away. I held my gaze steady, willing them to look at me.

"Tamar," I whispered.

Their eyes settled on mine, finding some sense of reality, and their breathing steadied. Their look was desperate and broken and lost.

"Tamar, it's okay. It's not your fault. You are not to blame, and you have done nothing wrong."

I wasn't sure if they understood my words. I couldn't truly tell if they could hear me. But they were focused on my face at least. Their trembling had slowed. That was a start.

I pulled them close, wrapping my arms around them and letting them feel my warmth. They buried their face into my shoulder and I felt the wetness of tears.

"Tamar, you are safe. Safe and free and loved. There is nothing for you to fear and there is no guilt for you to feel. Let it go. Let go your anger and your pain. Give it to me and let it go..." I continued to murmur such phrases, stroking their back and willing their heartbeat to calm and slow.

Tamar reached a moment where they could breathe normally again, and pulled back slightly to look at me. I let them, holding them by the shoulders at arms length.

"Who are you? Why did you come here?" they asked, suddenly shy.

"I am a friend, and I came to you to help you understand. You are not broken. There is nothing wrong with you." I took a chance, feeling that they had reached a place of enough peace. "What your father said—what he did—he was wrong. You are perfect the way you are and there is no evil in what you feel." I looked deeply into their eyes.

Tamar swallowed and scrubbed wetness from their cheeks and nose. They nodded seriously.

"You are a *nyssa*, did you know that?"

The child looked at me for a moment, then shook their head slowly, eyes wide.

"It is a special thing to be," I said. "Come, let me tell you what that means."

I stood, taking their hand and helped them to their feet. Together, we walked away from the crumbling house, out towards the peace of the pear orchards. As we walked, I spoke to them about their nature, and their power. I taught them what they were, and how they could reach their potential.

It was a lifetime. It was months and years. It was mere heartbeats.

When I withdrew from Savat's memories and returned to my own body, my leg seared my mind anew and I lost all awareness and couldn't breathe for several moments. The pain roiled my stomach and pitched the room in a dizzying spiral.

I pulled the pain and fear and violence from the ongoing battle outside the fortress walls and with a determination drawn from my very depths, brought my shattered leg into some semblance of health. Enough that the pain faded to a dull ache and it could support some of my weight, at least.

Savat sat with their back against the wall; knees drawn up and head bowed, sobbing quietly. They would keep for a few moments longer. I reached out with the power that flowed through me, finding Eelie far below in the dungeon cell. They were still unconscious from their fall.

I spun fine tendrils through them, healing the damage that they had received in our fight, and in its ending.

...the world is broken...

I stood beside them as they walked past me out of the roiling conflagration that had been the squalid tenement in Fin-Torfall. They didn't look back. The fire was beginning to spread to nearby buildings.

They left nothing behind but ashes. Nothing of their sister Medi, nothing of the horrors of Jame's attentions. They thought they left nothing of themself.

There was nothing. The world was broken.

I reached out and touched their shoulder, holding them still. They didn't resist—there was no intention for the moment; no self. They were simply an empty husk devoid of mind and purpose.

"Eelie," I said. I waited.

It took a long time before the child turned to me. Longer still for their eyes to find me.

"You are strong and powerful," I said, using a trickle of power to seat the words deeply in their mind. "You are also wounded and in pain. Your pain and your injuries are not your fault. They do not disfigure the beauty that is within you, and they cannot destroy your strength, unless you let them."

The words felt inadequate; impotent. There was nothing I could say to ease the grief, I knew. I knew also that a part of me didn't want to. A part of me wanted them to keep their pain and suffering and self-hate for what they had done to Sem.

They nodded at me, seeming to find something in my words. Then they looked back at the burning embers for a moment and began walking again. They were leaving Fin-Torfall behind, and maybe they would find the peace they sought somewhere else.

The power still flowed through me like a raging river; like the relentless tide breaking upon the shore. It was time to end that torrent.

I reached out with my mind, splitting the power twice and twice and twice, doubling and doubling until I had tens of thousands of fine threads of power, each finding an individual mind in that turbulent mass of belligerent soldiers. Black-clad and gray, I found them and I delved into their minds, damping their anger, their fear, and their hostility. I found their compassion and their calm, and I stoked them.

I found the leaders and I nudged their minds to desire calm, urged them to armistice.

There was injury and trauma and pain in abundance, strewn across a mile and more of battle lines, and I eased the worst of what I found. I drove a rolling wave of peace and solace over the land.

As I worked, I felt the power diminish. The slowing of the battle was constraining its source. The less the warriors raged, the less pain they caused and the less I could influence them. I drew my focus higher up the ranks to the leaders, directing the power I had left to try to stop the fighting.

I found the mind of the Blackcoat general, and whispered a relentless mantra of peace and surrender deep into his consciousness. I gave him the certainty that his lord wished the war to end. I reminded him of his wife and child and how much he wanted to hold them again.

I found Feren's mind, and I spoke to him in words and in feelings. *It is over. Let it be done. Savat has surrendered to me, and poses no more threat to the lands. His armies will stand down if they're given quarter.*

I felt his mind react in wonder and joy at my presence.

You have done well, I sent him. *Thank you.*

I let go of the last threads of pain and power, and came back to my own consciousness. Horns were sounding, brightly calling inscrutable signals over the battlefield.

Savat was watching me, silent and guileless.

"I'm—I'm sorry," they said in a small voice. "I don't... know what to say. What I've done..."

"Do you remember what I told you all those years ago, after your breaking?" I asked.

They looked at me for some moments, then nodded.

"You have begun your healing. Only begun. You will need to find more compassion and forgiveness for yourself still. It will take time, and it will take patience and kindness. I know of a place you can find that."

They looked at me, eyes wide. "You can't mean..."

I nodded. "Reft."

"They'll never accept me. Not after this. Not after..."

"I think they will," I said. "What matters more is whether you're ready to be accepted and to accept yourself. When you're ready... they will be there."

Savat looked into the embers of the fire, losing themself in the shimmering glow.

"Eelie is waiting for you below. They will need your help, and they need even more forgiveness and compassion. I've done what I can, but there is much healing for you both to find."

The signals were changing now, the horns blowing longer and less frantically.

"The war is ending," I said. "They will be coming for you soon, seeking justice or vengeance for their dead. I don't have the heart for any more bloodshed. Find Eelie. Leave before they find you. You both need justice and redress as much as the Torfallin do. Find it together."

Savat looked at me a long time, their eyes haunted. They opened their mouth once and twice, but ultimately said nothing. They rose shakily up to their feet and looked around at the ruins of the sitting room. Their eyes rested on the bodies of Tanith and Sem for several moments. Then they walked out.

I pulled myself up, testing my leg delicately. It hurt and I didn't dare put my full weight on it, but I was whole enough to stand at least. I picked my way across the glass-strewn carpets, limping slowly to Sem's body. It took a few moments more for me to figure out how to lower myself without straining my knee.

Sem's face was relaxed and at peace, finally. I had never noticed the pain and the tension they carried every moment I had known them until now, when the burden was gone. I leaned my head against their still chest and held them for a long time.

"Thank you, my friend," I whispered. "Thank you for what you taught me and what you gave me. I will do my best to be worthy of it."

We stayed there together until my heartbeat and breathing lost the ragged edge of fresh pain. Then I got to my feet slowly, still favoring the good leg. I worked my way around the room, picking up Sem's swords, cleaning the blades and returning them to their scabbards.

First one, then two.

On the couch by the fire, I found a woolen lap blanket. I took this up, shaking away the loose fragments of glass and carefully rolling up the swords in it to make a snug bundle that I tied closed by its corners.

With a deep breath, I slowly made my way down out of the fortress, step by unsteady step, and worked my way through the now open gate and away from the battlefield. I passed through confused masses of soldiers and prisoners. I walked east, into the rolling hills that rose gradually into a rough, mountainous trail.

Somewhere in that direction, there was a horse and two mules waiting: Artem, Beatrice, and a gray mule that would never now be given a name. I had nothing but the threadbare and bloodstained black clothes I wore and the bundle of swords under my arm. My leg ached and throbbed with each step, and the small rocks and broken ground bit at my bare feet.

The sky to the east was beginning to lighten with the coming dawn.

We're almost at the end of our time together. Just over this next pass, Reft awaits you. We should reach it in no more than two days. I know you feel anxious at our arrival, but you know now that I've walked the very path you do.

Understand then when I tell you: That place is not the beginning of your journey and it may not be the end. Where your path leads is ultimately up to you. You needn't listen to my maundering any more. I know you've grown tired of my voice and of my tale.

You ask yourself why I didn't create a Bridge to take us directly to the mountain? Why have we spent months traveling across the endless miles of road and river and stone from your parent's cottage on the shores of Slié?

It would have saved time. It would have saved you having to listen to me ramble. It would have saved me pain, limping all this way on my bad knee.

I didn't, because the journey matters. Our time together

matters. My pain *matters*.

The story matters.

Each life and every choice is as unique and varied as every leaf on every tree. What matters in a tale is not the words or the lesson. Skipping to the end of a journey only cheats you of each miles along the way, and it's the miles that are the important part. The miles make up who you are.

Stories don't have to have neat endings to be true. They don't need to explain or satisfy or uplift us. Stories help to tell us what is important, and also help us to understand the cost of what we value.

It's important that you understand—you who I have cared for these past months. You should know the paths your future may take. You should know *why* those paths exist—and who gave their lives before you so you could make this journey. More, you should know that the paths are many and varied: long and short and easy and labyrinthine.

There will be others along the way, like me, whose lives may join yours for a time and then diverge. You may find your paths will recross someday. You may never meet again.

And that's okay.

Life is change, and all paths—as all stories—come eventually to an end.

You'll also forge your own paths. As carefully as you may walk along in someone else's footprints, you'll still leave your own behind you. They may diminish, growing faint in the unrelenting march of time.

But those footprints may also become a sign for someone else to follow.

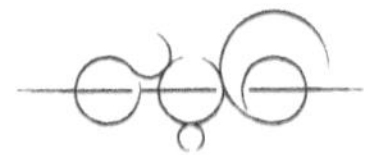

Acknowledgements

The list of people I need to thank for the existence of this book is largely the same as those I owe for the existence of book one. My partner who put me up in a hotel to give me the space I needed to finish this book, and who has put up with a lot as I worked to get it published. Everyone on the writing discord server that acts as my writing community, especially Candace, Amara, and Mireille. My therapist and my beta readers: G Stalica, Jordale, Samantha D, and Sara Codair. Of course, I also have to thank my editor Shannon, who has read this book through almost as many times as I have.

It takes many threads to weave a story such as this. All the more because when I started writing Arin's story three years ago, I thought it would be one book. This is not to say the story itself grew, as I had it mostly outlined from near the beginning. I knew how the end of this book would play out even then.

What I hadn't expected was how strongly the richness and depth of Arin's voice would take over the narrative. From the start, I knew that writing in first-person would mean that certain events would be missing from the narrative, because Arin themself wasn't there to witness them. After all, I could only write what Arin noticed and thought was important to narrate.

Arin, it turns out, is an incredibly curious and inquisitive character. When their voice took over, there was nothing for it but to write down what they saw, what they felt, and what they believed.

In short, I wasn't prepared for how different Arin's voice could be from my own.

Of course, Arin and all of the characters in their world are fictions. But I expect that many of my readers will be able to find echoes within their own memories of the same pain suffered in this fantasy world. For you, I hope that I was able to do your experiences some justice and that you might find solace in knowing that you are not alone. I see you. I'm with you.

If you are someone who read and were moved by this story and yet, perhaps like Feren, those echoes were foreign to your experience, please know that there are people in your life—even if you don't know it right now—that you can stand up and fight for. Please take Arin's words to heart:

Being an ally is not enough.

It's time to be something more.

About the Author

K. N. Brindle has worn many different hats in their life, which is impressive considering how difficult it is to find one that fits their extra-large head. They've worked as a graphic designer, and in the industrial design and architecture fields. They've built telecom equipment. They've been an app developer and a software architect, and have taught software engineering. They're most recently a licensed therapist.

They are fine with any pronouns when used with respect, though they *really* hate being called "sir."

They live in the southeastern U.S. with their partner, children, and just the right number of cats.

Introducing the next exciting novel
in a new science-fiction universe
by K. N. Brindle

"FILL ME IN. What are we walking into?" Jes said.

Windy thought for a moment before answering. "I don't know the seller's name. My contact is an intermediary. A bilge-monkey who works station mass transfer. Says he can hook us up with the seller."

"And how do we know it's not a set-up or a shake-down?"

"We don't. But he knows I've got a record of the conversation, and that not all of us are going to be there. We don't make it back out and the record goes to station security."

Jes shrugged uncomfortably. They wouldn't second guess her, but they hated working blind on the shady side of the law. They usually played on their instincts, but those instincts needed *some* context.

Jes and Windy hit the outgoing transit tube and rode it to the down-transition point, transferring to a small, ugly tube car that didn't even deign to blare ads at them. With a minute to spare, they got off on deck four—the lowest deck on the station that didn't require pressure suits—and wound their way through the narrow, twisting passages.

Here and there, a light was out or threatening to be soon. More often than not, tool carts or half-empty supply crates or piles of industrial refuse blocked the already narrow access. Some panels were missing from the passage walls and once, they had to step across the yawning gap of an open deck plate.

"Where is this guy?" Jes asked.

"He's supposed to be waiting for us just ahead," Windy replied.

They turned a last corner and saw a stick-thin man in a grimy utility jumpsuit—more grease-stain than the light blue it was meant to be.

"You came," he said. His voice was wheedling and tried hard at a threat that just didn't carry.

"We came," Windy said. "Where's your guy?" she asked him. She was able to put more threat in her voice than he could muster.

His hands came up, placating. "No worries, no worries. All good. The boss is in his office, right through there." He gestured to the hatch beside him.

Windy and Jes waited for him to open the hatch, then stepped through into a small, battered management office. Just enough room for a narrow terminal desk with a chair on either side facing each other. The space was shockingly well-lit after the gloomy passages, but the extra light didn't help the cabin to be more appealing.

Windy tensed as she recognized the man who occupied the desk. She heard a sharp breath from Jes behind her and knew they had recognized him too.

"My, my, my. If it isn't Jes and Windy; Click and Clack. You two still thick as thieves?" He smiled at them, but his voice had an edge.

"Harry," Windy said.

"Chief," Jes added, stepping into the tight office. They looked around briefly. "You've done well for yourself."

The former Chief Engineer of the Antares Drift arched his back against the frame of his chair, stretching. "I have. I run this deck. You might say this is my world down here. What happens is whatever I want to happen."

"It's... some kind of world," Jes said, looking over their shoulder to the darkened and neglected passage behind them.

Harry seemed to miss the implication in Jes's voice, or at least ignored it. "And now you two have come to me. What can I do for you, my good friends?"

"You know what we're looking for?" Windy said. "Your friend out there told me you could get it for us."

"All business? No time for an old crewmate?" Harry turned the corners of his mouth down in an exaggerated frown. "I'm hurt, Windy. Hurt. Oh, I have just what you need." He leaned back in his seat, resting his head against the bulkhead, then leaned forward and opened a hatch under the desk and pulled out a small metal-shielded frame with a wide interface port. It was rectangular, and roughly the size of a dinner plate.

"Question is, do you have what *I* need?"

"Maybe," Windy said, looking at the device. "What's your price?"

"Hmmm." Harry made a show of considering. Jes and Windy both knew that he had already set his price. "Well, you know, lucky for you I happen to know a little of what you've each got in your accounts. A little *residual* knowledge, you might say." Harry grinned at them. "How about you sign over your claim and shares from our last haul on the *Drift*? You get to fly a new ship; I get a little more comfortable down here. Maybe extend my... kingdom."

Windy felt the blow, and cursed at herself for not nailing

down the price beforehand. There was no way either of them would part with what little they had left to live on.

"Try it out," Harry offered. He placed the chip on the desk. "You brought a reader, I presume?"

Windy stared at him for a moment, then pulled a handheld device from her pocket. It was little more than a socket for the interface port with a power cell attached. She plugged it in and a small green indicator lit up on the end of the reader. Her eyes went glassy as she directed her implant to connect to the reader and scan the chip.

As the data filled her head, her eyes twitched from side to side. She dumped the ident public key into a registry search. The identity on the chip listed itself as registered out of *Alnasl L5* with no owner of record.

Windy sighed when she saw the ship's name. "You've got to be kidding. '*Heart of Gold*?' You couldn't find a chip with a more cliched name?"

There was a long-standing joke among spacers that every single world, station, and jurisdiction boasted its own registry entry for a ship called "Heart of Gold." In the years since the advent of the SDR, every comet jockey and spacer who managed to scrounge together enough to finance a ship of their own seemed to come up with the same clever idea.

"I can't help but note that you're standing here trying to buy a ship chip of questionable provenance," Harry said. "You want something flashy? To be noticed and remembered, maybe? Or do you want to slip into comfortable obscurity?"

She sighed. It was all moot anyway. "We're *not* giving you our residuals," Windy said. "What do you think we're going to do with a ship chip and no ship to plug it into?"

"Not my problem," Harry said with a shrug. "You want it, or not?"

"We'll take it," Jes said from behind her.

Windy turned to them in shock.

"But you're not getting accounts from both of us." They stepped forward, squeezing around Windy's bulky frame into the compartment. "I'll sign my shares over to you."

"Jes, no," Windy whispered. "We'll find another way."

They ignored her, staring Harry down.

"It's not enough," Harry said. He shook his head and reached out to take the chip.

Jes extended their right hand out over the desk, placing their left over the device. "You get my shares, and we walk out of here with the ship chip. More: we owe you a favor. Once we get our ship under us... I'm sure you can come up with something to call in a marker for. We have a deal?"

Harry sneered at Jes. "Come now. Half what I asked, and a marker *if* you manage a ship? What do you take me for?"

Jes smiled. "I take you for a man who runs four-deck and can let a little bit of credit slide on the potential for a bigger payout down the line. Or am I misremembering that you got your kicks landing a little wager here and there?"

Harry's sneer slipped fluidly into a wide smile. He grasped Jes's offered hand and shook. "Deal."

Jes's eyes went glassy for a moment as they dipped into their implant interface, transferring the shares. "Done."

"Always a pleasure, Jes. Don't be a stranger now," Harry said, grinning.

Jes took the device from the desk, pressing it into Windy's hands.

"See you 'round Chief."

"Round and round, Jes. Round and round, I will be seeing you."

They backed out of the office and past the bilge-monkey,

who had been leaning against the bulkhead through the whole negotiation. He watched them retrace their path through the dimly-lit corridors.

Windy waited until she was sure they were out of earshot. "Jes, what the fuck did you just do? How are you going to live without those residuals?"

Jes was silent for a moment. "Did we need that chip?" they said.

"Yes, damnit. But... what good is it going to do? We're not ready to take her out yet. Jes... We may never be ready. You know that, right?"

"We *are* going to do it." Jes's voice was firm; resolved. "Do you believe that, Windy?"

She hesitated. "I—I want to. But Jes—"

They reached the grim transit car and Jes stepped inside, turning to face her. "It's just money. I've got enough set by to last me a few more weeks. After that... who knows? Maybe we'll find an SDR. Maybe we'll stumble onto something fantastic. Or maybe I'll move in with you."

"Like *hell* you will. I'll not have you crowding my bunk; damping my pull. This woman has *needs*."

Jes met her eyes. "We're going to make it, Ada. This is the plan. We've got the hull. With this chip we've got a working nav-comm beacon that can echo clean. The skip drive and Q-comp are good enough to get us out of this particular sky. From there, we're free. Find jobs as we can and live how we want to live—"

Windy stared at Jes for a moment. They only used her first name, Ada, when they were being desperately serious. She shook her head. "In a half-scrap rust-bucket that was dumped in the recycler by its last owner?" Windy said.

Jes smiled at her wistfully. "You know what they say: 'One

person's trash is another person's—'"

"'—tragic descent into desperation borne of a willing adherence to fantasy that will ultimately lead to abject poverty or ignominious death?'" She cut in. She squeezed into the car beside them. She punched in Jes's deck number and the car began to move.

Windy was clutching the chip module with both hands as they accelerated up the transit tube. "Yeah, I think I've heard that one before."

In a single conversation, Jes Moran lost a ship, a job, and a marriage. Now, with not much more than a cool head, a few clever scams, and an odd assortment of friends—a seasoned spacer, a washout young pilot, and an alien engineer on the run from a vicious cabal—they might just have a shot at a future.

A rag-tag crew is one thing. A skip-ship cobbled together out of parts rescued from the recycler, though? Well, when you're at the bottom of the ladder, you grab for the rung you can reach.

When a hot tip for a big score finds its way to Jes's ears, a plan starts to come together. But the ship is barely space-worthy, and the crew isn't the only interested party. The cargo could set them up for life if they can get to it in time. It could also make them a target. Everyone is playing for keeps. But there's one thing that nobody bargained for:

Jes Moran *really* doesn't like to lose.

COMMON
ACCORD

K. N. Brindle

Follow K.N. Brindle for news and updates at
www.knbrindle.com

www.ingramcontent.com/pod-product-compliance
Lightning Source LLC
Chambersburg PA
CBHW032347310726
48973CB00007B/1894